A ZODIAC TACTICAL/INJURED HEROES CROSSOVER

CODE NAME:
GEMINI

JANIE CROUCH
DANIELLE M HAAS

CODE NAME: GEMINI

Chapter 1

It had been a long-damned time since Andrew Zimmerman had sat in Zodiac Tactical's active mission room.

Honestly, he never thought he'd be here again.

He looked around at the three other men in the room with him—brothers in every sense of the word but biological. Hell, one was even biological, Andrew's twin Tristan.

The other two he'd known for over a decade. Had served with them in the Navy SEALs—mission after mission. Then even more since getting out of the military and working in the same security company together.

There was nobody he would trust more to have his back in any kind of battle than the men sitting in this room.

Still, they all had to be wondering why Andrew was here. He sure as hell was.

Ian DeRose, owner and founder of Zodiac Tactical walked in the conference room. "Let's do this."

He pressed a button and the door slid closed behind him. The rest of the security measures that button provided weren't as easily visible. But Ian had basically just sealed them in a room that could not be hacked or monitored from any outside force either in this building or further away.

Ian had learned the hard way that enemies were everywhere.

Andrew had learned that same lesson—although his education had come at a much higher price.

He sat here now trying to keep the exhaustion off his face. The nightmare had been back last night, stealing his sleep. His subconscious fucking with him because he was coming here today to the active mission room.

Everybody knew Andrew Zimmerman didn't do active missions anymore.

"We're battening down the hatches in here so you can plan Wavy's surprise birthday party, aren't we?" Landon Black, Ian's right-hand man asked, grin as usual on his handsome face.

Ian cracked a smile. "God knows an ultra-secure room would be the only way of pulling something like that over on my wife. But no, we've got an actual mission."

Andrew kept waiting for everyone to look over and ask why he was here if they had a mission. Andrew hadn't been in the field for three years.

Three years and eighteen days to be exact.

Since the night his wife was murdered.

His nightmare last night had brought back all the details—as if he could forget. The smoke. The agonizing heat from the flames and his wounds. Hearing his screaming baby daughters lying in the grass beside him.

Kylie's death.

Andrew not being able to do a fucking thing about any of it except beg the angel who'd saved him to save Kylie instead.

An angel he wasn't even sure had even been real. Definitely hadn't been real enough to save his wife.

"You okay, bro?" Tristan leaned over and whispered the

words. Ian and Landon were still cracking jokes about how their wives could run a security company of their own.

Andrew nodded at his brother—face so similar, but not quite identical, to his own. "Yeah. Just wondering why I'm here. You know anything?"

"No. I got the message this morning too. Alyse and I just got back in town a couple of days ago from her shoot."

Tristan said it casually like he wasn't married to one of the biggest movie stars in the world. To everyone else Alyse Peterson was America's Glamor Princess, to Tristan she was just Alyse.

And the love of his life.

Andrew didn't begrudge his brother his happiness and he very much liked his sister-in-law. Not to mention his girls thought their Aunt Alyse walked on water. Especially when she did their makeup.

"You're going to that wedding, right?" Tristan asked. "Your friends in Tennessee?"

"Tucker Clayman and Elizabeth Gilmore. Yeah, the girls and I are leaving tomorrow." Yet another reason Andrew didn't know why he was here.

"Ok, let's focus." Everyone sat up straighter at Ian's words as screens came up out of the conference room table in front of each person. "We've gotten intel to suggest that the Volkov Cartel is back in play."

Andrew froze, jaw tightening into granite. He could feel everyone's eyes on him. "Are we certain?"

Ian nodded. The image on the giant screen changed to a man in his late-thirties with slicked-back black hair, dark eyes, and thick goatee. "Allow me the unfortunate pleasure of re-introducing Roman Volkov—aka, the Wolf. He took up the reigns of the Volkov Cartel after his father died."

Andrew stared at the picture in front of him—a reintroduction wasn't necessary. Roman Volkov hadn't been the one who tossed a homemade grenade through Andrew's living room window that had ultimately killed Kylie, but he'd definitely given the order.

"I thought he was dead." He forced the words through gritted teeth.

"We'd all hoped that was the case." Ian shook his head. "But we were never able to confirm proof of death three years ago."

"For those just meeting this wish-you'd-died-the-first-time asshole, give us the lowdown." Sarge was the only one who hadn't been actively helping Zodiac take down the cartel at that time.

Ian flipped to the next slide. "The Volkov Cartel has been on and off law enforcement's radar for a decade. They have their fingers into all sorts of bad guys pies: drugs, money laundering, information sales. The reason they've been so successful at staying ahead of law enforcement is because they never have a home base."

"Constantly on the move?" Sarge asked.

Ian nodded. "One big city to the next. New York, Miami, Los Angeles. When they showed up in Denver three years ago, law enforcement asked Zodiac to get involved as support."

"A number of us went undercover—mostly support positions to gather intel and help the main law enforcement players." Andrew forced the words out. "I volunteered since Callum Webb was leading the team."

Everybody around the table murmured in agreement. Not much more needed to be said in that regard. Callum worked for Omega Sector—an elite federal interagency task force—but was basically Zodiac Tactical family.

He'd risked his life trying to get word to Andrew that Roman Volkov had ordered hits on everyone he suspected was a traitor—including Andrew.

Unfortunately, word had come too late.

Andrew leaned back in his seat. The nightmare last night had been enough to bring all those memories to the surface. He didn't want to rehash them again. Not even with the men he thought of as brothers.

Ian took back over. "We all know that mission ended up being a clusterfuck. Omega lost four agents. Zodiac lost two team members and..."

Everybody very deliberately didn't look at Andrew.

And *Kylie*. She hadn't been law enforcement or involved in the mission in any way other than having the bad luck of being married to Andrew.

Ian cleared his throat. "The Volkov Cartel also took a big hit. Most of their senior members were killed or arrested. We thought Roman was gone too, but evidently that's not the case."

The screen flipped to the next image. "When his father was alive, Roman the Wolf was the main enforcer for the cartel. His job entailed making sure everyone stayed in line. He tended to do that in the most brutal way possible. Once Dad died and he took power, he was even worse. And the bastard loved leaving a calling card."

Another slide dominated the screen. A close-up of a dead body with X's carved over the eyes and a shot of vodka by the head.

"Not very subtle," Tristan muttered.

"Worse," Ian continued, "This image is only from a few days ago. Dead guy is a former associate of Roman's—a low level player who was trying to take over some of the Volkov's previous territory."

Landon let out a whistle. "It looks like the Wolf is definitely back."

Shit.

Tristan scrubbed a hand over his face. "It took Omega Sector years to pinpoint the cartel's location the first time. The

Wolf was always one step ahead of them—obviously had eyes and ears on the inside."

Ian nodded. "Which is why we're all here today. There's a possible lead on Roman Volkov's whereabouts, and Omega Sector wants us to move on it to make sure word doesn't get back to the Wolf. Nobody outside of this room will know what's going on."

Andrew sat up straighter, shaking off the image of the dead henchman. "What sort of lead are we talking about?"

Ian pressed the button again and the image shifted. "This sort."

A grainy video of a woman played. The shadows blocked the details of her face, but her dark hair spilled down a slender shoulder. She was petite—and fit in a way that came with a disciplined workout routine. She kept her shoulders straight, posture perfect, despite an air of unease with every step.

She was darting her gaze back and forth, glancing over her shoulder every few seconds like she was scared and being followed. But even when she moved the shadows still kept her face hidden.

Andrew shook off the feeling that something about this woman felt vaguely familiar. "Who is that? Someone dumb enough to get involved with Roman?"

"Even better. This is Tasha Volkov, the Wolf's sister."

"*What*?" Andrew leaned in closer to the screen and watched the footage again. "Nobody has ever mentioned a sister before."

"Nobody knew about her. Jenna Franklin and the geek crew accidentally discovered her."

Jenna Franklin and her computer crew didn't miss much. This sister must've been very well hidden.

Ian leaned back in his chair. "They're still gathering info. What's important is that now we know she exists."

Andrew wasn't really paying attention to the conversation.

He couldn't drag his eyes away from the footage playing on repeat.

Roman Volkov was alive and this woman—*his sister*—was the way to get to him.

A way to finally get justice for Kylie.

The feeling that he knew this woman faded into nothing. There was no way he'd ever met her before.

This woman by her very genes was the devil incarnate. The Volkov Cartel had kept her identity and existence a secret for a reason.

Not that the reason mattered to Andrew.

"What's the plan?" He looked up from the screen.

"You are," Ian said.

Andrew could feel the other men in the room stiffen. Everyone was aware that Andrew hadn't been on an active mission since Kylie's death. He had two little girls and couldn't take a chance on making them orphans.

He watched the footage again before reluctantly shaking his head. "I can't go off hunting this woman. I can't leave the girls alone for that long."

Acid burned in his gut at the thought of sitting this out, but he didn't have a choice.

"We don't need you to hunt her down. We just need to you to go to your friends' wedding as planned, but do a little work while you're there."

Andrew sat back in his seat. "I'm not following you."

"We've gotten word that Tasha Volkov is currently in Pine Valley, Tennessee."

Andrew blinked. "Are you fucking kidding me right now?"

Ian shook his head. "Nope. As far as Jenna can tell, Tasha Volkov being there is not tied to you in any way. There's no reason to think she'll know you at all."

That was probably true. Andrew hadn't had a prominent undercover role. Definitely had never met the Volkov sister.

Ian crossed his arms over his chest. "We need you to find this woman while you're at that wedding and put a micro transmitter on her phone. We want to track her—listen to her calls and conversations—until she leads us to her brother. Take down the Wolf once and for all."

He watched the footage again. At first, she'd seemed vulnerable and nervous. But knowing what he did now, he just saw evil.

"Bugging her is our best plan?" It seemed too slow. Too patient.

Ian raised his brows. "What else did you have in mind? Knock her out and drag her back to Colorado so we can interrogate her?"

Andrew clenched his jaw. Actually, that didn't sound so bad to him. This woman's comfort was not his priority. A little interrogation might make him feel better. "I've heard worse ideas."

"No, we keep this as simple as possible. You're already invited to the wedding, so you have a reason to be in the area without rousing her suspicions. Plant the transmitter and we'll go from there."

"Fine." He stood up. This briefing had taken a lot longer than he'd thought. "Is that all? I need to grab the girls and pack."

"Yeah." Ian rubbed the back of his neck. "Look, Andrew, if you don't want to do this—"

"I'll do it. You guys just make sure we're ready to move when we find out what she knows. Looks like we'll be taking down two Volkovs this time. And this time we'll do it permanently."

Tristan stood up next to him. "Hell yes we will."

Andrew secured the files he needed and headed out of the conference room—he'd be studying these all night.

Tristan caught him in the hallway. "Hey, you sure you're

up for this? If you have doubts, we can come up with another plan. You'll already have your hands full traveling with the girls."

"I'll handle it. We don't want to spook the sister by bringing in extra people."

Tristan pulled him in for a quick hug. "Despite working, try to have a good time, okay? These are people you care about getting married."

A good time? What started out as an invitation to an out-of-state wedding for an old friend had turned into an assignment that carried more weight than any job he'd ever had. Add two hyper and often mischievous four-year-olds and only one adult to keep them in line for a whirlwind trip, and a *good time* was the last thing he was expecting.

"Yeah, good time. Roger that," he still replied.

Tristan rolled his eyes. "Give Elizabeth and Tucker my regards."

"I will."

He'd worked with the former FBI profiler years before and had kept in contact, meeting her fiancé Tucker a handful of times more recently. Elizabeth also had a young daughter and they had bonded over being single parents—getting their girls together as often as possible.

The elevator doors opened at the end of the hall, and he said goodbye to his brother before hurrying to step inside. Thankful for a few seconds alone, he pressed the button for the floor where the daycare center was located and leaned back against the mirrored wall. He prepared himself for the best and worst part of his day.

The part when he set eyes on his sweet daughters, after a long day of working in this office. When he struggled against the guilt and loneliness that always plagued him as he watched the other kids being kissed and cuddled by doting mothers.

Something his girls would never have.

The door slid open, and a squeal of laughter made him smile. His girls. He would know that sound anywhere.

Caroline was the louder of the twins, her joy for life infectious as hell—and loud. So very, very loud.

And no doubt Olivia was egging her on, snickering behind a table or wall as her sister stole the spotlight. A light Olivia often hid from, preferring instead to be the brains behind whatever operation the two of them concocted.

He made a beeline for the day care, face down and pace hurried. He didn't have any small talk in him today. Not with a headful of information and a heart full of emotions all fighting to take top billing. He needed to mentally and emotionally prep for this mission.

Not to mention he needed to get his children, get home, and get packed before staring down the barrel of a full travel day with two little girls.

If Kylie was here, she would have doted and fussed and handled traveling with the cute little monsters like it was a grand adventure. Instead, the girls were stuck with him—a single dad who was in over his head and constantly wondering how he was messing things up for them.

The door to the daycare opened and bright bursts of color greeted him. Framed drawings and coloring sheets hung on the walls. A short cubical with square inserts housed spring jackets, rain boots, and lunch bags. Parents huddled at the entryway, laughing about weekend plans and waiting for their kids to storm through the swinging door that led to the open play area beyond. He was once again grateful Ian had opened a daycare in the Zodiac Tactical building. No doubt part of the reason had been for Andrew himself—after what had happened, he'd needed to have his girls nearby if he was going to be able to work at all.

A familiar squeal crinkled his nose. He couldn't help but shake his head and chuckle.

"Daddy!" Caroline and Olivia's sweet voices mingled together. They pushed through the crowd and launched themselves into his arms.

His chuckle grew into a full-blown laugh, and he nearly toppled onto the tiled floor. For an instant, his heart was as full as his arms and he pressed a kiss to each sweaty forehead. His sweet girls were robbed of their mother, but he'd make sure they always knew safety and comfort and love.

And after he found the Volkov sister and completed his assignment, they'd all finally know justice for the woman they'd loved and lost.

Chapter 2

"Daddy, are we there yet?"

Andrew gripped the steering wheel and prayed for patience for the hundredth time today.

He followed the instructions the GPS spit at him and turned onto the quaint town square of Pine Valley, the whole Tennessee town vaguely resembling Mayberry. "Almost."

"Ice cream!" Caroline squealed, piercing his eardrum when she saw the sign just south of the square. She kicked her legs, her feet connecting with the back of his seat in a frantic rhythm that matched the pounding in his head.

"Can we get some, Daddy?" Olivia chimed in. "Pretty please?"

A moment of weakness for the girls' sweet pleas almost had him slowing and finding a parking spot in front of the ice cream parlor. It actually wasn't a terrible idea. He could use the time to scope out the town. Hell, he might even get lucky and spot his target right away so he could get his assignment done and enjoy the rest of the weekend.

But the schedule for the next two days was too tight. Best to get to Crossroads Mountain Retreat—where the wedding would take place tomorrow and where he and the girls were being put up for a couple of nights.

"Maybe later today," Andrew said, surveying the area with eagle eyes. "Besides, Audrey is waiting for you. Don't you want to see your friend?"

The girls clapped their hands and cheered, immediately launching into a discussion about Audrey—the bride Elizabeth's daughter.

He chuckled at their enthusiasm. They'd been troopers all day. Waking up at the ass crack of dawn to board a plane where they shoveled snacks in their mouths and watched their tablets for the few hours' long flight from Denver to Tennessee.

Being trapped in the car for the drive to Pine Valley hadn't been high on their list after their feet had hit solid ground, but he'd bribed them with chocolate and the promise of as much time as they wanted with the friend they rarely got to see.

He made a mental note of the different shops he passed. He'd been to Pine Valley before but hadn't been in active mission mode like he was now. He'd just been an overwhelmed single dad on his way to see friends.

Of course, he was *still* that.

Quiet streets made up the town square with a white gazebo in the center of the grassy knoll. Young couples sat on benches along the sidewalks and a cluster of women pushed strollers with the speed of power walkers.

In a town this size, everyone would know everyone—be involved in the juicy gossip. And a young, attractive woman moving in would be a hot topic, no matter how far she tried to stay under the radar. Hell, after asking a few questions, he might have a location on the Volkov sister before the wedding even started. Then he could slip away, bug her phone, and spend the rest of his stay enjoying friends and a nice wedding.

The GPS chirped more directions. He blocked out the

giggling banter between the girls as he drove up a mountain and found the lane that led to Crossroads Mountain Retreat. The tension bunching the muscles in the back of his neck loosened as he parked. He'd made it with all three of them in one piece.

"We're finally here," Olivia said, a hint of exhaustion in her little voice.

"Holy moly. It's like a castle." Caroline fiddled with the straps on her car seat. "Gimme out, Daddy."

"Whoa there. Hold your horses, munchkins."

Caroline giggled. "I don't have a horse."

He turned with his hand fisted, arm extended toward his beautiful daughter. "I've got one right here in my hand for you, sweet cheeks. Wanna hold on to it while I figure out where we're supposed to go?"

Her browns eyes went wide, and she nodded. "Uh huh."

He grabbed her little hand and placed the pretend horse in her palm before sealing her fist shut.

"Me, too." Olivia reached her arm forward.

Repeating the process, he kept his mouth pressed in a firm line and all hints of amusement from his voice. "I'm trusting you both to keep those horses under control. Don't let them loose in the car, okay?"

"Okay," they said in unison.

He bit back a grin and shut off the engine before hopping out of the car, leaving the door open. He stretched his arms high over his head.

"Well look who it is." Tucker Clayman's gruff voice turned Andrew toward the wide, wraparound porch of the lodge. He jogged down the steps. His hair was buzzed short, and his gray T-shirt showed off the black ink of his tattoos circling his biceps. He clapped a hand on Andrew's shoulder. "It's about damn time you got here. God forbid you took off a few more days and came down earlier."

Shrugging, Andrew rubbed a hand through his tousled mess of hair. "What can I say? I'm a busy guy."

"Daddy, don't forget us!" Caroline called from the car.

Laughing, Tucker opened the back door. "Hey there, little ladies. Long time no see. Want me to spring y'all loose?"

"Yes." Again, the answer came out in unison.

"Yes, what?" Andrew asked, eyebrow raised.

"Yes, please!"

"Even if y'all hadn't said please, I'd still get you out." Tucker winked in the girls' direction as he unhooked the complicated buckles of Olivia's seat. "Audrey's been asking about you both all morning."

Andrew opened Caroline's door and managed to free his squirming daughter at the same time Olivia climbed out. He closed the door and rounded the back of the car to tackle their luggage. "You lucked out, man. Looks like you're going to have a gorgeous day for the wedding."

"I lucked out in more than just the weather. Seriously, look at the woman I'm about to marry."

Andrew swept his gaze past the blossoming trees and distant peaks of the Smoky Mountains to the striking woman with the wide smile gliding from the three-story log cabin styled building.

Tucker was right. He was a lucky sonofabitch to be marrying Elizabeth Gilmore. She and Andrew had worked together multiple times, and his heart had broken for her when her husband was killed while she was pregnant with Audrey. But it wasn't until Kylie had been killed that he understood everything Elizabeth had lost.

A partner. A lover. The dream of a life filled with love that would never come true.

But nothing hit harder than knowing your child would never know the other half of them—would never create precious memories with someone who loved them so damned much.

Audrey, Elizabeth's five-year-old daughter, ran ahead, not stopping until she had Olivia and Caroline spinning—the three of them a tiny tornado of squeals and laughter. The innocent sound of pure joy warmed Andrew's heart and made the hassle of getting to Tennessee well worth it.

"Good luck getting these three away from each other," Elizabeth walked over and hugged him. "I'm so glad you could make it."

"There's nowhere else I'd rather be."

Especially if it meant finding Tasha Volkov and putting down the Wolf for good.

"Let's get y'all settled inside." Tucker grabbed the handle of one of the suitcases while hooking a duffle over his shoulder.

The girls ran off together like a gaggle of hyper ducklings, leading the way to the lodge.

"It was nice of your friend to let us stay here for a couple nights," Andrew said to Tucker. "There weren't a lot of options for lodging in town."

Tucker walked to the lodge and placed the luggage inside the door. "You and the girls will be in one of the cabins by the lake, so just leave everything here until we head out back."

Andrew set the bags on the floor and let out a low whistle. "You better tell me those cabins are as nice as this place because this is damn impressive."

Mahogany floors stretched from wall to wall. Burgundy rugs broke up the open space with patches of seating scattered around the room. A stone fireplace stretched three-floors up, where dark beams zig zagged along the ceiling. Windows made up the entire far wall, letting sunshine pour in along with amazing views of the lake and green-tipped mountains.

"The cabins are smaller but the view's just as nice." Elizabeth grinned then dropped to her knees and opened her arms. "Now, you two girls come give Auntie Liz a hug."

The twins hurled themselves at Elizabeth.

"Mommy, can Olivia and Caroline get their nails done, too? Daddy, please? Can they? Can they?" Audrey darted her pleading eyes from Tucker to Elizabeth.

A dagger sliced through Andrew's chest at hearing Audrey call Tucker *Daddy*. Audrey would have two parents now. Elizabeth, his broken-hearted single-parent buddy, would no longer go through this world alone. And as much as he wanted that for Elizabeth—and for Audrey—he couldn't stop a tiny pinch of jealousy.

"Daddy, I want pretty nails," Caroline said, wriggling her fingers.

"Yeah, me too," Olivia echoed.

Clearing his throat, he focused on the conversation. "Girls, I'm sure Auntie Liz has a ton of things to get done before the big day tomorrow. We don't want to take up all her time."

Elizabeth stood and wrapped an arm around both girls' shoulders. "I really don't mind. Audrey and I have a whole afternoon of girly fun planned. I'd hoped these two could join us. Pamper them a little after such a long travel day while giving you some alone time."

He hated to dump his daughters on the bride-to-be, but the arrangement couldn't be more perfect. They'd be safe and happy while he gathered intel on the Volkov sister. "You sure?"

"Positive."

"Do you need their car seats or anything?"

"Nah, everything we'll need is right here at the lodge. You girls ready?" Elizabeth lifted her hands as if she were about to take the children on the adventure of a lifetime.

"Yeah!" All three girls yelled and jumped up and down, scampering away.

"I'm exhausted just watching that." Tucker slapped a hand on his shoulder. "Want to grab a drink on the deck?"

Tucker was from Pine Valley. Andrew would pick his brain for any usable information, then he'd make an excuse to head into town and see what he could find. "Sure. A beer sounds great."

Tucker dipped his chin toward the double doors that led to the deck. "You head on out. I'll grab the beers and be there in a minute."

Andrew ignored the clusters of people sitting in small groups or milling about the room. He stepped outside and breathed in deep, the cool, mountain air filling his lungs. Commotion at the far end of the deck caught his attention. High-top tables were being set up around the space and flowery garland—wedding decorations—strung in any free spot.

Weddings weren't really his thing, but this one was already shaping up to be beautiful. How could it not be with the Smoky Mountains giving such a lush backdrop.

He was turning back toward the deck doors when a cluster of people on the lawn caught his attention as they moved toward the lodge, yoga mats in tow. Specifically, the woman with long blonde hair at the back of the pack, not talking to anyone else.

Something about the set of her shoulders, the way she walked with her posture perfect but as if she wished to remain hidden set alarms blasting in his brain.

He'd spent most of the night last night studying the video footage Zodiac Tactical had provided. The details of the woman's face had been obscured so he'd memorized everything else about her—how she held herself, her gait, her posture.

The hair color was wrong on the woman walking across

the lawn now, and he still couldn't see her face, but he knew without a shadow of a doubt that this was her.

This was the woman who—inadvertently or not—had led to Kylie's death. This was the woman who was going to help make sure Andrew got justice for that.

No matter what.

He already had the micro transmitter in his pocket ready to be placed, but the overwhelming urge to crush it and find other means—*much more ugly means*—of making Tasha Volkov tell where her brother was danced through his mind.

He gripped the banister in front of him to stop from leaping over it and dragging Tasha away, repercussions be damned.

This woman was responsible for his wife's death.

He looked down at his hands, his breath beginning to saw in and out as before his eyes they became covered in blood.

A window smashing. An explosion stealing his senses. Flames erupting.

Fear strangling him as he fought to get the ones he loved the most out of the burning house as smoke invaded his lungs and stole his air until he collapsed.

Unable to move or speak or do a fucking thing to help himself or his family.

Someone getting the girls out then pulling him from the flames despite his silent screams to leave him and help Kylie instead.

Andrew blinked hard, trying to bring himself back to the present.

His chest tightened, and he squeezed the railing until his knuckles turned white. He pulled air in through his nose as his breath hitched higher in his throat. Dots invaded his vision and sweat clung to his hairline. The ripples on the lake behind the lodge warbled—past and present blending in a way he couldn't separate.

"Hey there, buddy. You okay?" The deep, husky drawl snapped Andrew back into the moment.

His eyes opened. Grip loosened. The blood was gone from his hands. He forced a breath in then out.

"Yeah, I'm fine," he finally managed to muttered.

A broad-shouldered man with shaggy brown hair and a couple days' worth of scruff on his jawline stood beside him. "You sure? Around here there's certainly no shame, nor much shock, if someone is struggling with past demons. After all, helping with that is what the Crossroads Mountain Retreat is for."

Andrew took in another steadying breath. He wasn't here to fight his demons.

He was here to capture one.

He looked back out at the woman he was sure was Tasha Volkov. She'd stopped to talk to another woman just beyond the main building "I'm sure. Thanks though."

The guy shrugged and leaned his forearms over the railing. "Good to hear. Just wanted to offer a helping hand if one was needed. I'm Lincoln by the way."

Andrew finally faced the guy and gave a brief nod of greeting, while keeping an eye on Tasha. "Andrew Zimmerman. You a guest here for the wedding?"

Lincoln snorted out a laugh. "Nah. I live here with my wife. She owns the place."

A local. That was good. He might have some insight. Andrew needed to keep him talking. "It's quite a place. Been married long?"

"Not at all, but don't have any complaints so far."

Andrew couldn't help but grin. "And the two of you met here?"

Lincoln nodded. "I was forced to come when I was injured on the job—I'm a police officer. Fought coming here tooth and nail, figuring this place was all some new age hocus-pocus bullshit that wouldn't help. But Crossroads healed me in more ways than I realized I needed. And it led me to Brooke."

Love was fairly oozing from the words. Andrew couldn't help but be happy for the guy. "Glad it worked out for you."

"You're here for the wedding?"

"Yeah. Known Elizabeth for years. Met Tucker a few times. So decided to come for the festivities." Andrew leaned as casually as he could against the railing "Any idea who that is? The blonde in the green shirt?"

Lincoln glanced over his shoulder. "That's Tasha."

She hadn't changed her first name.

"Got a last name?"

Lincoln narrowed his eyes, as if unsure he liked the question. "Bowers."

An alias. Andrew wasn't surprised. It wasn't like she was going to wear a neon sign proclaiming that she belonged to a family of terrorists and murderers.

The need to use violence against her to get information pressed at him again, but this time he tamped it down. No doubt those thoughts were what had triggered his little PTSD incident a minute ago.

He needed to keep himself under control. Focus on the mission *within* the given perimeters.

"She work here?" he asked.

"She works at Serenity Mountain Studio, the yoga studio downtown. But she helps out with classes here from time to time. Since this is a busy weekend, I guess she's leading a class or two."

Andrew forced himself to smile and talk about other things so he wouldn't make the cop any more suspicious.

But the hunt was on, and Andrew had just stumbled upon his prey.

Chapter 3

The overwhelming sensation of being watched crawled up Tasha's spine like a line of army ants. Her heart rate spiked, and she swallowed the ball of fear lodged in her throat. She fought against the impulse to drop everything and run.

Her yoga group, still chatting as they walked back to the lodge, would find that a little odd.

If there was one rule Tasha lived by, it was to draw as little attention to herself as possible. That had been generally easy in Pine Valley when her only responsibility was sitting behind a desk at the yoga studio.

But things had changed a little in the last few months. As she'd helped her boss by leading more classes—both at the studio and here at Crossroads—the constant terror in the pit of her stomach had dissipated just a little. Enough for her to feel as though she didn't have to keep running. Didn't have to keep looking over her shoulder and sleeping with a gun next to her pillow.

Putting her Glock in the top drawer of her nightstand had felt like a huge victory a week ago. Even if it was a sad commentary of her pathetic life.

But she'd take pathetic and scared over being in her half-brother's hands any day.

The hairs at the base of her neck lifted along with her gaze as she attempted to discover what was setting off her internal alarms. The deck stretching along the back of the lodge was full of wedding preparation. Strangers milled about and set up the area where Tucker and Elizabeth would celebrate their nuptials. She spotted Officer Lincoln Sawyer on the far end, standing next to another man.

She wasn't close enough to clearly see his face, but something about him struck a nerve. She could tell he was watching her—completely still as he did it. She hurried her pace across the lawn, needing to get out of his sightline.

"Hey, Tasha. Over here."

Tasha had done her damnedest to stay separate from the people in Pine Valley, but somehow a number of them had slipped through the chinks in her armor with their friendliness. Laura Metcalf was one of those. The other stood by the side door and waved a hand high. Her long, blonde hair was pulled into a messy bun at the top of her head. An apron was tied around her slim waist with a dusting of what looked like flour spread across her cheek.

"Thanks for the fun class, everyone." She reached the concrete patio under the deck and relaxed now that she was safely away from the eyes that had been following her. "You can drop your mats in a pile by the door, and I'll take care of them. Hope to see y'all again."

She internally cringed at the fake accent she used along with the local vernacular. She'd learned the hard way to do whatever it took to fit into a new town. In Tennessee, that meant using y'all all the damn time and drawing out her words with a soft lilt for emphasis. It was getting easier to do, even if it sounded foreign to her own ears.

As foreign as the blonde hair that greeted her when she looked in the mirror.

The colorful mats piled up one by one along with goodbyes from the guests. She scooped long, foam mats into her arms.

"I'll take half." Laura grabbed the rest from the ground. "No need to clean them all by yourself."

Tasha huffed out a laugh. "Yeah, because wiping down seven yoga mats takes a toll on me."

"Well, giving you a hand gives me another chance to talk you into coming to the wedding tomorrow."

Tasha sighed and opened the door, letting Laura in first before following behind. A blast of cool air chased away the heat covering her skin from the workout. "You know I was only invited because I teach classes here at Crossroads from time to time. Tucker and Elizabeth don't really want me at their wedding."

Not to mention the idea of being in a room full of strangers was enough to make her skin itch.

"You were invited because you're a part of this community. Whether you want to be or not, you're one of us now." Grinning, Laura wiggled her eyebrows then led the way into the state-of-the-art gym here in the lodge.

Laura was the kind of person who wanted to help friends and strangers alike. The other woman definitely had her own demons—ones she hid behind a bright smile. But even with her personal sadness Laura always tried to help others. It was one of the main reasons why Tasha was still in Pine Valley.

There was someone who finally cared about her.

Yeah, the blonde could be a little overbearing with her friendliness, but it came from a good heart.

Tasha wasn't sure how to get out of this wedding conversation, and honestly wasn't sure she even wanted to. She definitely knew Elizabeth and Tucker and were so happy they were getting their forever. She would know a lot of the guests too. Maybe going wasn't such a bad idea.

She rushed past the free-standing weights and cardio equipment to the cleaning station. She sprayed the mats with disinfectant then wiped them down before stacking them neatly in the corner. She always liked being in this gym.

Regular workouts and sparring had been found to help the emotional healing process of some people suffering from PTSD, so Crossroads had put significant money into making sure theirs was top notch.

"Come on," Laura said in a sing-song voice. "You've lived in Pine Valley for a while now, and I can barely coax you from of your house for a girls' night out."

Tasha rubbed her hands up and down her pants and rolled her eyes. "It's not exactly a girls' night out when you're my only friend."

"Which is why you need to come tomorrow. It'll be the perfect opportunity to get to know people a little better. You can be my plus one."

"Nobody cares about that."

Laura swatted her hand through the air. "You'll be sparing me the humiliation of attending solo. Please? Don't make me beg."

She laughed. "This isn't begging?"

"Kind of." Laura scrunched her nose. "See how much I want you there? I won't stop hounding until you agree."

Biting the inside of her cheek, Tasha ran through her usual list of excuses: having a class to teach today, having an early class to teach the next day, needing to handle some errands. None would work. Laura would call bullshit on all of them.

"Tash," Laura said softly. "You're too young to hide away."

Heat rose from her neck. Crap. Before coming to Pine Valley, she hadn't stayed in one place long enough to make a friend like Laura. That'd always been fine. Staying safe was more important than creating bonds with people around her.

But she liked Pine Valley and the life she'd carved out here. If she wanted to keep it, she needed to step out of her comfort zone just enough to not screw everything up. If she said no now, Laura would push for a reason. Start asking questions Tasha couldn't answer.

"Fine. You've talked me into it. I'll go. And especially because *you're* too young to hide away too."

That sadness flashed behind Laura's eyes but it was gone before Tasha could read more into it.

Laura shot her a smile. "We're going to have so much fun. I promise."

A deep rumble of laughter turned Tasha toward the door. Lincoln, Tucker, and the man who'd been watching her stepped into the gym. The man stopped, his gaze meeting hers.

She dropped the mat she was cleaning as she was able to finally see him clearly. Terror and confusion spun circles in the pit of her stomach, making her nauseous.

His dark hair was a bit longer and the scruffiness along his jawline gave him a hard edge.

But it was *him*. The man who'd changed the course of her life even though she didn't even know his name.

The need to run slammed into her again.

She forced herself to remain steady. The three men were in front of the door. She had to play this smart if she wanted to get out.

She didn't know what the man was doing here. She only knew that if he'd found her, it was only a matter of time before her brother did too. And when Roman came for her, he wouldn't stop until she was dead.

"Hey, there's the groom." Laura shot a big grin over at

Tucker. "I just talked Tasha into being my plus one for tomorrow. Better late than never."

She walked toward the three men, and Tasha followed digging deep into her mind for her self-defense moves in case she needed them. Tucker and Lincoln were both fully capable of taking her down, but they had no reason to.

Unless the man had told them who she really was. Who her family was.

Her best bet to get out would be to push Laura into the three of them and make a run for it. Use her speed to her advantage and hope for the best.

The man was holding a beer and didn't seem poised to make an attack. But he was watching her with brown eyes she hadn't forgotten for three years.

Tucker smiled. "Good. Although you know you don't have to be a plus one, Tasha. You did get your invitation, right?"

Tasha nodded, still staying slightly behind her friend, her weight balanced evenly, ready to move in any direction necessary. She didn't want to have to shove Laura—didn't want the last thing she did to her friend to be that—but if that was her only choice, she'd do what she had to do.

That was one thing she'd definitely learned in the past three years: do what you have to do to survive.

"Ladies, this is Andrew Zimmerman." Tucker held up his own beer bottle towards the man still starting at Tasha. "He and Elizabeth have known each other for... hell, how long, man?"

Andrew Zimmerman.

She finally had a name. Three years ago, she'd only had an address and the knowledge of how evil her brother had truly become.

"Almost five years," Andrew responded.

Five years.

Tasha relaxed the slightest bit. He'd known Elizabeth long

before that night that had destroyed everything. Long before Tasha had known the truth about her family.

"Nice to meet both of you," Andrew continued, his deep voice so much different than when she'd heard it once before.

"Andrew and his daughters flew in from Colorado. The girls are with Elizabeth and Audrey doing nails and stuff."

"Nice to meet you, Andrew." Laura shook his hand. "Is your wife here with you?"

"No, she's deceased." His eyes finally dropped from Tasha to look at Laura.

Tasha flinched even though she'd already known his wife was dead.

"I'm so sorry," Laura murmured, before stepping back and giving Tasha a nudge.

Message received: *gorgeous single dad* alert—*proceed with no caution whatsoever.*

Laura was as unsubtle as she was friendly.

Laura and Tucker began talking wedding details, with Lincoln and Andrew chiming in occasionally. Tasha relaxed just the slightest bit more. Now that those brown eyes weren't pinning her, she could think a little more clearly.

An insane coincidence. The international banker who'd had business with her brother—and been collateral damage when Roman had gone on the rampage—also happened to know Elizabeth and Tucker.

Andrew wasn't here for Tasha at all. Didn't remember her.

Didn't know the price she had paid three years ago.

He'd been too busy paying his own price.

When there was a slight gap in the conversation she squeezed Laura's elbow. "I've got to get going. One more yoga class to teach today."

Laura reached over and kissed her on the cheek. "I'll see you tomorrow." She leaned in closer to Tasha's ear. "Wear something sexy. What a hunk!"

Tasha's smile was more of a grimace as she stepped back. The men didn't seem to have heard her, thankfully.

Andrew stepped over and pushed open the door for her. His brown eyes found hers again and for a second she could swear he knew who she was.

And that he hated her with every fiber in his tall, fit body.

She shuddered, unable to help it. Her instincts screamed once again for her to run.

Then he smiled, and whatever she thought she'd seen vanished. "It was nice meeting you. Maybe I'll catch you at the wedding."

He turned back to Tucker, Lincoln, and Laura.

No, this man didn't know who Tasha was at all. That was just her own paranoia.

It had to be.

Chapter 4

The next afternoon, Andrew straightened his tie in the mirror and gave himself one last check before shepherding the girls to the ceremony.

Another night of not much sleep, partly from having two wound-up little girls in the room with him, but mostly from knowing Tasha Volkov was in his sites.

That had definitely been her yesterday. He'd already sent the name Tasha Bowers back to Zodiac for them to run it. Not surprising, nothing had come of it. No credit cards in that name. No registration with the DMV. It was just the alias she was using here.

He'd asked around a little more as best he could without rousing suspicions, but no one seemed to know much about her. She'd done a good job of burying her past. Keeping a low profile. Enough of an online presence to not look suspicious, but nothing too personal. No photos or sharing of memories. Definitely no mention of her family and very few friends.

Now that he had no doubt that Tasha was his target, he just needed to figure out how to get close enough to complete the mission.

He was still fighting the urge not to completely deviate from the plan. He could grab his sidearm, force her away from the wedding, and demand she tell him everything he needed to know about her family.

Not that he would even need to use a weapon to take Tasha. The woman was tiny, couldn't be much more than five feet tall and barely more than a hundred pounds. He had nearly a foot on her.

He fisted his hands at his sides. Her delicate nature shouldn't matter. Neither should those blue eyes that took up damned near half her face.

She was his enemy. That was the only thing he needed to remember.

"Daddy, how do I look?" Olivia spun in a circle, her dress whirling around her.

Andrew forced his attention back into the room. "Beautiful, my princess."

"What about me?" Caroline mimicked her sister until they twirled around the room like a pair of spinning teacups.

"Fabulous. One and all."

He had to get a grip. Plotting possible violence against Tasha while his twins danced like ballerinas crossed some sort of line. He breathed in deep, calming the constant beat of adrenaline against his skull.

He needed a clear head today. No making mistakes or going rogue. Both would lead to consequences he couldn't afford.

"Come on Daddy. Audrey's waiting." Olivia grabbed one hand—Caroline taking the other—and pulled him toward the door of their cabin.

"Okay. Let's go."

Warm sunlight streaked down from the blue Tennessee sky. He kept a firm grip on his daughters, so the little dirt magnets wouldn't mess up their light blue dresses before the wedding started.

The ceremony was set up a short walk away from the studio-style cabin they were staying in. People were already milling around talking.

"Daddy, look! A doggie!"

The twins dropped his hands and ran forward. A giant black dog sat beside Tucker, who stood at the end of a long white runner that stretched from the path along the lake to a flower-covered altar. The Smoky Mountains made a perfect backdrop to it all.

Andrew shook Tucker's hand and grinned at his girls being licked by the Labrador Retriever. "Who's this? Your best man?"

Tucker grinned. "One of them. This is Otto. He's been by my side for the good, the bad, and the ugly. Couldn't think of anyone better to stand with me while I marry my other best friend."

"Elizabeth's okay with that?"

"Are you kidding? She and Audrey insisted he be up here. But I'll have my buddies Chet and Wade up here to. You know, so I don't look like a total weirdo."

The girls giggled.

"Tell Otto bye," Andrew said. "We need to find our seats."

They fawned over the dog for a few more seconds then helped pick three chairs on the bride's side.

Andrew scanned the crowd. Most of the seats were filled. It was a small group, twenty to thirty tops. He spotted Laura buzzing around, but where was Tasha?

He glanced over his shoulder. Bingo. She was seated in the back row.

Her blonde hair was twisted into some fancy bun at the nape of her neck. She wore a black cotton dress, but damn it, there was nothing simple about it. The neckline dropped low enough to show off the curve of her breasts and the silhouette hugged her torso.

A blast of shame slammed against him and forced him forward. What the hell was that? *Attraction?* There was no room for any kind of attraction. Tasha was the enemy. Plain and simple.

Unable to help himself, he twisted around once more. Tasha's eyes, still swallowing her whole face, latched onto his.

She didn't look away. And why would she? She didn't know who he really was. She just thought he was some *hunk* attending his friends' wedding—at least, according to Laura's whispered words yesterday when she thought no one heard.

That was his best bet—pretend to be just another wedding guest, another man interested in striking up an innocent conversation with a beautiful woman. Grab her phone when he could and plant the transmitter.

Simple.

He lifted the corner of his mouth in a half-grin at her. Friendly. Charming.

She dropped her gaze to her lap, but not before he saw a tiny smile.

He righted himself, facing forward once again. He'd initiated contact and now it was time to watch his two friends get married. He hooked his arm around each of his girl's tiny shoulders and forced Tasha to the back of his mind, at least for the moment. He wanted to savor watching Elizabeth, Tucker, and Audrey get their happily ever after.

Then it would be time to take down the Volkovs. Starting with Tasha.

~

TASHA TWISTED the program in her hands. She forced herself to stare straight ahead, no matter how badly she wanted to glance over at Andrew and his two adorable girls.

She blew out a long, shaky breath. She'd been on the verge of cancelling more than once today. Putting herself in a situation where she was this close to someone from her past was a huge mistake.

But…she was curious. About Andrew. About his girls. About his life after that horrible night.

Intrigue had her paying way too much attention to her hair and makeup as she'd readied herself for the wedding. She didn't know anything about Andrew Zimmerman except he was in international banking and had ties with her half-brother three years ago.

The fact that Roman had put a kill order out on Andrew had to mean Andrew wasn't a criminal. A lot more reason to like him.

And she couldn't deny that wasn't the only thing she liked. Everything about his physical appearance was appealing: thick dark hair, deep brown eyes, a warrior's jawline—strong and uncompromising.

And then when he'd smiled at her a few minutes ago, his whole face had become more inviting. And watching him put his arms around his two adorable daughters was definitely not lessening the attraction.

It was so strange to think he'd had such a huge role in her life—every single day of the past three years had been a reminder of him in some way—while he hadn't even known she existed.

Laura swooped in from nowhere and took the chair beside her. "Sorry I'm late. I was helping Brooke make sure everything was perfect in the lodge for the reception. Hopefully now I can sit back and enjoy. Or at least relax before I take Audrey for the night."

Grateful for the interruption, Tasha relaxed her grip on her program and focused on her friend. "You two will have a blast."

Laura beamed. "We will, and I have a feeling I'll be exhausted tomorrow. We've had a few slumber parties and the child never wants to sleep. Unless she's exhausted from the day, she'll want to stay up and watch movies while I feed her tons of junk food."

"I bet she'll be tired. Especially after the dancing, not to mention the emotions of the day."

"Good point," Laura said, smoothing a stray piece of hair in her low ponytail. "Brooke will be there too to help out. We're staying at the lodge. You should join us."

"We'll see."

Tasha didn't have any intention of joining the little slumber party, but she'd figure out an excuse later. Preferably when Laura was distracted and couldn't throw out a hundred reasons for Tasha to stay. She had to keep her wall up around Laura, as hard as that was.

Hell, she kept a wall between her and everyone. It was the only way she could survive.

Music floated in the air, forcing Tasha's attention to the processional. Audrey skipped down the aisle in a fluffy white dress with matching ribbon tied in her blonde hair. She held a basket and threw red rose petals on the ground, a smile on her sweet face.

Pressure squeezed Tasha's chest. Pure joy radiated from the little girl's face. Audrey made it to the alter and threw her arms around Tucker before turning and facing the crowd, Otto now by her side. She waved to her friends—Andrew's daughters—in the congregation.

The wedding march began, and Tasha rose to her feet with the rest of the wedding guests. A gasp caught in her throat as the bride came into view. Elizabeth wore a strapless, cream-colored gown. Delicate lace hugged her torso before a light silk flowed out at her waist. Beams of sun streamed down like a spotlight on Elizabeth, who stared straight ahead—eyes only for Tucker.

The slippery tentacles of envy curled in the pit of Tasha's stomach. She'd never looked at someone the way Elizabeth looked at Tucker. And chances were, she never would.

She swallowed down the unwanted thoughts and focused on the positive. She was safe. She was the happiest she'd been in years. And she had a community of people who actually seemed to want her around. Something she hadn't had since her mom died when she was young and her dad had shipped her off to boarding school.

And especially since she found out what her family truly was and had lost nearly everything trying to stop her brother's madness.

Elizabeth floated by, clasping a loose bouquet of wildflowers, then stopped beside Tucker. She held out a hand to Audrey, who nestled between the two of them.

The music stopped. Tasha settled back on her seat. She listened closely as words of love and commitment, family and faith, bonded the trio.

Tears dotted the corners of her eyes. Weddings always got to her—not like she'd been to many. But there was something extra special about witnessing two people find their ways to each other after each suffering so many hardships. Each losing so much only to end up with something so damn special was magical.

But it also made Tasha's soul break just a little. Because even though she'd been through her share of troubles, there was no pot of gold at the end of some imaginary rainbow for her.

Laura placed a hand on Tasha's, stopping her continued twisting of the wrinkled paper. "You okay?"

Tasha nodded. "Yeah. Fine. It's beautiful."

The officiant announced the new husband and wife right before Tucker captured Elizabeth in his arms and kissed her.

Tasha clapped along with the cheering guests and returned to her feet as the couple each grabbed hold of one of Audrey's hands and ran down the aisle, the little girl between them.

"They make the most precious family, don't they?" Laura lowered her pressed together palms to her chin.

"It's nice to see things work out." Tasha couldn't help but let her gaze travel to Andrew and his daughters. Things hadn't worked out for him and his wife.

Nerves knotted her stomach, and she turned her back on the striking man and his precious little girls. She may want nothing to do with Roman or any part of her *heritage*, but she'd never wash away the stench of death and destruction that clung to her by being born into such a horrible family.

The tears in her eyes grew, and she dashed them away with her fingertips, grateful she could use the wedding as an excuse for the emotion she couldn't hide.

Damn it, she hadn't let herself get bogged down in the pathetic tragedy that was her life since she'd moved to Pine Valley. But all it took was one glimpse of a man connected to her past to send her crashing to the dark place she'd crawled out of months before.

A place she'd vowed never to return.

Maybe Andrew had crossed paths with her again because the universe was trying to tell her something. She'd moved hundred miles away, lived with one eye constantly open, and she still couldn't outrun her past.

It was always going to show up—just a matter of when.

The knowledge that she'd never truly escape the clutches of her brother sat like a boulder in her chest. Andrew's appearance here just solidified it.

The only way she'd ever be free of her family would be over her dead body.

Chapter 5

The ice in Andrew's glass clattered as he swirled the scotch. If he was only allowing himself one drink tonight, he was making damn sure it was a good one. A droplet of amber liquid beaded on the side of the glass and slid down onto the white cloth covering the high-top table on the deck.

Decorations coated the area with explosions of white, green, and a generous array of flowers. Lights strung around the railing and draped overhead would set a magical mood once the sun went down.

But no amount of décor could compete with the splashes of orange and yellow across the blue sky. The clear lake mirrored the peaks of the mountains, and the gentle breeze made the trees dance along with the smooth jazz that played while the guests mingled and waited for the newlyweds to arrive.

Andrew loved the stark grandeur of the Colorado Rockies but these Smokies had an entirely different sort of beauty.

"Daddy, can we have cake?" Caroline asked, bouncing up and down on her tiptoes. "It looks so yummy."

"And so pretty," Olivia said. Her dark eyes were wide, her mouth hanging open.

He chuckled, afraid drool would soon drip down his child's chin. "We can't have cake until Tucker and Elizabeth cut it. It's a wedding rule."

The girls groaned.

Lincoln and a petite woman with long brown hair grinned nearby, clearly overhearing the exchange from their spot at the railing. Lincoln turned toward him. "If you want to keep them happy until then, I'm sure Chet has some sweets you can use to bribe them."

The brown-haired woman on his arm slapped him. "You don't mention candy to a child without the parents' permission first. I'm Brooke by the way." She stepped away from her husband's side and offered a slim hand.

Andrew wiped the condensation from his palm before shaking it. "Andrew. It's nice to meet you. And thanks for the backup, although I'm afraid for this trip any kind of limitations on sugar have flown right out the window."

"So where's the candy?" Olivia turned in a full circle with her fisted hands on her hips.

"Liv, don't be rude," he scolded.

Olivia winced. "Sorry, Daddy."

Brooke laughed. "Chet's the cook here and he has a whole table of goodies waiting."

The twins' mouths formed matching o's.

Andrew shook his head, already dreading the sugar crash he saw in their future.

"If you don't mind, I can take them. Laura's helping set things up. You'll be able to see them the whole time." Brooke gestured to the closest window where he spied a giant man with a bushy beard straightening displays of cookies and cupcakes.

"Go ahead. Girls, be good and listen to Ms. Brooke."

He watched his daughters dart inside and go straight to the burly man with a white apron tied around his waist.

"Chet's not as scary as he looks," Lincoln said, taking the seat beside Andrew.

Snorting, Andrew took another sip of scotch. "I'm more worried about whoever those two little monsters are able to con into doing their bidding."

He kept an eye on his daughters as they talked their way into a cupcake and cookie each. Laura met them in front of the dessert table and crouched down to talk to them.

Knowing they were safe, he let his gaze drift. He noted a few familiar faces from the day before, but no sign of Tasha. Irritation clawed at his neck, and he loosened his tie. Just because she'd attended the wedding didn't mean she planned to stay. Damn it. He hadn't thought she'd leave early. If she didn't show for the reception, he'd have to concoct another plan.

"Are the girls having a good time?" Lincoln asked, breaking into his thoughts.

"They love it here. Part of that is because of Audrey, part is they think the lodge is a castle. They haven't even seen the pool."

"I'm surprised Audrey hasn't shown them that yet. She lives in that thing. But I suppose they had plenty to keep them busy yesterday."

"Does Audrey spend a lot of time here?"

"She's like the little mascot. We all fell in love with her when Elizabeth brought her here to keep them safe. Tucker fell head over heels at first sight, but I'm sure you know that story."

Andrew nodded, already aware of how Elizabeth had been forced to face her past when a stalker came after her and Audrey. Tucker had been the last person she wanted to trust since a part of her blamed him for her first husband's death, but in the end, he was the perfect man to keep her safe.

A murmur circulated around the guests. Lincoln stood. "Looks like the happy couple are about to be announced. Your girls will be thrilled to finally get some of that cake."

A quick glance toward the window showed Olivia with white frosting smeared across her cheek and Caroline twirling as Laura and Brooke laughed and clapped. "I think they've had plenty. Let's hope Audrey can distract them from shoving more in their faces."

The double doors to the lodge swung open as the DJ in the corner asked everyone to rise and welcome Mr., Mrs., and Miss Clayman. Cheers erupted. Tucker carried Audrey onto the deck while Elizabeth hoisted her bouquet in the air like a prized trophy.

Andrew was happy for his friends, ignoring the little ache in his heart.

A crowd of people clustered around the makeshift dance floor. The DJ announced the first dance, and Tucker led Elizabeth and Audrey to the middle of the crowd. He held them both close as the music played.

Everyone watched and Andrew caught a flash of blonde hair across the room. Tasha stood in the corner, her back to him, and swayed along with the music as she stared out into the rugged land beyond.

She was here. Adrenaline rushed through his veins. The target was in his sights, and he wouldn't lose track of her again until his mission was complete.

"Daddy! We want to dance!" Caroline clamored.

Laura was now holding both girls' hands as they walked to him.

"Yeah!" Olivia's grin was huge. "And can we spend the night with Audrey and Miss Laura and Miss Brooke? They invited us. We didn't pester."

They'd had multiple talks about the girls not using their weapon of choice: pestering.

Olivia glanced up at Laura like that last statement may not be entirely factual.

If that was the case, Laura didn't rat them out. "Brooke and I are on Audrey duty tonight and we'd love it if your girls could hang with us. I think it would help Audrey too so her mom and new dad can have their wedding night."

He glanced over at Tasha in the corner. Not having to worry about the girls would make planting the transmitter on Tasha's phone a hell of a lot easier.

"As long as you're sure," he said to Laura.

The girls both let out squeals of delight.

"My pleasure." Laura grinned.

"Dance with us, Daddy!" Caroline chanted, jumping up and down.

"Dance with them for a little while, then I'll take over. We're going to have a grand night." Laura raised an eyebrow. "And maybe if I have the girls, it will give you a chance to dance with...*other people*."

He knew exactly who she meant.

The thought of holding Tasha in his arms was both repugnant and yet somehow inviting.

The rest of the guests were starting to take to the dance floor and Andrew led the girls out there. He kept an eye on the blonde head in the corner.

This was the beginning of the end for her, she just didn't know it yet.

TASHA BREATHED in deep and stared at the tiny waves lapping along the lake, allowing the cool wind to blow across her face.

Somehow being outside helped her remain centered. Maybe it was the knowledge that she wasn't trapped within four walls, that she could run if needed.

If Roman showed up to kill her.

Coming here tonight had been a mistake. The longer she stayed the more she knew it was true. Getting close to anyone —even Laura—was a mistake. Trying to fit in this community was a mistake. Constantly finding herself looking at Andrew Zimmerman was definitely a damned mistake.

It was time to move on. She was just trying to gather the strength to do it.

"Please tell me you don't plan to stand here alone all night." Laura appeared out of nowhere and stood beside her.

Tasha shrugged. "Started feeling a little claustrophobic." That was a good as excuse as any.

Laura bumped her shoulder against Tasha's. "But if you don't come back inside, you'll miss seeing the handsome Andrew dancing with his daughters. And that might just be the cutest thing ever."

Unable to resist, Tasha turned and leaned against the railing. She searched the now crowded dance floor until she spotted Andrew spinning his girls around in big circles. Their pretty dresses spun in the air as they giggled, and Andrew's grin was wide.

"He definitely is handsome, I'll give you that." Tasha sighed. Gone were the days where she could giggle with a friend about an attractive man. And definitely not about Andrew.

Laura wrapped an arm around her. "Come inside and have a drink. My last one before I take over babysitting duties. But don't worry, I'll still give you a ride, or line up someone else."

Tasha rubbed her forehead to try to ease a little of the stress there. She hadn't wanted to come this afternoon. Laura had offered to come pick her up before she'd even had a chance to cancel.

She quietly sighed and followed Laura inside.

"I don't even know what you like to drink." Laura tossed the question over her shoulder as she approached the bar. "How is that even possible?"

Because knowing someone's beverage of choice was close-friend territory and Tasha couldn't allow that.

"I'll just take a white wine."

"I'll do the same. Something light before I take over watching the girls for the night."

"Girls? I thought it was just Audrey."

Laura was grinning as she got the wine and handed Tasha her glass. "Change of plans. Brooke and I added two more little ones to the party." Her grin got wider. "Hi, Andrew. Taking a break from dancing?"

The muscles in Tasha's shoulders went rigid. She didn't need to turn around to know he was standing right behind her.

"Yeah, the girls are done for the night, I think. Brooke has all three."

"That's perfect. I was just on my way to hang with them. Now that you're here, Tasha won't have to have her drink alone."

Laura leaned in to Tasha's ear and dropped her volume way low. "P.S.— I left a condom under your pillow when I picked you up. Just in case. You're welcome."

Words of protest jumbled in Tasha's open mouth, but she couldn't get any of them out before Laura patted her shoulder and strolled away, giggling like a schoolgirl.

Damn it.

Andrew's deep rumble of laughter curled her toes. "She's very friendly."

Tasha let out a half sigh/half laugh. "But not very subtle." And he didn't know the half of it.

JANIE CROUCH & DANIELLE M. HAAS

Releasing a long, steady breath, she finally turned around. He was closer than she'd anticipated, his broad chest inches from her. He'd lost his tie and rolled his shirtsleeves to his elbows—a lethally sexy combination that made her mouth dry. His dark hair was tousled, as though he'd ran his hands through it countless times.

What would it feel like to run her fingers through that gorgeous head of hair? To roam her knuckles along the corded muscles of his forearm? Her stomach twisted and heat crashed against her cheeks.

"Are you okay?" he asked, eyes narrowing. "Do you need to sit down? You look a little flushed."

He nestled her elbow in his warm palm and led her to a seating area away from the commotion of the reception still going at full force.

She settled onto the couch cushion and took a too-big sip of her wine before situating the glass on the coffee table in front of her. The fruity taste coated her tongue and burned down her throat, before calming her nerves. Her elbow tingled from where he'd touched her.

When was the last time a man had touched her at all? Much less in a way that had her wanting to move closer.

No. She couldn't get caught up in the romance and happiness surrounding her. Couldn't allow her mind to wander to the *what-if*'s and *wouldn't-it-be-nice* fantasies.

Especially not with this man.

"Tasha?"

The soft sound of her name snapped her back to the moment. She forced a smile. "Sorry. I zoned out for a second."

He grinned and sat on the seat beside her, his knees angled toward hers. "I get it. Weddings are fun but make for long days. Especially when the day starts before dawn."

She winced and clutched her bag tightly on her lap. "Yikes. Not a morning person, huh?"

"Not when I barely slept on a too-small couch. Believe it or not, that was better than the bed with two squirming rugrats." He chuckled and took a sip of water.

"Yoga would be good to stretch you out a little."

He wrinkled his nose.

Laughing, she held up her palms, leaving her bag on her lap. "Sorry. Hazard of the trade, I guess. Always trying to recruit new people."

He grinned. "Nah, I get it. I'm sure it'd be great, but not really my thing. Like to do anything else other than yoga?"

She struggled to find something she could share. "Uh… gardening."

If you could call the four plants in her tiny bungalow gardening. She'd had a garden at home before she'd found out what the Volkov family business really was.

Amazing how she missed her garden more than anything.

"Gardening. Really?"

"Is that surprising?"

He rubbed the back of his neck. "A little. My grandma gardened. I always picture little old ladies kneeling on those little foam mats, complaining about dirty nails and mulch in their hair."

The image brought out more laughter. "Well, gardening isn't for everyone. I like figuring out ways to make my space beautiful. How to mix and match the unexpected to create something magical. Leaving a small piece of myself behind for the next person to discover and love."

He frowned. "Do you leave things behind a lot?"

Shit. She'd let more slip than she should have. "No more than anyone else searching for their place in life I suppose." Flustered, she rose and searched the room for Laura. Damn it, this was a terrible night not to have her own mode of transportation. She needed to get out of here.

Andrew stood. "Did I say something wrong?"

"No, it's just getting late and I have early classes to teach in the morning. I should get going."

"You just downed a glass of wine pretty quickly," he said, dipping his chin to her empty glass. "You might want to wait a little bit before you get behind the wheel."

"I didn't drive. Laura did. She was going to take me home before coming back to help with Audrey. And now, I guess your girls too." This was about to get even more awkward. "Um, do you mind if I borrow your phone for a second?"

He looked even more shocked than she'd expected. "*You* want to borrow *my* phone?"

A nervous laugh spilled from her lips. "I want to look up the number of a cab company and call for one."

"Where's your phone?"

"I, um, forgot it," she lied. Her burner phone was mostly for emergencies only. She used it occasionally, but didn't carry it with her. Better to stay off grid as much as possible. "It's at home."

He shook his head like the thought was unfathomable.

"What?" she asked.

He shook his head and smiled, although the smile didn't seem quite genuine. "I, uh... Most people are just glued to their phones, that's all."

That was because most people had friends and family they wanted to stay in touch with. Or social media accounts where they wanted to upload cute pictures. Tasha didn't have any of those.

"Not me, I guess." She shrugged.

"I can take you home."

She blinked up at him. "What? No. You're here with your friends, and you have the girls. You don't want to leave to drive me into town."

"The girls are with Laura and Brooke—totally not interested in me. Honestly it would be no bother. And seriously, do they even have cabs in a town this small?"

He had an excellent point. She tried to find a good reason to tell him no and refuse his offer, but nothing came to mind.

He reached out and touched her elbow. She could almost feel the heat of his fingers through the thin fabric of her sleeve.

She wanted him to keep touching her.

What harm could it do? One short car ride where she could pretend that this was an attractive man being chivalrous, who was attracted to her too. She could pretend like she'd never met him before and failed him in worst of ways. She could pretend like he'd like to keep touching her as much as she'd like him to do so.

For one short car ride she could pretend like her life was normal and she wasn't exhausted, lonely, and scared nearly every day of her life.

What could it hurt?

Chapter 6

For the first time Tasha regretted all the locks she'd had installed on the front door of the little bungalow she rented downtown. Her sweat-slicked palm made inserting the key in all the small holes more difficult than it should be.

"You didn't have to walk me to my door," she said over her shoulder as she struggled to get into her home.

The car ride into town had been filled with more conversation and laughter than she'd expected.

Andrew himself was more than she'd expected.

He shoved his hands in the front pockets of his pants and gave a little shrug. The faint glow of the moon beamed down on him, making him look almost boyish. "I promised to see you home safe. Can't do that if you're standing outside in the dark by yourself, trying to get in to the fortress of solitude."

She was glad the porch light wasn't on so he couldn't see the blush creeping into her cheeks. "A single girl can never be too safe."

Finally, she unfastened the last lock. Hesitation had her turning the knob slowly.

He stood on the little stoop, smiling down at her.

"Do you want to come in for some coffee or tea?" She couldn't stop the words from escaping her lips.

She held her breath, afraid he'd make some awkward excuse and walk off. But also, equally afraid he'd say yes.

His smile grew. "Yeah, thanks. Better make it decaf though."

"I can handle that." She swung open the door and stepped inside, flipping on lights as she moved through the living room to the kitchen beyond. "Come on in."

The tiny house was old, the small rooms separated instead of the modern open concept builds. Neither the heat nor the air conditioning worked well and it was all in need of a better paint job, but she didn't mind. It was clean and close to work. And most importantly, the rent didn't cut in to much of her very limited finances.

Andrew stayed so close behind her she could almost feel the heat of his body with every step. Her nerves were so jittery, even decaffeinated coffee would be too much for her system. She set her bag on the laminate counter and busied herself readying the coffee pot.

Leaning against the counter, he hooked his ankles and watched her. "This is nice. Have you lived here long?"

She snorted. *Nice* wasn't the word she'd use to describe her shabby surroundings. The only thing she knew about Andrew was that he was in International Finance—even though she wasn't exactly sure how that had tied to Roman. Regardless, he was probably used to higher quality things. Not the avocado-colored refrigerator that hummed so loudly she could hear it when she slept or the two-person table she'd saved from a salvage yard, then restored.

"Thanks, it's nice enough. I've been here awhile," she said, making sure to keep her answer as vague as possible.

"How about yoga? Always been into that?" He leaned an elbow onto the counter behind him.

"I like things that can quiet my mind. It's why I like gardening as well." She hoped he didn't ask to see it. Her current four potted plants weren't very impressive as far as gardens went.

But she could throw them in her car at a moment's notice if she needed to get out of town.

"How about family? Got anybody nearby?"

"My mom...isn't far from here." That wasn't totally untrue. "Beyond that, none to really speak of."

She turned to get mugs from the cabinet. She didn't want to talk about her family. Couldn't stand the thought of talking about her family with him after what had happened.

Her fingers tightened around the mugs. What was she doing, talking to Andrew like he truly was some handsome stranger she'd just met at mutual friends' wedding.

Talking to him like he wouldn't be running for the hills right now if he knew she was Roman's half-sister.

Her back still turned to him she reached over to get a spoon out of the drawer next to her.

"Is that your phone in with your silverware?"

She spun to find him way too close to her. She let out a breathless laugh. "This place is pretty old. This is the only drawer in the kitchen that works. If I keep it in here whenever I'm home, I know I won't misplace it."

She'd learned the hard way a couple years ago to make sure she had an exact place for everything so she could pack up and leave in under a minute. She had a bugout bag—a backpack—in the coat closet near the front door that held some clothes and all the cash she could spare. She could grab it, the Glock, and her phone, and rush out immediately if needed.

"That's certainly one way not to lose it."

He was so close. Those brown eyes filled her whole line of

vision. His scent—a subtle cologne mixed with something uniquely *him*—was pulling at her.

Before she even knew what she was going to do, she'd closed the distance between them, her lips meeting his.

It had been so damned long—literally *years*—since she'd been close to a man like this. Honestly, she hadn't even wanted to. Just surviving had taken up all of her energy and focus.

But she wanted this man.

Until he stiffened and began pulling away.

God, what had she done? She was such a fucking idiot. She didn't even open her eyes as she began to apologize. She blamed Laura and the whole *condom-under-the-pillow* statement earlier planting ideas in her head.

"Andrew, I'm so sorry. I don't know what I was think—"

Her words were cut off by his mouth crashing back into hers. Her mouth open as she let out a surprised squeak and his tongue took advantage. The mugs in her hands clattered to the counter as he devoured her lips.

This…this was beyond anything she'd ever felt, even back before she'd found out the truth about her family and lived a carefree existence doing whatever she wanted.

His fingers slid into her hair, destroying the bun she'd fashioned for the wedding. He tilted her head so he could better access her mouth. Her hands trailed up his arms and wrapped around his wide shoulders.

It wasn't until his fingers found the zipper at the back of her dress that reason came back to her. She couldn't have him take her dress off here in the kitchen as much as she wanted him to. There was too much light. He would have too many questions about the scars that riddled her shoulders and back.

Questions there was no way she could answer.

He pulled back when he felt her stiffen and ran a hand through his hair. "I took it too far. I—"

"No, you didn't." She forced the words out quickly before

she got too nervous to say them. She *wanted* him. "I just would rather take this to the bedroom if it's okay with you."

His brown eyes were tortured now. He was going to say no. This wasn't what he really wanted.

She wasn't what he really wanted.

She forced a smile. "Don't worry about it. No harm, no foul. I—"

Her breath came out in a squeak once more when his hands slid down her sides, then back up, pulling the soft material of her dress with it as he went. As soon as it was past her knees, he reached down and scooped her up in his arms, taking her weight.

"Which way to your room?"

His eyes looked different—harder, more intent—for the second she saw them before his mouth locked on hers again. She tilted her head in the direction of the bedroom. This place wasn't that big. He'd find it.

His lips stayed pressed against hers as he easily carried her weight. Thankfully he didn't turn on the lights as he lowered her to the bed and continued to slide her dress up her legs.

His mouth made its way back to hers but somehow the kisses felt different. More deliberate.

What did that even mean?

It wasn't like it was bad. The opposite in fact. Every stroke of Andrew's tongue in her mouth caused heat to course through her whole body. And his hands sliding up her thighs and peeling off her plain cotton panties wasn't helping quench that heat.

His lips moved down her jaw before stopping. He let out a groan. "I don't have a condom."

"Actually, I do." She silently thanked Laura for her obnoxious meddling, while praying she'd been telling the truth.

He froze. "Right. Of course."

She slid her hand under the pillow and sure enough it was there. She held it up.

It was light enough for him to make out what she was holding, but not enough for him to be able to make out any details about her body. That was good. Although she wished she could see his eyes again like she could in the kitchen.

She heard the condom wrapper rip and she stiffened. They were both still nearly fully dressed.

"Andrew, I—" She faded off. She wasn't sure what she wanted to say. That she wanted more? That it had been a long time for her? That she wanted him to kiss her again like he had in the kitchen?

Because his lips were on hers again, but it still felt different. Good, but...*different.*

His hand slid under her dress to cup her breast, his lips moving back to her throat and she forgot what she was going to say anyway. She focused on the feeling of having him close. Having his breath mingled with hers.

His hand slid down her thigh and spread her legs so he could fit his trim hips between them. A second later he pushed inside her, filling her to the hilt.

Pain froze her to the bed. She'd thought she'd been ready, but she wasn't.

He froze. "Tasha?"

"I'm sorry. I— I—"

She breathed in and out for a second. It wasn't so bad now that her body was adjusting to his length. A moment later he reached between their bodies and touched her, giving her the pressure she needed to let out a groan.

All the pain disappeared as her body softened at his touch. His lips found her throat once again, sucking gently with the same rhythm his fingers were strumming between her legs.

Then he began moving his body once more. Her arms

wrapped around his shoulders as she hooked one leg around his hips.

Yes, *this*. Maybe it wasn't exactly what she'd wanted but it was so much more than she'd had in so long.

He slid his fingers from her clit and hiked his arm under one knee, giving him deeper penetration.

She breathed out his name as his thrusts came faster and the heat in her body built back up pushing her higher and she silently tripped over the edge. She gripped his shoulders and buried her face in his neck as the tiny shockwaves ran through her.

Yes. She wanted more. More of him. More of this.

It took her a second to realize he'd stopped moving. Had he finished? Maybe he was just really quiet during sex. His breathing was as labored as hers. But he felt stiff. Tense.

"Um." Lord, she had no idea how to broach this subject. "Are you okay? Is there something you'd like, um, me to do? To help you...finish?"

He lifted his weight up onto his arms and pulled out of her. "No, I'm...great. It's fine."

She must've been mistaken. "Okay. Good." God, this felt so awkward.

"I'm just going to get some water."

She covered her eyes with her arm as he got out of bed, not that she could see him anyway. Maybe while he was gone she could figure out what to say.

Maybe if she explained that it had been a long time for her. Even joke about how Laura had been the one to leave the condom under her pillow. Surely that would break the ice.

But there was no sound of running water from the kitchen. The only sound she heard a minute later was her door being opened and Andrew leaving.

Chapter 7

"We've found two more of Roman Volkov's calling cards and are fairly certain a break-in at a pharmaceutical lab was orchestrated by the Volkov Cartel also."

Andrew was back in the Zodiac active mission room.

And if anything, he was more exhausted than he'd been the last time he was here a month ago.

The nightmares about Kylie's death were back, stealing his sleep every evening. But this time the faceless angel that had saved him and the girls that night had a face.

Tasha's.

After what happened between them in Pine Valley a month ago, Andrew couldn't even begin to process how fucked up it was that it was Tasha saving him in his dreams.

He scrubbed a hand down his face and tried to concentrate on what Ian DeRose and Callum Webb were saying. It could basically be summarized in one sentence:

Roman Volkov and his merry band of terrorists were back in full swing.

"Where was the pharmaceutical lab?" Ian asked Callum.

"Cincinnati."

"What was taken?"

"Opioids that will make a pretty penny on the black market."

Ian ran his hand through his dark hair. "How about Roman's murder victims? Where were they?"

"One was in Dallas." Callum thumbed through the file in front of him. "The other was in Atlanta. Cartel is bouncing around, as usual. We only know the victims were related because of the infamous calling card."

Andrew hadn't been part of tracking the Volkovs over the past month. He'd done his part. He had the girls now and they were solely his responsibility. No more active missions.

Especially since the last active mission with Tasha had been…*definitely* not his finest hour.

What the hell had he been thinking?

He hadn't been thinking. That was the problem.

And then he hadn't been able to *stop* thinking about her since then.

He wasn't proud of what he'd done—how he'd handled the whole situation—even if planting the transmitter on his way out the door had meant a successful mission.

"The bug you planted isn't working," Ian said.

Okay, maybe it hadn't been a successful mission.

Andrew shook his head. "I planted it on her cell phone. I am one hundred percent sure it was hers."

Because she kept it in the silverware drawer. That had somehow been…*endearing* to him.

Right before everything had completely unraveled.

He hadn't told anyone at Zodiac Tactical exactly how he'd gotten the transmitter on Tasha's phone. Definitely hadn't brought up the fact that he'd slept with her to do it.

Not that any of his colleagues would have judged him for it —they'd all had to make ethically questionable decisions over the course of their career. But the whole situation already

Code Name: Gemini

made him feel like an asshole and sharing the details with his friends would just make it worse.

What the fuck had he been thinking?

"No, the transmitter functions," Callum said. Andrew had to drag his attention back to the conversation at hand. "We've been able to gather intel from her phone based on its transmissions."

He scrubbed a hand down his face. "What sort of intel have you gotten from it?"

"Mostly completely innocuous. Local numbers that check out with businesses and established contacts of hers based on what you've told us."

When he arrived home after the wedding, Andrew had done a complete debrief about the mission. He'd included the fact that she'd invited him into her home, but had left out the sex. In the report, he'd listed any person he was aware of having contact with Tasha.

"Mostly calls or texts to and from a Laura Metcalf."

Andrew nodded. Not surprising. "Anything useful whatsoever?"

Callum leaned back in his chair. "Tasha has checked a couple of known chatrooms and websites that are connected to Roman and the cartel."

That was a start. "Anything that we can move on?"

"Unfortunately, no. Every site she accessed that was tied to the cartel was either outdated or one we were already aware of and monitoring. She hasn't made any attempts to communicate or contact Roman directly. At least not with that phone."

Andrew could feel frustration eat at him. The man who had ordered Kylie's death was still alive and still actively committing crimes.

And damn it, he needed what had happened a month ago between him and Tasha to not be for nothing.

63

He rubbed the back of his neck. "It's possible she has another phone."

Callum nodded. "We've already considered that, and it's definitely a possibility. But, given that she has utilized this phone to hit certain websites that are red-flagged makes us think a secondary phone is unlikely."

Ian leaned back in his chair. "Callum and I both feel like Tasha is still the best bet for good intel. Is there anything you've thought of in the past month you might not have mentioned in the initial debrief? You know the drill—no detail is too small."

Andrew took a calming breath in through his nose and blew it out through his mouth, trying to think of Tasha neutrally.

Not what she felt like underneath him.

Not what the smooth skin of her inner thighs felt like under his fingers.

Not how she'd felt wrapped around his—

He cleared his throat. "The suspect seemed relatively well-liked, although all indications are that she is a loner. The Laura Metcalf phone calls don't surprise me–Laura definitely appears to be Tasha's closest friend."

Ian nodded. "And these people in Pine Valley…you trust them?"

Andrew shrugged. "I'm really only close with Elizabeth and Tucker, but would trust that who they choose to associate with would be non-criminals. The Crossroads Mountain Retreat has been around for years and has done a lot of good work for former law enforcement and military—people suffering with PTSD."

"That doesn't mean people linked to the retreat might not be criminals," Callum pointed out.

Andrew nodded. "Agreed. But honestly, the people associated with Crossroads is not where I would spend my time looking."

Callum nodded. "Okay. Tasha's cover in town is a yoga instructor. Do you see how that would be useful to the cartel in any way?"

Andrew shook his head. "Honestly, no. But it does give her access to a number of different people. Maybe there's a target there she's attempting to find out more about."

He watched as Callum and Ian shot each other a look, as if that was a topic they'd already discussed.

With a nod, Ian leaned forward and pressed the intercom button on conference table phone. "Can you send Isaac in? Thank you."

Andrew sat up straighter. "Isaac Baxter? Isn't he stationed in Europe?"

"He returned stateside last week. After some discussion, Callum and I thought that he might be a good fit for the next part of this mission."

A weight sunk in Andrew's chest. He didn't know Isaac well, but he already had a good idea of what the plan was if Isaac was being called in to help.

"We feel like getting someone in Pine Valley for a couple weeks to truly get close to Tasha is the best bet," Ian continued. "Someone who can infiltrate her daily life and find out what she's doing and how she normally contacts her brother. Obviously, it's not with her phone so maybe they meet face-to-face or something."

Isaac walked in and offered everyone a friendly smile. The guy looked like a fucking movie star. "What's going on, boss? Landon said you had a mission for me. Something about the Volkov Cartel."

Ian nodded. "We've got the long-lost Volkov sister hanging out in a tiny town in Tennessee. We need to use her to get to her brother."

"Andrew got a transmitter on her phone but that hasn't

provided us much intel," Callum added. "We need somebody who can work with her on a daily basis. Get intimate with her."

"A Romeo mission." Isaac's smile fell just slightly.

"I know they're not your favorite," Ian said. "And if we had more time and if Roman Volkov would fucking stop killing people, we would go about this in a more appropriate manner. But, unfortunately, that's not a luxury we currently have. We've got to move hard and fast and this woman is the best route."

It didn't take a genius to see that Isaac wasn't thrilled with this idea but he was still going to agree.

"I'll do it." The words were out of Andrew's mouth before he knew he was going to say them.

All three of the other men turned to stare at him. None of them said anything.

"I've already met Tasha and connected with her," he continued.

Connected could mean quite a few things in this situation, but he wasn't about to elaborate.

"Sending somebody else in now on a Romeo mission might make her suspicious since I was just"—Andrew forced himself not to grimace—"*flirting* with her at the wedding."

Ian glanced over at Callum and then back at Andrew. "To be honest, you were our first choice but we didn't think…" He faded off with a shrug.

"That I'd be up to it? That I'm capable of handling a situation like this on an active mission?"

"No." Ian's response was tight. "*You* took yourself out of the field, not me. I've never doubted your abilities. But what about your girls?"

"If we're talking about a couple of weeks, I'll leave them with Gavin and Lexi. Lexi's been asking to take them to

Disney World and the girls will be beside themselves with happiness."

His brother and sister-in-law hadn't had any children of their own yet and considered the girls good practice for when they finally did.

"Andrew, are you sure?" Callum asked. "When we say we didn't want to ask you it's truly not because we didn't think you were capable. Asking someone to seduce the sister of the man who killed their wife seems too much to ask of anyone."

Andrew should come clean right now and tell them the full story of what had happened at Tasha's house a month ago. If anything, it would help ease their worries about whether he could do this.

But he couldn't force the words out.

He was…*conflicted*.

Yeah, he was ashamed he'd slept with the sister of the man who'd had his wife killed.

But more, he was ashamed at how he'd done it. How bad it must have been for Tasha.

Wham, bam, and not even a thank you, ma'am.

He shouldn't care how poor the experience was for her—that wasn't what was important. But somehow, he did.

"I'll handle it," he forced out. "Nothing is more critical to me than taking down Roman Volkov."

"You left things good between you and Tasha?" Callum asked. "With a plausible reason for why you'd be back a month later showing up again?"

"I'll handle it," he said again. He was going to have to start with an apology and hope that was enough to get her to talk to him at all.

Ian studied him, eyes narrowed, like he could tell there was something Andrew wasn't admitting. But he didn't press. "Okay, we'll work up the full plan while you get your daughters situated. We've already manipulated her situation to put some financial pressure on her. She picked up a shift at the local diner."

Andrew nodded. That wasn't an uncommon practice when trying to get a perp to do something. Breaking up their comfortable life was often a good first step.

Isaac will run backup for you on this mission, but will stay out of sight unless needed."

Andrew glanced over at the younger man who nodded.

"Whatever you need, man." Isaac offered a friendly smile again. "Honestly, I'm happy not to take point."

It looked like Andrew was going back to Pine Valley.

Back to Tasha Volkov.

A FEW HOURS later Andrew was wading through the mounds of dresses and swimsuits that cluttered the pink rug in Olivia and Caroline's room. His head spun as the girls chattered excitedly about their trip to Disney World.

They hadn't even blinked at the thought of losing Dad for a couple of weeks.

"I don't want my Belle dress, I want my Cinderella one," Olivia said, a small whine in her voice.

Caroline fisted her tiny hands on her hips. "But that's my dress. I'm always Cinderella."

Andrew had to swallow a laugh, or he'd be forced to deal with the girls' wrath. Their argument might seem silly to him, but to his twins, which princess they dressed up as while visiting the most magical place on earth was a big deal.

"Why can't you share?" He asked as he picked up clothes and folded them before placing them in a giant suitcase on Olivia's bed.

After his world had been turned upside down and his home destroyed, he'd opted for a place tucked away from as many people as possible. Security was his biggest concern, and both his property and house were decked-out with state-of-the-art equipment that he could monitor from anywhere.

But the girls had decorating jurisdiction over the room they shared. Which meant pink rugs and walls, frilly white curtains, and princess bedspreads. The home was big enough for them each to have their own space, but they chose to stay together. A decision he loved because if the worst happened, they'd be in one place where he could scoop them both up and carry them to safety.

Never again did he want to feel like he wasn't in a position to get his family to safety.

"Share?" Caroline asked, brows pinched. "How can we share who we are?"

He struggled not to smile. "But isn't that the fun of make believe? You can change who you are every single day. You have plenty of dresses. You could each be a different princess every single day."

The girls turned to stare at each other, shrugged, then grinned—clearly on board with his solution.

If only his own life were so simple. If he could just change who he was every day depending on his mood or what was on his agenda.

"Daddy, I wish you could come with us. You're going to miss eating in castles and riding all the fun rides." Olivia snuggled up beside him and hugged his legs.

He held his daughter close. "I wish I could too, baby girl."

But even more he wanted to put an end to the Volkovs.

Olivia and Caroline would forget he hadn't tagged along with all the fun their aunt and uncle would heap on them.

"My bag's all packed," Caroline announced from across the room. She beamed with pride, her backpack at her foot overflowing with stuffed animals and coloring books.

"Good job," he said, not wanting to ruffle her feathers by

telling her she needed to take some things out. He'd finished getting them properly packed after they went to bed.

Tomorrow he'd turn his precious daughters over to his brother, knowing Gavin was more than capable of protecting them.

Then he'd find a way back into Tasha Volkov's life.

Chapter 8

Tasha wiped off the dirty table in the Chill N' Grill and glanced out the window before hurrying by the cluster of people waiting to be seated. She flashed a quick smile. "I'll be right with you folks."

They nodded then returned to their conversation.

April showers hadn't let up for the past week, perfectly matching Tasha's mood.

When she'd moved to Pine Valley six months ago, she hadn't expected much. That had changed slowly over time, providing her with some friends and a place where she didn't feel like she constantly had to look over her shoulder.

A place where her luck was finally turning.

Then Andrew Zimmerman had crashed into her life the month before, with his unremarkable sex, and cast some kind of bad omen over her very existence. And her luck had turned to shit.

Various repairs from breakdowns of damned near everything had meant her savings had dwindled down to nothing, making the money she earned teaching yoga harder and harder to stretch. She'd had to pick up another job that paid in cash and didn't ask many questions.

She rushed back over and sat the people by the door, handing them menus before delivering food to another table.

Lucky for her, she'd gotten to know the grill's owner, Wade McKenzie, over the past few months and he'd agreed to give her several waitress shifts a week. He'd raised a brow at her request for cash payments, but had agreed when she'd made something up about a bank account issue she'd hoped to get fixed soon.

So here she was, the girl who'd gone to some of the most exclusive boarding schools in Europe and worn all the best designers for most of her life, now a part-time waitress.

And fine, maybe she couldn't blame Andrew Zimmerman for all her bad luck, and certainly not for this ongoing rain, but that night a month ago had seemed to start the downward spiral.

She brought water refills to yet another table.

Then, if her low funds and bruised ego weren't enough, she'd discovered chatter of Roman's renewed interest in finding her. She'd gotten on her burner phone and ancient laptop and accessed some sites she'd first discovered when she'd learned the truth about her family and their terrorist ties.

On that chat room there were multiple posts of Roman searching for her. They were disguised as pleas for her to come home, encoded by referring to her as "Birthday Girl" since Tasha meant birthday in Russian.

A shudder tickled her spine. Roman would only have one reason for wanting to unite with her: to make her pay for going against the family. Definitely not to *celebrate* her.

Her half-brother had always hated her, his jealously over their father's relationship with Tasha's mother driving a constant wedge between them. Then the jealousy had festered over the years, growing into a toxic hate she was helpless to stop.

Then three years ago she'd gone up against him directly then run.

She had no doubt if Roman found her, it wasn't going to be for a joyful reunion.

She pushed the thoughts away and wiped down a table that had emptied then walked back toward the kitchen.

"Earth to Tasha!"

Blinking back to the present, Tasha found herself face-to-face with Laura who was sitting by herself at the bar. Rain dotted her hunter green jacket.

"Hey, you. Sorry. My brain is in a dozen different places."

"I can tell. How have you been? I feel like we haven't had a chance to talk much since Tucker and Elizabeth's wedding."

Tasha tossed the towel she was holding over her shoulder, and grimaced. "Sorry. Things have been crazy."

And she'd known that Laura would push about Andrew—want to know all the details about him taking her home. She'd managed to keep her friend at bay by saying it hadn't worked out, and then try to mostly avoid her all together.

Tasha didn't know why she was keeping what had happened between her and Andrew a secret. Laura would be the first to bring over a bottle of wine and talk shit with her about a bad lay.

But somehow Tasha didn't want to do that.

She didn't know why. Maybe because of what her family had done to his. Maybe because she'd thought about him so often for the past three years, even though she hadn't known his name. Maybe because she'd found him so attractive when she'd been afraid that part of her—the *passionate* part of her—had withered and died in the constant fight for her own survival.

Yeah, the sex had been adequate at best. And yeah, she

was glad she would never have to see him again. But still, she didn't want to share the details of that night.

She didn't want to share how disappointed she'd been. Not necessarily with the sex—that could've been fixed with a little effort and communication. But with him running away without a word.

Laura squeezed her hand. "I'm sorry you're having to work here. I know Zoe wishes she had more work for you at the yoga studio so you didn't have to get a second job. She mentioned something about you becoming a certified trainer so you could teach more classes."

Tasha wished she could take her boss up on that offer but becoming certified as a trainer in another fitness area meant taking classes, which meant her name and information in one more database. Something she couldn't risk.

She forced a smile. "Yeah, maybe at some point. Right now I'm happy here and like staying as busy as possible."

Okay, so that was a lie. Picking up shifts after teaching made her feet ache each night and the muscles in her neck scream. She might be in better shape than most, but perfecting downward dog didn't help much with hauling around heavy plates and dealing with demanding customers.

But she did like being busy. At least then she didn't have time to sit around and think about...*people*. Or disappointments.

"Sorry, I've got to go," she said before Laura could get in another word. "We're swamped. I need to go grab a table's order."

Laura nodded, as if understanding Tasha didn't want to be pushed right now. "I'll make Wade grab my order. We can catch up later."

"I'd like that." She flashed a quick smile then changed direction to the group of middle-aged women who'd come in the door and were brushing off rain. That area was going to need to be mopped soon.

"Hi, ladies." Tasha offered them a smile. "Four of you today?"

"Yep," a round blonde said. "It's been one hell of a morning for all of us, and with the rain coming down in buckets, we'll probably be here for a while."

Great. Nothing like a group setting up camp during one of the busiest times of the day. The most she could hope was they left a big tip.

"Not a problem," she said, ushering them to the table by the fireplace. She hated the large buck head mounted above the stone hearth but complaining about taxidermy—especially the kind killed and stuffed by the owner's father—was a sure-fire way to stick out in Pine Valley.

"Menus are on the table," Tasha continued as the women situated themselves around the table. "I can grab drinks now or come back."

"I'll take a tall drink of that." The leggy brunette wiggled her eyebrows and flicked her wrist toward the door.

Tasha turned and froze.

Andrew Zimmerman had just stepped inside.

"Hubba hubba," one of the ladies said behind her. "I haven't seen him around town. I'd have noticed that for sure."

"Oh shush." Giggles by all. "Benji would die if he heard his perfect little wife ogling another man."

"There's nothing wrong with looking."

Heat climbed to Tasha's cheeks, and she tore her gaze from Andrew. She couldn't even wrap her thoughts around how she was feeling.

He looked good, that was for sure.

After what had happened between them, he definitely wasn't here for her. Her best plan would be to avoid him altogether.

Definitely not let him know that he'd hurt her with his actions.

Grabbing her order pad, she turned expectedly back to the ladies. "Sorry gals, I can't get you any of him but how about some water? Or maybe a mimosa to warm you from this wet cold front we can't escape?"

All four women squealed and nodded.

"Perfect. Let me get those for you, then I'll come back to take your orders."

She caught a glimpse of Andrew making his way to the bar. Straight toward Laura.

Shit. Laura would tell him Tasha was working. She had no reason not to.

Of course, he might not even ask at all. She didn't know which was worse.

She couldn't hide until he left and still expect to make any decent tips today. She'd have to confront him.

But damn it, she'd do it with her head held high and pretend like he hadn't bruised the hell out of her ego.

Lifting her chin, she tucked her order pad back in the dirty apron tied around her waist and weaved through the tables to the bar before he could get to Laura.

As if sensing her, Andrew turned, and their eyes met. His widened slightly then he lifted a hand. His face pinched in a way that told her he might be as uncomfortable with this encounter as she was.

Good.

"Andrew Zimmerman." Her lips pressed in a tight line. "Never in a hundred years did I think I'd see you in here today. At all ever again, actually."

He flinched slightly and she knew her point had hit home. "I was in the mood for some good atmosphere. I hear this place is the best in town."

She snorted although he wasn't wrong. The Chill N' Grill

was a staple in Pine Valley. The food was always good, the service friendly, and the beer cold. Not to mention a honky tonk atmosphere that made costumers feel like kicking up their feet and having a good time.

She raised one eyebrow. "You came a long way for lunch. Are the girls with you?"

"No," he said, shaking his head, still looking sheepish. "This was a trip I needed to do alone, or at least this part of it. They don't need to see their daddy groveling at a nice woman's feet, begging her forgiveness for being an ass."

She froze. That wasn't at all what she'd thought he was going to say.

"I don't think that's necessary." She crossed her arms over her chest slowly. "We both knew you were only in town for the weekend."

"That's not what I mean, and you know it." He took a step closer and all other sounds in the restaurant seemed to fade to nothing.

"Actually I don't. I don't know anything about you, do I? I found that out pretty quickly."

His full lips pressed more firmly. "I shouldn't have done what I did."

She tilted her head to the side and stepped slightly closer so no one else could hear. "You'll have to be more specific. You shouldn't have been so bland in bed or shouldn't have left without saying a word?"

He flinched again.

Damn it, she needed to stop. What good was this doing? What was done was done.

She ran a hand over her ponytail and twirled the ends around her finger. "Listen. What happened wasn't a big deal. No harm, no foul. It's nice seeing you again, but I need to get back to work."

He rested a hand on her forearm to stop her from leaving,

and the familiar zing of energy zipped through her body.

"My taking off on you was a big deal, and it has eaten me up inside ever since. I need you to understand something." His voice thickened, and he cleared his throat. "You're the first woman I've been with since my wife died."

All of Tasha's righteous anger fled. So he had had a reason for acting the way he did. It was totally understandable. She closed her eyes for a beat. "Andrew, that's got to be so hard. I don't know what to say."

"Not much for you to say. For me, there's a lot. A lot I want to explain. To apologize for. Hell, maybe even to do over. Do you think we could grab dinner tonight?"

"I can't."

"Because you don't want to, or because you have plans? I'm in town a few more days. Maybe we can meet tomorrow instead."

She shook her head, hating how much she wanted to agree to dinner. But she'd already risked too much the night she'd slept with him, only for him to crush her. She didn't want to go through that again.

"I have classes to teach tonight, and I'm booked solid tomorrow. I appreciate the apology and explanation, but really, there's no need. Honestly, maybe you did us both a favor. I've never had a one-night stand, and it was bound to be awkward. You spared us that."

He ran his fingers through that thick hair. "It's not just how I left. It's how I treated you. I pulled away, pulled back. I got in my head. I felt guilty, like I was cheating on Kylie. I didn't want to stop, but I didn't know how to keep going. I ended up making a mess of things and ruining a great night with an amazing woman."

She finally smiled. "Thank you. You didn't need to come down here to tell me that, even if it's nice to hear, nonetheless.

But I really do need to get back to work. I have mimosas to make and orders to take before heading to job number two."

"Okay," he said, finally taking his hand off her arm. "But like I said, I'll be around. If you change your mind, I'm doing some work at Crossroads, so I'll be staying there."

"Have a good trip." Unable to resist, she pressed a quick kiss to his cheek then walked away without another look.

A heaviness pressed down on her shoulders, despite learning it wasn't her fault he'd ran away without an explanation or goodbye. His life was complicated and messy.

Just like her own.

But their two lives could never intersect. Could never be joined in a way that would maybe give them both what they wanted—what they *needed*. So there was no reason to delay the inevitable. Andrew Zimmerman needed to stay out of her life for good, even if every ounce of her being screamed to see him again.

She walked by Laura, who snagged her hand and forced her to stop.

"Was that Andrew you were just talking to? Are you all right? You look a little shaky."

She didn't want to lie to her friend. Not in this moment. So she gave as much of the truth as she could allow. "Yeah, that was him. Says he's in town for a few days. He wants to have dinner but I told him no."

Laura's mouth fell open. "Why?"

Tasha glanced over her shoulder at Andrew as he walked out the door. "Because spending time with Andrew is a hazard I can't afford."

Chapter 9

Slivers of downtown Pine Valley were visible through the sheet of rain outside the rental car as Andrew directed Isaac to Tasha's small house.

"That's the one," he said, flicking a finger toward the white bungalow with black shutters and a weather-worn front door.

"You sure she won't come home any time soon?"

"She said she has a couple classes to teach once she finishes her shift at the restaurant."

"Did you make plans to see her later tonight?" Isaac asked as he drove a little further down the block so they wouldn't be parking right in front of her place. The storm was keeping almost everyone inside, but they didn't want to draw undue attention to themselves while Andrew broke into Tasha's place.

He didn't want to mention that Tasha had turned him down cold. But he couldn't blame her for how she was feeling.

Bland in bed.

He gritted his teeth at her words, although if that was the worst thing she said about him, then he was getting off pretty damned lightly.

Worrying about that should be way down on Andrew's list

of priorities. Good sex had not been part of the mission parameters. He'd done what he'd needed to do to get that transmitter on her phone.

But Tasha was right. It had been bland at best.

He hadn't been lying when he told her it had been the first time he'd had sex since Kylie died. And he hadn't been lying when he'd suggested it had messed with his head.

It had. It still did.

And yet here he was, back, ready to do it with her again.

And if he was honest with himself: *wanting* to do it again. And not just to get intel, although he would do that.

But this time, he damned well wouldn't be *bland*.

"No, she was reluctant to commit to anything."

"You okay?" Isaac asked, wiping a wisp of sandy blond hair from his forehead. The shaggy cut made him look more like a surfer than a skilled agent who worked with an elite team at Zodiac Tactical, but anyone who underestimated him for it did so at their own peril.

"Yeah. I'll be fine. Just keep an eye out and let me know if I need to get out quick."

Flipping the hood of his black jacket over his head, he darted into the rain and ran up the narrow sidewalk to the concrete stoop. He knew better than to go through the front door—she had that fortified heavily enough to withstand a siege. The back door was equally problematic.

But the window off the small living room? He'd noted that as a potential security vulnerability last time he was here—the lock on it was new, but the window itself was old and on hinges that could easily be popped out. He walked straight to it and with a couple of well-placed taps, was inside the bungalow a couple minutes later.

Somebody from a family of criminals should know more about fortifying herself. Having all the locks in the world didn't help if there was a different chink in the armor somewhere.

"I'm in," he said into his comms unit.

"Ok, you're still completely clear out here."

"I'm turning on visuals so you can see." They'd agreed that two sets of eyes could only help. Andrew's unit transmitted what he saw to Isaac's screen inside the car.

"Roger that, visuals coming through fine."

He walked around slowly so Isaac could get a feel for the place. Not wanting to draw attention to the empty home, he kept the lights off even though the onslaught of rain casted the living room in shadows.

Andrew might have been here before, but he'd been so caught up in his mission he hadn't paid much attention to the details. Details that now jumped out at him.

The small room held an old couch, a tube television straight from the 1990's, and a skinny stand in front of the bay window with a smattering of potted plants. No pictures lined the walls, no mementos or trinkets cluttered the space.

Interesting. His path had crossed with Roman Volkov, and his father, more than once. Both men were known to enjoy the finer things in life. No way the Wolf would only surround himself with the bare minimum. Why would he let his sister?

He'd assumed Tasha's day jobs were cover, her fortune safely tucked away. But maybe they'd agreed to stay radio silent while the dust settled. That would explain why Zodiac Tactical hadn't heard anything while monitoring her phone over the past month.

Not wanting to waste any more time, he made quick work of hiding bugs around the room—under a lampshade by the couch, in the corner of the ceiling under the thick crown molding, and at the side of the television set.

"These coming through okay?"

"Yeah, although makes me feel like shit. So intrusive."

"I get it, and don't disagree," Andrew said. "But you saw

Roman's fucking *calling card*. The man is a psychopath—his whole organization is. If this saves lives, then it's worth it."

Illegal maybe, but worth it. They'd worry about the legal ramifications once they found out where the Volkov Cartel was hiding and were ready to take them down.

"Living room's done," he said to Isaac as he moved into the kitchen. "The house is small. A couple more rooms left."

"I've got to be honest; this place isn't what I was expecting based on the intel I looked at on the Volkovs."

Andrew nodded. "Agreed. Place is clean, but old. Furniture is all worn, and she doesn't have much of it."

"No decorative items. Nothing personal or frivolous."

Andrew walked into the kitchen, forcing himself not to remember that kiss that had started the whole mess right up against that counter.

He opened her cabinets then the fridge. "Hardly any food either. Some canned goods and boxed processed crap. Fridge is almost completely empty."

"She must eat out most the time or something."

"Maybe." A mess of opened mail cluttered the small table. Curious, he ventured over and scanned the fanned-out paperwork. "Do you see this?"

It was multiple handwritten notices of overdue bills—rent, electrical, water. Multiple warnings that she was going to be evicted if she didn't pay—all made out to Tasha Bowers.

"Why would she be so behind in her bills?" Isaac asked. "That's way more than the financial pressure Zodiac was putting on her. It doesn't seem smart. Brings unwanted attention."

"Why wouldn't Roman just give her the money to pay the bills off? Why would Roman let her live like this?"

Tasha was Roman's sister. No way he'd sit back and watch her struggle to survive, unable to make rent, with shit furniture and nothing in the fridge. Andrew definitely wouldn't let his sister Lyn live that way.

But then again, his family weren't criminals in a dangerous cartel.

"I don't know. Something feels off, right?"

"Yeah, maybe." Andrew placed a video device near the back corner of the fridge. The kitchen was so small it could record the whole thing.

"Okay," Andrew continued. "I'm making my way into the bedroom."

"You're going to put video there, right?"

"I'll place it but we'll leave it off. If audio suggests we need to see what's going on we can activate the cameras remotely."

He didn't know why he was respecting Tasha's privacy in any way. Still, it was a thin line between gathering intel and being perverts.

He placed two more bugs in the hall—one close to the bathroom the other above the doorframe to the bedroom—then entered Tasha's most private space.

The bed was neatly made, a crisp blue blanket and a couple of pillows covering the mattress. Again, nothing other than what Tasha needed appeared inside. No luxuries at all. He peeked under the bed then opened the closet.

A couple long-sleeved shirts were hanging up, a casual dress, and the dress she wore to the wedding.

"That doesn't seem like a lot of clothes," Isaac said. Again, Andrew couldn't disagree.

He opened the cracked dresser. "One pair of jeans and a couple pairs of yoga pants. I don't see any extra shoes or jewelry or anything. Don't women love that shit?"

"Depends on the woman, I guess."

Andrew snorted. "Fair point." Kylie hadn't been big on the girly, frivolous things either. Except shoes. His wife had had a weakness for shoes he'd never understood but always indulged.

Blowing out a shaky breath, he forced his thoughts from Kylie while he was in Tasha's bedroom. He didn't want to intertwine the two women any more than he already had.

He walked over to the nightstand and opened the drawer. A Glock 19 rested there. Andrew carefully lifted it and found it loaded. "Okay, that's more like what I was expecting to find."

He placed it back the way he'd found it, then turned and placed the transmitters in the bedroom. Finding the weapon squelched any remorse he might've had about invading Tasha's privacy.

She was a criminal. He needed to remember that. Whatever sick attraction he had to her didn't mean anything.

"Okay, bedroom is done."

"Decided to turn the video on?"

"I've decided to do whatever the fuck I need to do to bring down the Volkovs."

Isaac was silent for a moment. "Roger that."

Andrew walked back out to the living room. "I'm going to go through her laptop really quick."

"Okay, but hurry. You've been inside for a while now."

Andrew glanced at his watch. More time had passed than he'd realized. He opened the old laptop as he sat on the lumpy couch. He did a simple backdoor hack to get him past her initial security screen and brought up her internet browser.

"She left a lot of tabs open. Her email is up, but nothing exciting. I'm going to look at her search history."

"Okay."

He searched but didn't find anything useful. "Nothing on here we haven't already seen from her phone usage."

"Put a micro transmitter on there and put it back," Isaac warned. "The rain's slowing down and a few neighbors have ventured outside. Small town people are going to freak out if they see you leaving her place at all, especially through a window."

Andrew placed the transmitter that would let them know her full internet search history then put the computer away. Isaac was right, he'd already stayed too long.

"Okay, I'm done. Am I clear to leave?"

"Yeah."

He walked to the window then looked back. "I feel like I'm missing something here. Like you said, the way she's living doesn't seem to make sense."

"That's why we placed the bugs. So we can get a clearer picture."

"Yeah, but just like bugging her phone I'm not sure any of this gear is going to get us the answers we need."

"Then how do we get them?"

Andrew knew the answer right away, even if he didn't like it.

"*Me*. I need her to open up to me. Talk to me about who she is, about her life, and be there when she slips."

Because she would.

"How are you going to do that?"

Andrew climbed back out the window and closed it securely behind him so she'd have no hint anyone had been in her place.

Tasha keeping her distance wasn't an option. He needed to get close to her.

"I think it's time for me to take some yoga classes."

Chapter 10

The muscles in Tasha's neck screamed. She wasn't sure if it was the extra shifts she'd been covering at the Chill N' Grill or the tension of her mounting bills that were to blame. Either way, it sucked. She'd worked for nine days straight.

Ignoring her discomfort, she flashed the local handyman a smile and slid his check onto the table. "Always nice to see you, Bob. Have a good rest of your day."

He tipped the bill of his red ball cap and grinned. "Best part of the day is behind me now that I've seen you."

She chuckled and shook her head. "I'll make sure to not tell your wife you said that."

Shrugging, he laid a few bills on the table without looking at what he owed. "You do that, and she'll skin us both." He shot her a wink and stood.

If Bob Truly wasn't nearly eighty years old, she might take his kindness for flirting. And he acted the same regardless of if his wife was with him or not. He was a town staple, puttering around with his rusty toolbox wherever he was needed, spreading kind words to whoever was lucky enough to cross his path.

She palmed the cash and counted, frowning as she called out after him as he headed toward the door. "You left way too much Bob."

He didn't even turn around, just waved a hand through the air and walked out into the bright, sunny afternoon.

Her heart swelled. Add this tip to what she'd made over the last few days, and she'd finally be able to make up what was owed on her rent. Her utilities were another problem, but she wanted to give herself one second to enjoy this tiny victory before worrying about the rest of her issues.

The door stayed open a beat before Andrew walked through, his gaze searching her out as soon as he crossed the threshold.

Her breath caught in her throat as irritation and excitement swirled inside her. This was the third day in a row he'd shown up at the restaurant, not to mention taking her yoga classes. Hell, he'd even stayed for the expectant mother's class, which would have drawn complaints if he hadn't looked so delicious in the joggers and fitted T-shirt he'd worn.

None of the mothers-to-be had shown any inclination that they didn't want him there.

Tasha glanced around, half-wishing for another server to sweep in and seat him. The other half of her squealed like a giddy school-girl that he'd come back after her repeated refusals to go out with him.

He'd asked her out each time they met, and each time she'd politely refused.

Getting too close to him was dangerous, even if she was oh so tempted. He was still the first man she'd been attracted to, and the first one she'd been anywhere near intimate with, in years. She'd enjoyed his company at the wedding—before the evening had turned to shit—and spending a little time with him would be a nice escape.

No string, no attachment, no problems.

But Andrew Zimmerman would always present a problem —she couldn't forget that. She'd be smarter all the way around to keep her distance.

Yet here he came with his sights set on her, striding forward, dragging his aviator sunglasses off and hooking them on his heather gray T-shirt that was just as perfectly fitted today as it had been in class last night. Jeans hung low on his hips this time rather than sweatpants. The muscles in his arms bunched as he lifted a hand to wave at Wade behind the bar as he approached.

Her fingers itched to touch the man. Those shoulders, that chest. She had to wipe them on her apron to make sure they didn't reach out on their own accord.

He shot her a charming smile as he leaned against the bar. "Long time no see."

She struggled against returning the smile. "Maybe it's time for me to do a little research on stalking. See if I need call the police."

The smile turned into an adorable pout. "But that would be mean."

He sat down on one of the barstools and she handed him a menu, although he probably had it memorized after being here so often over the past three days. "Why are you here again?"

"What can I say? I'm persistent when I see something I want."

Cocking her head to the side, she studied his chiseled jawline and those brown eyes. "And what exactly do you want from me?"

The question had plagued her since he'd shown back up in Pine Valley and throughout all his obvious attempts to get near her.

His apology had been appreciated, and accepted. It should've ended there.

She didn't know why he was being so appealingly persistent. It didn't make sense. He lived in Colorado while she was in Tennessee. He was only here temporarily. And it wasn't like the sex between them had been good enough to ignore those other factors.

"I want your time," he said with a small shrug. "That's all I've ever wanted. But I can take a hint."

She raised a brow. "Can you?"

"Might take me awhile." He wrinkled his nose in a way that made him look much younger than his thirty-some years. "I'm sorry if I overstepped or made you feel uncomfortable. You're just..." he raised his hands then let them fall. "Different."

"Different? Not sure if that's a compliment or not."

He chuckled. "Trust me, it is. I wanted to stop by today and say thank you." He handed the menu back to her.

"You're not staying?"

He shook his head. "Not today."

Which meant he wasn't going to ask her out again either. She swallowed her disappointment. She hadn't agreed to dinner or ice cream or any of his other offers, but him asking her had been the highlight of her day.

Even if she was only just now able to admit that to herself.

"Are you going back to Colorado?"

She hated the tightness in her voice. What was wrong with her? She barely knew this man, and what she did know should keep her far away. She very definitely shouldn't be choked up at the thought of never seeing him again.

"Nah, not yet. I have some more time here, but I've decided to leave you alone. Save you the trouble of getting that restraining order."

She forced out a smile. "You know I was just kidding about that."

He winked at her. "Regardless. Thanks for putting up with me. I hope you enjoy your day. I know I'll be enjoying mine— doing something I haven't done in years."

"What's that?" She asked, unable to keep her curiosity at bay.

He beamed. "I'm going on a picnic. Sounds dumb, I know. But hey, why the hell not, right?"

"A picnic?" That was the last thing she'd expected him to say.

"Yep, a mid-afternoon picnic. Got a basket packed and everything. Going to a lake out on the south side of Crossroads property. Tucker told me about it. Evidently it's pretty remote. A nice place to go to just enjoy nature."

"That sounds…really nice." Like something straight out of a romance novel. Tasha knew exactly where he was talking about.

He shot her that charming grin again. "Going to study the Smokies properly so I can compare them to my Rockies back in Colorado. See if I can decide which mountain range I like better while enjoying a gorgeous afternoon."

"That seems very relaxing." And damned if she wasn't jealous. Of him getting to enjoy the mountains and of the mountains getting to have him nearby.

"I hope it will be. I'll see you around. And I promise not to annoy you anymore." He turned toward the door.

"See you," she whispered, completely mortified to hear the twinge of tears in her voice.

He'd given up. He'd taken her no for an answer. Why in the world should she be upset with that? It was what she wanted.

Right?

He stopped and turned back toward her. "I'm not going to

invite you to go, because I meant what I said about not continuing to bother you. But I'll be at the lake around 3:00 and just in case anyone else shows up, I'll make sure my basket has enough for two."

He left without another word. All she could do was watch him go.

Chapter 11

"She's not coming."

"She'll be here," Isaac replied into the comms unit in Andrew's ear. "No woman can resist a romantic picnic."

Andrew wasn't so sure.

Tasha had rebuffed his every advance over the past few days. Even showing up at her yoga classes hadn't seemed to score him any points. All it had earned him was sore muscles he hadn't even realized he had.

He'd stuck around to chat after each class, but that hadn't led to anything. He'd damned well memorized the menu at the Chill N' Grill from eating there so much, but those little moments with Tasha hadn't given him anything he didn't already know.

They were no closer to discovering the whereabouts of the Volkov Cartel than they'd been over a month ago when they'd first found out Tasha existed. The transmitting devices they'd put all over her house hadn't provided any details either.

Tasha came home from one or both of her jobs, warmed up some sort of meager meal then generally passed out in her bed. She'd done nothing to suggest she had any sort of life whatsoever, much less any contact with her brother.

Today was the last chance Andrew had. Time was ticking away too damned quickly and there'd been another body with Roman's calling card found in Houston yesterday.

If Tasha didn't show up here this afternoon, then they needed to regroup and see about someone else working her. Probably Isaac with his charm and good looks and no history of crappy sex followed by fleeing the scene.

Yet the thought of Isaac getting anywhere near Tasha made Andrew want to put his fist through a wall.

"Do you see anything yet?"

"Nope." Isaac popped the P as he said it. "But give her more time."

"She's not coming."

The disappointment sitting on his chest was only partially to do with the case.

"Want me to come be your date?" Isaac asked with a laugh. "I put some damn good shit in that basket."

Andrew wasn't sure what was worse. Sitting and eating alone or sitting and eating with Isaac. Neither option did anything to erase the feeling of being a complete idiot.

He peeked inside the basket. "Champagne? Seriously?"

"What? A little alcohol might loosen her lips a bit. And nothing shouts romantic picnic more than champagne and grapes and all that junk."

Andrew snorted. "All that *junk*? I'm sure you'll make someone a very lucky lady one day, Mr. Romance."

"I can make you a lucky man right now if you want help drinking that booze."

He chuckled under his breath. "I don't need that sort of lucky."

"*Lucky* by enjoying my sunny disposition and charming

personality, asshole. You only wish you could get lucky with me any other way."

"I'll take my chances of looking like a lonely loser and enjoy all this myself."

"Oh, I don't think you look like a loser at all."

Andrew stiffened at the teasing feminine voice behind him and turned around.

Tasha stood there wearing the pale blue summer dress he'd spotted in her closet, the color the exact shade of her eyes. A white cardigan was thrown over top. Her blonde hair flowed down her back, the subtle wind pushing tendrils across her face.

"Hi." He jumped to his feet. "I didn't think you were coming. Didn't hear any cars." Hadn't been warned by his asshole of a partner.

She rubbed her arms where they were crossed over her chest. "Yeah, I parked over at the lodge and walked."

"You look beautiful." The words were out before he could stop them.

She gave him a shy smile and tucked a long strand of hair behind her ear. "Is it okay if I crash your party?"

"Not much of a party. Just me talking to myself." He swept a hand toward his basket. "And enjoying the contents."

She stepped onto the red and black checked blanket and peered into the basket. "Two champagne flutes. I guess I was a foregone conclusion."

"No, not at all. Just a desperate hope. Can I offer you a glass of bubbly?"

"Sure." Her smile was still shy. "That sounds amazing."

"Told you," Isaac said in his ear. "Damn good shit."

Andrew didn't respond, merely reached up and turned the comms unit off in his ear. Isaac would be able to see them through his binoculars from where he'd hidden the car.

Andrew set out the flutes then secured the bottle, cracking open the top with a loud pop.

Tasha giggled, the sound lifting his spirits more than it should, before clapping a hand over her mouth and stopping the sound.

He shook his head. "Don't stop that lovely laugh on my account." He poured her a glass and handed it to her.

She let out a small sigh. "I can't remember that last time I had a picnic."

He unpacked the grapes and cheese and a thick hunk of bread Isaac had packed. "Me either. Unless you count sitting on my kitchen floor with plastic tea cups filled with mystery liquids I don't even want to attempt to identify."

She wrinkled her nose but laughed. "You make is sound like your daughters have tried to poison you."

"I wouldn't put it past them. They're rotten to the core." He winked, just to make sure she knew he was kidding, then took a sip of champagne. Bubbles tingled his tongue.

"They were little darlings at the wedding. Why aren't they with you on this trip?"

"They went on vacation with my brother and sister-in-law. They preferred a trip to Disney World with two people they have wrapped around their fingers over coming with me on a business trip. Go figure."

"That's wonderful you have a brother who takes your daughters on vacation. Do you have other family?"

He nodded and popped a grape in his mouth. "Another brother and a sister."

"Four of you. That's a lot."

"Yep. Always a full house. How about you. Any siblings?"

She took another sip of champagne, looking away. "A brother—technically a half-brother."

Bingo. Half-brother. That was new news. "Do you get to see him often?"

"No. We've never been close."

He wished he could see into her eyes to try to figure out if this was some well-rehearsed line or if it was the truth.

"I'm sorry."

She shrugged one shoulder. "You know how it is. Family drama."

Drama tended to happen when the family was full of criminals.

"I know. But even with drama, family is still family, you know? Got to keep them close."

Hopefully talking about hers would get her in the mood to contact Roman. But he had to balance that with not giving her cause for suspicion.

"Yeah, I guess."

"What about your parents? What do they think about the family drama?"

She shook her head. "My mom died when I wasn't much older than your daughters."

"That had to be tough."

She dropped her gaze. "Yeah. My dad didn't know what to do with a little girl, so he chose to let others deal with me. I spent a lot of time in boarding schools. He thought it was for the best, and maybe he was right."

That was why law enforcement hadn't known about Tasha's existence until recently. She hadn't been around much.

"Are you close with him now?"

"No." She looked up at the mountains. "He died about four years ago. But even then we weren't close."

She was telling the truth about that. Andrew knew for a fact Marcus Volkov had died around that time period. Roman had taken up the reigns of the cartel. Maybe keeping the conversation focused on her father was the right way to go.

"I'm sure it was hard for your dad to know if he was making the best decisions for you. I'm constantly asking myself if I'm doing right by my girls. If I'm messing things up or raising them wrong. I feel like I can't give them everything they need."

"All any child needs is to be seen and heard. To be loved. I might not know you well, but I know you do those things for your twins."

Those blue eyes were warm with sincerity. It loosened something inside him, melted some of his resistance toward her. Nothing about this woman suggested she was anything like Roman or the cartel.

"Thank you. That means a lot."

She reached over to grab a grape and it brought them a little closer. His knee brushed against her leg. He longed to reach out, to run the tip of his finger along her jawline or take off that damn sweater of hers and touch her soft skin.

He reeled himself back. He needed to work the mission, not get drawn in by beautiful eyes and soft words.

But still, he didn't pull away.

"You mentioned before you were new to Pine Valley." He grabbed his own grape. "Where did you live before here?"

She shook her head. "For the past few years I've sort of lived all over. After I graduated from boarding school, I came back to the States, but my family moved around a lot. We didn't stay in one place for long."

"Sounds like you come from a military family," he said. "Always moving from base to base."

"My family was definitely not military." Her laugh was sad. "More like nomads."

He needed to keep up on this angle.

"Where were you before here?"

She looked away again. "Spent a little time in Houston. Some in Nashville."

Andrew stiffened. Both of those were cities where there had been activity from the Volkov Cartel recently.

He wanted to push, ask what her family did, but he was afraid that would set off too many alarms.

"You like living that wandering life?" he managed with a smile. "That's all the rage right now—buy a camper, see the country, post your pictures."

She pulled up her knees to her chest and wrapped her arms around them. It brought them even closer. "No. Honestly, I think I'd prefer a home base. I love the community here in Pine Valley. I've actually made some friends."

"But this is only temporary for you?"

Andrew knew the cartel couldn't house itself here. Like she'd said, Pine Valley was too much of a community—the people here would recognize multiple strangers. It was too small. Too intimate.

"Probably. Seems like it always works out that way."

"Where do you think you'll go?"

"I have no idea."

She looked over at him and there was such a sadness in her eyes that it froze him for a moment. He couldn't stop himself, he wrapped an arm around her shoulder and pulled her close.

He needed to push. *Now* while she was vulnerable.

But hell if it didn't leave a bad taste in his mouth.

"Surely you've got somewhere in mind if you're not staying here."

"St. Petersburg, maybe."

"Russia?" Volkov was definitely a Russian name, but as far as Andrew knew the family didn't have any actual ties to the country of their heritage. Plus, he couldn't press about the Russian name since as far as he was supposed to know her last name was Bowers.

God, this situation was about to become a complete clusterfuck if multiple international law enforcement agencies had to work together to shut down the cartel.

"No," she let out a soft laugh. "Florida. That's a little closer."

St Petersburg.

Andrew reached up and turned his comms unit on in his ear. "St. Petersburg, huh? I do hear they have gorgeous beaches. You ever been there before?"

He knew Isaac would get the info and make sure the Zodiac Tactical team started researching it right away. They'd have men on the ground there within the hour.

"No, I'm more of a mountain girl myself." She rested more fully against him with a little sigh.

"If you like mountains, you should see the Rockies then. Colorado is beautiful."

Shit. Why had he said that?

"Careful, brother," Isaac murmured in his ear.

Andrew reached up and switched off the comms unit. He didn't want to take a chance on Tasha hearing Isaac when she was this close. Not to mention, Andrew didn't need a witness to all the ways he was fucking this up.

"Maybe," was all she said.

He needed to get this back on track. "When do you think you'll head to St. Pete?"

She shrugged. "When it's time. I'm not sure yet."

When it was time. That had to be a sign that she was waiting for some sort of signal from Roman.

"So, you have three siblings. How about your parents? Are you close with them?" she asked.

He knew it was her attempt to change the subject, so he let it slide.

"With my dad. My mom died when I was young. She had heart problems."

Ones his sister had inherited—Lyn's husband Heath carried around a portable defibrillator everywhere they went.

They all teased Heath about his man purse he carried the

defibrillator in, but Heath didn't care. He'd almost lost Lyn once due to complications with her heart, and was determined it wouldn't happen again.

"I'm so sorry."

"Mom's death was a long time ago."

Tasha's voice got a little softer. "Can I ask you a personal question? You don't have to answer if you don't want to."

"Sure. I'll answer if I can." And maybe her asking a personal question would enable him to do the same later.

"Do you ever take the girls to visit their mom's grave?"

That wasn't what he was expecting. "I have a few times, so they can put flowers up and we can talk about her. They were so young when she died, they don't really remember her."

Save Kylie!

Andrew blinked away the memory that swallowed his subconscious in a wave and threatened to overwhelm him— him begging his imaginary angel that night to leave him and save Kylie instead.

"Do you—do you think it helps them?"

He took in a deep breath and forced himself to focus on the here and now. "I think so. It certain helps me when I visit my mother's grave. Even if it's just a chance to take a moment and really remember her without a bunch of distractions."

"Yeah," she whispered.

"Can I ask you a personal question now?"

"Sure. I'll answer if I can," she repeated his words back to him.

"How did you end up in a tiny little down like Pine Valley?"

"I was…" She faded off then started again. "I ran out of gas here and then decided to stay."

Sharing time was obviously over if she was making up stuff like that. Fine, he wasn't going to push and risk blowing his cover. They had more information now than they'd had an hour ago. They would focus on St. Petersburg.

He should pack up the picnic and leave, but couldn't make himself do so. Maybe it was the champagne, maybe it was the sunshine flowing over the beautiful mountains surrounding them, but he just wanted to stay here a while.

Stay with Tasha in his arms.

"Well, I'm glad you ran out of gas." He leaned back and smiled down at her. "Because if you hadn't we never would have—"

His words were broken off by her lips softly pressing against his. Before he could even decide whether it was a good idea to take things further, she pulled back.

"Thank you," she whispered.

"For what?"

"For asking me out. For planning this picnic, even though you didn't know if I would come. For sharing about your life. It means a lot to me. More than you know."

"You're worth all those things." Andrew had to tamp down his guilt at the wide smile that covered her face at his words.

She believed him.

The problem was, he was starting to believe his words too.

Chapter 12

Tasha smoothed her palm over the pale blue dress and put on the same white sweater she'd worn on her picnic date with Andrew yesterday. She hated she didn't have another one, but she didn't have the luxury of owning a closet full of clothes like she had in her previous life.

A life where she'd been a spoiled princess whose world was built on the destruction of others.

She might not have been aware of who her family really was—or the horrible things they'd done—for most of her life, but that didn't make sleeping at night any easier now.

She supposed she should be grateful her father had sent her to boarding school. It had sheltered her from the truth. But once she'd become and adult, and come home, she should've figured it out.

She'd been so damned oblivious—happy to go on international trips and shop at all the most expensive boutiques. She'd never questioned where her family's money had come from. Never questioned why'd they'd moved around so much.

Her father had been dying of cancer when she'd accidentally walked in on a conversation between him and Roman that should've clued her in. But she'd still refused to accept the truth. Even after her father had died a few months later and Roman had taken over the family *business*, she hadn't left, convinced she'd misunderstood in some way.

It was only that night when Roman had discovered law enforcement had infiltrated the cartel, and had ordered hits on anyone he wasn't completely sure was loyal that she'd finally taken action.

Roman hadn't cared if the kill orders he'd given were on people who had betrayed him or not. Innocent, guilty…it didn't seem to matter to him. The only thing that had mattered to him was showing his power.

As if his sick calling card—X's carved over the eyes and a shot of vodka left by the dead person's head—wasn't enough of a show of power.

Roman had taken great pleasure in showing her that. Laughing as he watched her lose the contents of her stomach.

She'd known she had to leave. But when she'd heard about the list of people Roman was having killed that night, she'd tried to help. Gone from place to place trying to stop the hits. Not that she'd been able to do much good. Andrew and his girls had been the only ones she'd been able to save.

Roman had found out about her betrayal and had been chasing her ever since. Wanted her dead. He would've found her long before now if he hadn't had to also hide from the damage law enforcement had done to the cartel.

But even without her so-called betrayal he'd always hated her, had always been jealous of the relationship their father had shared with her mother.

And now Tasha was an enemy he'd destroy no matter what.

She needed to remember that. To hold on to the truth of

what her life was with an iron fist and stop giving into the fantasy Andrew brought with him.

Picnics and soft kisses and sweet words. He'd more than made up for the bland sex a month ago, and hadn't put any pressure on her at all for it to happen again.

Which, honestly, had just made her want it—want *him* —more.

But that wasn't what was important right now. Right now she was going to do something she should've done months ago. And it centered around something Andrew had asked: how had she ended up in Pine Valley?

She'd only been stretching the truth a little bit when she said she'd run out of gas and stayed—it had been more like she'd run out of money.

But there had been a reason she'd been in this part of Tennessee. Something the daily work of trying to survive and make sure Roman didn't find her had caused her to lose sight of.

She turned from the mirror and walked out her front door, reattaching all the locks, then climbed into her junky old car. She was soon heading out of town.

She hadn't gotten far before her phone buzzed in her purse. Tasha had made sure to grab it before heading out in case she had an emergency. At a stop sign, she pulled it out and glanced down at the screen and concern rippled through her.

> Call when you can. Just want to talk.

She dialed Laura immediately and hit the speaker phone button before crossing the intersection. Her friend had been there for Tasha so many times, it was time for Tasha to help her for a change.

"What in the world are you doing up?" Laura asked, her

voice a little too bright. "Are you teaching one of those sunrise classes at the retreat again?"

"No way. I only do those when Zoe absolutely can't. I hate waking up that early."

"Then why are you awake now?"

"I could ask you the same thing." Tasha merged into the light traffic then took a sharp left, away from the highway. Instinct, and experience, always had her driving like a lunatic.

She never knew if she was being followed.

A beat of silence pulsed from speaker. "I couldn't sleep."

"Any reason why?" Tasha asked gently. She'd heard the whispers around town. Knew that Laura had just left a bad situation and was on her own for the first time in her life.

"It's still tough getting used to the new place. Every noise freaks me out. Maybe I should get a dog or something."

"I've heard worse ideas."

Tasha had considered a pet a couple of years ago. Something to move around with her. Someone to talk to, even if it couldn't talk back. But in the end, not knowing where she'd be and for how long seemed like too much of a disruption for another living thing. So she kept plants. They were her friends, her babies, her confidants.

Even if that made her a weirdo.

"Same, but I don't want to talk about my inability to decide on a pet. I want to hear every detail from your picnic date with the hunky Andrew yesterday. How'd it go?"

She glanced in the rearview mirror. She noted the black truck a good distance behind her and made another left that weaved her through a neighborhood.

"Great. *Too* great."

After chatting and flirting all afternoon, and that one quick kiss, she'd been tempted to invite him back to her house. But this time she knew him much better than that night after the wedding. She'd been embarrassed by how run down her house was. She hadn't wanted him to witness her tattered furniture and meager lifestyle. Plus her cupboards and fridge were so bare—extensive groceries had been a luxury she couldn't much afford over the past couple weeks—that she definitely wouldn't have been able to offer him anything.

Laura laughed. "Too great? How is that possible? A date can't be too good."

"It was pretty damned good," she said with a snort. "But I don't know why I'm encouraging this between me and Andrew. There can't ever be anything between us."

The sound of running water gurgled through the speaker. "Why not? Hell, he came back out here to see you. I'm convinced of it."

"First, he came to Tennessee to help friends not see me. Second, he lives in Colorado. Has a life with two little girls to look after. Our worlds are way too different."

"They don't have to be," Laura said.

Tasha tensed as she looked in the mirror again. Was that the same truck still behind her in the distance? It was hard to tell in the dim dawn light plus the fact that pickup trucks were a dime a dozen around here.

But it was a reminder of why she should be paying attention to her surroundings instead of talking to a friend right now.

A reminder of why she shouldn't have friends at all.

"It is what it is." Tasha kept her glancing in the rearview mirror. "He's only here for a few more days. I'd be stupid to get attached."

In more ways than one.

She took a right out of the neighborhood and then swung around and did a sharp left. She grimaced as the tires squealed, but Laura didn't notice.

"Sometimes you have to just trust yourself and take a chance. It's something I'm trying to learn."

Tasha took another turn, back to the right and hit the gas. She reached the next curve and took it quickly.

If that truck was following her, he was going to have to make some pretty aggressive moves and she would know it. She was now on a straightaway.

"Tash, are you there?"

"Yeah, I'm sorry. Just thinking." And watching for people trying to kill her.

"Well, I hope you'll take a chance with Andrew. What have you got to lose?"

The list was way too long, even if she could explain it.

"I'll see how it plays out. I don't really think he's interested."

She relaxed a little when there was no sign of the truck behind her, then took the next left onto the highway. Her exit was only a few miles ahead.

"I've seen how he looks at you. He's definitely interested."

If he knew the truth he wouldn't be. "Maybe."

"It's hard to let somebody in when you've been hurt, but sometimes it's the best thing for us."

"I hope you'll be willing to listen to your own advice too, sweetie."

Tasha didn't know all of Laura's history but knew it had been painful.

They both fell into silence, Laura lost in thought, Tasha still keeping an eye out behind her. She'd lost that truck, or, more likely, it had never been following her in the first place.

Her exit loomed to the right. She took the turn and found the road to the cemetery. "I hate to do this, but I need to get going."

"You never did tell me why you were awake so early. Where are you?"

The gates to the cemetery came into view, and her chest tightened. She hadn't been here since the day her mother was buried. But Andrew's words yesterday had compelled her to come.

She wanted to believe her mom was always with her, but she'd never felt her presence. Never saw her mom as standing beside her, wanting to give her guidance or strength. Maybe this could help—could make Tasha feel closer to the woman she missed every single day.

"I'm doing something I should have done a long time ago. I'm visiting my mother."

≈

"GEMINI, the suspect is on the move. I repeat, Tasha is in her car, on her way out of town."

Andrew jerked awake immediately at the sound of his Zodiac Tactical code name coming from the speaker next to the couch where he'd fallen asleep.

He'd been up most of the night running St. Petersburg scenarios with Jenna Franklin and the rest of the Zodiac computer team—trying to see if they could get ahead of Roman in some way. Ian DeRose himself was already on his way to the beach town.

So far the intel hadn't proven useful in any way. There had been no sign of the Volkov Cartel. Everyone at Zodiac Tactical was shaking down anyone who knew anything about the city, but none of their contacts had heard any chatter of Roman Volkov being anywhere nearby.

"Roger," he told Isaac. "I'm on it."

Thankful he was already dressed, so he ran to his truck from the RV they were using as command central, parked not far from Tasha's house.

He got in his truck and tore out of the parking lot. "Which direction?"

Damn it, they should've put a tracker on her car. But

they'd been afraid of detection and sure the contact with Roman would be through electronic means first, not just her taking off.

"South."

He took a left and punched the gas. "How far ahead of me is she?"

"A couple miles at most. I thought she was running out to her car to get something. Then she left."

Shit. Had Tasha panicked that mentioning St. Petersburg had given away something? Was she leaving for good?

"What was the situation in her house before she left? Was she packing everything? Did she take a bag with her?"

"No. She had a pretty restless night. Was up pacing, but not on her computer or phone at all. About an hour ago she showered then put on the dress she wore yesterday. I didn't know she was going to leave until she walked out the door. I'm not even sure *she* knew she was going to leave until that moment."

Ok, weird. "Roger. Let me know if anything changes at her place."

Honestly, Andrew hadn't been expecting this. It had felt like they'd created a bond between them yesterday on the picnic. For the first time he had some doubts about her involvement with her brother—*half-brother*—at all.

It had sounded like there was no lost love between them. And for at least the last month she hadn't made any attempt to contact Roman.

Hell, since learning about her existence there hadn't been any indication that she was part of the cartel. And if he was honest, Andrew would agree that nothing about her actions or personality suggested she was anything like her brother or father.

Andrew believed it to the point where at the picnic he'd been ready to believe her innocence.

When he spotted her rusted sedan ahead of him, he relaxed slightly. She wasn't going very fast. He had her now. It was just a matter of following.

Then almost out of the blue she made a sharp turn to her right. With a curse he sped up to follow. He barely caught sight of her before she made another tight left through a residential neighborhood. She was driving like a madwoman.

Or someone who knew how to lose a tail.

Another sharp turn took her out of the neighborhood, but a garbage truck backed out of a driveway and blocked his path. Shit. The large vehicle lumbered along, blocking his view. He swerved around the truck, but Tasha's car was gone.

He banged his hand against the steering wheel then grabbed his phone, calling Jenna Franklin's direct line.

"Jenna, Tasha Volkov took off and is headed somewhere, and I need to know where," he said without greeting. He knew the computer guru wouldn't be offended. "I last saw her on the corner of Elm Road and Middlebranch in Westchester, which is about five miles south of Pine Valley."

"Roger that. We're on it."

"Check routes that would lead to St. Petersburg. Maybe she decided to bug out."

"Call you back." Jenna ended the call. She'd be searching every traffic and security cam available in this area.

He got back on the phone with Isaac. "I lost Tasha—she somehow figured out she had a tail. Are you sure there was nothing that suggested she was going to leave permanently? Nothing on her computer? Phone?"

"I've already re-watched the footage," the younger man said. "I'm telling you there was nothing last night. She got home a little after dark, then didn't touch her computer or phone all night."

"Something happened that just had her driving pretty damned recklessly through a neighborhood."

"The only footage I haven't watched was her in the bathroom."

"Send it to me." They'd tried to be decent and give her privacy in the bathroom, but she'd just lost that privilege with this driving stunt.

Still, if anyone was going to see her in the shower it was damned well only going to be Andrew.

He pulled to the side of the road and waited for anything to point him in Tasha's direction. The footage from Isaac came first.

Andrew forced back any sort of guilt or distaste as he watched the bathroom video. He refused to look at her as a woman.

She was only a suspect now.

He hardened himself against a smile as she sung an 80s hairband tune while in the shower. But that, nor anything else in the bathroom suggested any sort of guilt or planning on her part.

He called Isaac back. "There was nothing in the bathroom footage. Check the other again to make sure you didn't miss anything."

"Roger."

Andrew's grip tightened on the steering wheel. This was his fault. He'd been out of the game too long, too afraid to be on an active mission because of the girls. And now he'd fallen for Tasha's pretty face. Not just that, her caring nature that always put him at ease for some reason—made feel as though he'd known her for years.

His phone rang. Jenna. "I'm not having much luck. She's very smart by staying in neighborhoods—not many cameras. I found one traffic cam where she rolled through twenty minutes ago, in Golden Ridge."

"Golden Ridge. Why have I heard of that?"

"It's a small ass town that holds a large pharmaceutical lab.

It was robbed last year, potentially by the Volkov Cartel, although we don't have confirmation."

"That can't be a coincidence," Andrew said, pulling back onto the street.

"I don't believe in coincidences," Jenna replied.

"See if you find anything else there. Then keep looking at routes south toward St. Petersburg."

Rage fisted his throat. Not only did he not know Tasha, but he also hadn't trusted the information given to him that warned she was dangerous. Of course nothing about her screamed criminal mastermind. That's how she'd stayed under the radar for so long. And he'd been gullible enough to buy her bullshit.

He slammed his fist against the horn, the noise booming into the quiet morning. She'd played him. Batted her eyelashes and flirted just enough to keep him wanting more. Keep him blind to the truth.

Not anymore. It was time to get the answers he needed no matter what.

Chapter 13

The door to the Chill N' Grill opened, grabbing Tasha's attention. She held her breath, hope mounting in her chest.

Only to be dashed when Andrew didn't hustle inside. Instead, two giggling teenage girls hurried in from the brewing storm outside.

Sighing, Tasha forced a smile and showed them to an empty table, promising to return soon to take their orders. She slipped a cash tip into her pocket from a nearby booth then cleared off the dirty dishes before heading to the kitchen.

The restaurant was thinning out, most people wanting to get home before the storm hit even worse, and Tasha was counting down the seconds to closing. She'd gotten back from visiting Mom's grave just in time to come in for her afternoon shift.

All day she'd waited for Andrew to show up so she could tell him about her visit to the cemetery—and how his encouragement had helped her do something she hadn't realized how much she needed.

After the picnic and the closeness they'd shared, she knew

he would understand how she'd felt about everything this morning. She wanted to tell him about it.

But he hadn't come in today.

She sat down her tray and wiped stray strands of hair from her forehead. What did she expect? He'd asked her out for days and she'd turned him down. Then she finally showed up at the picnic yesterday and now expected him to drop everything and talk to her just because she now wanted it?

The guy probably had emotional whiplash. She couldn't blame him.

The kitchen door swung open. Her boss, Wade McKenzie, sidestepped her and carried an armload of dirty glasses to the sink. "Rain's coming down, and it's so damn cold outside, it might freeze."

She looked outside the window. The wind was pretty bad, almost blowing the rain sideways. "*Freeze*? It's April."

Wade shrugged. "It happens. I'm going to close a little early. You can head home before the roads get bad."

"Thanks," she said. "Want me to tell those teenagers who just came in the kitchen's closed?"

"I'll talk to them. Then I'll call their parents and let them know they're on their way home. This is just going to get worse once it gets dark, I'm pretty sure."

She smiled, warmed by his concern over the young drivers. It was that type of kindness from the people in Pine Valley that made her want to stay here.

To make this as permanent a home as she could.

"Okay. I'm off tomorrow, but I'll see you the day after."

"Drive safe." Wade took his glasses back to the sink.

Stepping back into the dining hall, the chime of the bell announced a new customer. Tasha turned to tell them they were closing early but froze when she saw Andrew standing there.

She could swear she saw surprise in his eyes before he blinked it away. But that didn't make sense so she ignored it.

"Hey, you!" Her voice was breathy, but she didn't care. She was happy to see him. She rushed toward him, ready to throw her arms around him in a hug, their kiss from yesterday seared into her mind.

"Hi." He crossed his arms over his chest and stiffened as she got closer.

The temperature had plummeted and it had nothing to do with the weather outside. Tasha stopped in her tracks, her arms falling to her sides, excitement at seeing him dissipating.

He definitely wasn't happy to see her.

She wasn't sure what to do or say. She hadn't made a fool out of herself, but she'd come pretty damned close.

"I, uh…" She took another step back. "Wade just notified me we're closing early. Because of the weather."

Andrew was studying her with narrowed eyes. This was definitely not the same man who'd picnicked with her yesterday—bringing out parts of herself she hadn't shared with anyone. Definitely wasn't the man who'd kissed her like she was something precious.

This was more the man who'd snuck out of her house without a word after sex. She'd let herself forget he existed.

But she was remembering now.

"I didn't think you were here," he said.

What did that mean?

"Oh." She took another step back.

Andrew ran a hand over his wet hair. "I came by at lunch but you weren't here."

"I didn't have to work the lunch shift today."

Why did he seem so mad? Distant?

"Look," she continued. "Like I said, we're closing early. But I can probably get you something to go from the kitchen. I'm about to head home. It's been a…wild day."

He tilted his head to the side, studying her with those brown eyes. "What sort of wild?"

She took a breath. Took a chance, like Laura had said. "I was actually hoping you'd come by today so I could tell you about it. After our talk yesterday, I decided to go visit my mother's grave this morning."

"*What*?"

He looked so genuinely shocked she had to laugh a little.

"Yeah. She was buried in Gatlinburg. I've never been back to her gravesite so thought it was time. Actually, she was born not too far from here too in Martinsboro."

"You went to see your mother's grave." His iciness had melted away but there was still shock in his tone.

She shrugged. "Yeah. Is that stupid? I promise the weather was much better this morning when I sped out of here at dawn."

"You went to your mother's grave in Gatlinburg."

She had no idea what was happening in this conversation. "Um, yes."

She was saved by Wade coming back out from the kitchen. "Hey Andrew, how you doing, man? We're closing early. I'm afraid this rain is going to freeze over."

Andrew nodded. "Yeah, good idea. I'll make sure Tasha gets home. Her tires are damned near bald."

She couldn't even argue with that. New tires weren't in the budget.

"Okay, good. That way I don't need to worry about her." Wade gave them a wave as he went to talk to the teenagers who'd come in a few minutes ago.

Andrew nodded at her. "Let me know when you're ready."

She stared at him. "Are you sure everything is okay? You seemed...upset or something when you first came in."

He shrugged. "Must be this bipolar weather making me

cranky. But I'm good, I promise. Let's just get you home." He winked at her and gave her a smile.

Okay, she must have been imagining the distance. Or, like he said, the weather was making everyone a little nuts.

But she had to rub her stomach against the tingling there at his lingering smile.

This man didn't just give her the butterflies. He gave her the whole damn zoo.

RAIN DUMPED onto Tasha's windshield. Her wiper blades danced back and forth as she slowly pulled out of the parking lot and headed toward home. She only lived a short distance away, but her grip was tight on the steering wheel. She drove slow, cautious of the water flooding the street.

At least the storm kept her mind off Andrew and her mess of feelings. She had no idea how to decipher those. Hell, she hadn't even been aware she had those feeling until he'd seemed so distant and all of a sudden she'd been faced with losing whatever was budding between them.

She didn't want to lose it.

She wanted to get closer to him.

The thought was equally thrilling and terrifying.

She reached her driveway with a whoosh of relief. A quick glance to the side showed her Andrew had parked safely next to her. She turned off her car and made a run for the front stoop. Thank God for the narrow strip of roof covering her head or she'd have been soaked by the time she unlocked the door and made it inside, Andrew at her heels.

"Man, it's been a while since we've had a storm like this," she said with a nervous laugh. "And why is it so cold?"

Andrew lowered the hood of his jacket. "Guess the weather's usually milder here than in Colorado. A little frost on the ground in late Spring isn't uncommon there. Hell, I've seen snow fall in the summer up in the mountains before."

She cringed. "Don't say the S word. Not now."

A tiny half-smile poked through his gruff expression. "Don't like snow, huh?"

She lifted a shoulder. "I love it in the winter, where it belongs. Nothing beats a white Christmas or building a snowman."

"Do you get to do that a lot?" He tilted his head, eyes narrowed as if examining her every word.

"Not here. But I've lived in my share of snowy places." She shrugged out of her jacket and hung it on the hook by the door.

Andrew stood on the threadbare welcome mat, not coming inside.

He wasn't sure he was welcome, she realized.

"Do you want to come in?" she said. "Maybe for a cup of tea?"

It was sort of pathetic that he was the only one she wanted to talk to about what she'd done today. But she knew he would understand—he'd known much more loss than she had.

One dark brow quirked up. "If you trade tea for whisky, you've got a deal."

"Got to love bribing a man to spend time with me with booze." She smiled, shaking her head. "Take a seat and I'll be right back."

She hurried into the kitchen and searched her cabinets for something to give him. She wasn't a big drinker, aside from the occasional glass of wine, and didn't have any extra income for luxuries she didn't use.

Hell, she didn't have money for any luxuries at all.

Settling on the cheap bottle of white wine in the fridge, she unscrewed the cap and poured two glasses. The cups didn't match, and hers had a chip on the rim, but it'd have to do.

She found him sitting on her worn sofa, typing something rapidly on his phone. The cushions dipped low under his weight.

She handed him the glass. "Wine is all I had."

"Wine is perfect." He put his phone away. "So, tell me about this morning."

She sat beside him, trying to ignore how in bad of shape her couch was. She took a gulp of her wine, then sat her glass on the coffee table.

"I liked what you said yesterday about feeling closer to your wife when you take the girls to see her grave. I woke up this morning and knew that I needed to go to my mom's grave. I'm ashamed to admit I live so close but haven't been."

"Is that why you moved to Pine Valley? To be close to her?"

That was a good question. One she didn't necessarily have the answer to.

"Maybe on some level, but it wasn't a conscious decision. Mom was born near here and buried near here, but I've never really visited. So I went to the grave then drove through her hometown."

Andrew nodded at her to continue.

"It's not like Mom had any family left in Martinsboro. My dad and I made the decision to bury her in this area because… well, to be honest, he made the arrangements and I never bothered to ask why."

"You were young. That's understandable."

She picked at a fraying patch of denim on her knee. "But I should have. Should have asked a lot more questions, but sometimes it's easier to live in the dark. To not know all the answers."

"Answers about your family? Do you have questions about them?"

She had more questions than could be answered in this lifetime, but couldn't get into that, especially with him.

She shrugged. "Doesn't everyone have questions about their family?"

He paused for a long moment. "Did you find out any answers today?"

Had she? Not really. The dead couldn't talk. She would never know if her mother had known the truth about her father and what he did before she died. Hell, Tasha didn't even know the full truth. She only knew enough to know she didn't want to know more.

"No. No real answers, I guess. It was more a chance for me to talk than anything else."

"What did you talk about?" He turned to look more closely at her.

"Everything." About her father. About Roman. About how terrified she was all the time that Roman would find her and kill. About how she was tired of running and wondering if she could settle down in Pine Valley.

Andrew reached over and tucked a strand of hair behind her ear, and it was all she could do to keep from leaning in closer. "Tell me what you told your mother. Tell me about those secrets you keep, Tasha."

She blinked, surprised at his words. "Secrets?"

Oh God, had he realized she was hiding something?

He shrugged. "We all have secrets, I guess. But sometimes I feel like yours maybe… *weigh* on you. I'd like to help you shoulder them, if you'll let me."

She had way too many secrets, and would like nothing more than to lean on him. But she couldn't.

So she took a sip of wine and gave him a partial truth instead.

"I don't know that I really talked about any secrets. But I did tell my mother I'd met a man who pushed me to do something scary. Who encouraged me to take a risk. I cried and laughed. Hell, I probably looked like a crazy person. But I didn't care. When I walked away, I felt freer. Lighter."

"Good. That's generally how I feel when I visit Kylie's grave too."

"You love her." Talking about her in any way was dangerous but Tasha couldn't stop herself.

He shrugged. "I'll always love her. She was an amazing mother and wife."

"I'm sure she was," Tasha whispered.

"But don't get me wrong, she was also stubborn and a pain in my ass a lot of the time. Definitely no angel."

Tasha had no idea what to say. She didn't begrudge Andrew his obvious love for his wife, but also hearing about her was hard for multiple reasons.

"I'm so sorry for your loss," she finally said. The words would be inadequate under any circumstances, but for Tasha they were indefinitely more so.

"You've never asked me how she died."

Tasha stiffened. No, she hadn't asked because she already knew. But her lack of curiosity had to seem odd to him.

"I—I just figured you didn't want to talk about it with someone you'd…"

Ugh. She was making it worse.

He raised one dark eyebrow. "Someone whose house I should be embarrassed to even be sitting in given how I treated you the last time I was here?"

She cringed. "No! No, that's not what I meant. I just meant I figured it was none of my business."

His face relaxed into a smile. "I do still owe you an apology for that night."

"You already apologized."

He let out a rueful sigh. "My actions warrant more than one. Probably a dozen."

Before she could stop herself, she leaned over and kissed him.

"You had a bad moment." She said against his lips. "We all get them. I don't hold it against you, so don't hold it against yourself."

She started to pull back, but his hand reached out and hooked around the back of her neck, pulling her lips back against his.

And he took control of the kiss, his tongue seeking hers and inviting her to play, easing her until she was laying draped over his lap. His lips were hot and demanding on hers—both their breath soon ragged as she felt his hand on her hip, pulling her closer.

Yes, she wanted this. Wanted more.

"Let's go back to the bedroom." She could barely move her mouth away from his to say the words. She slipped her fingers into this hair, moaning quietly has he kissed across her jaw and then down the side of her neck.

She waited for him to pull back, lead them to the bedroom, but he didn't.

His hands came up and cupped her cheeks gently, as he kissed the side of her mouth before running his tongue over her lower lip.

Then he drew back just a fraction of an inch. "I want to. I want to take you back to that bedroom and do everything right this time. Show you how good it can be."

She smiled. "Then let's do it."

She shifted away, getting ready to stand. She didn't want to continue out here in the light. He hadn't noticed the feel of her scars last time, maybe he wouldn't notice this time either. But in the light he would definitely notice them.

Andrew didn't move. He looked away, almost pained, before returning his attention to her.

"What's wrong?" she whispered.

"Tonight, I just want to hold you. Would that be okay? For us to take things slowly? I want to be with you, to lay with you, and have you laying against me. Just…hold you."

She studied him. Maybe he was struggling again about his wife, about how to move forward. That was fine. At least he was attempting to do it the right way this time, rather than running out the door. She wouldn't demand an explanation for things he might not be ready to talk about.

She could give him that, at least. She leaned her forehead against his. "Holding each other sounds wonderful. It's been an exhausting day."

He nodded. "Filtering through family stuff can be exhausting."

"Trust me, I understand. My family is the most exhausting thing in my life."

Chapter 14

Hours later Andrew laid in Tasha's lumpy bed holding her soft body close to him. He'd never been this torn in his whole life.

She'd been visiting her mother's grave. Damn. Andrew had called it in to Zodiac on the way from the Chill N' Grill. Once they knew where to search, they'd been able to confirm it almost immediately. She'd been in Gatlinburg most of the morning.

Her whereabouts were accounted for. She hadn't been doing anything wrong. Hadn't run away to meet with her brother and plan some criminal activities.

Since Andrew had spent most of the day calling himself a fucking idiot thinking she'd played him, it had taken a complete shift in mental gears for him to accept that she hadn't been. He'd almost completely ruined everything by how he'd treated her at the restaurant before he'd pulled it together.

Tasha had gone to visit her mother's grave because of their conversation while on their picnic. She'd even thanked him for it.

She shifted, murmuring a little in her sleep and he pulled

her closer, unable to let her go, not to mention it was so damned cold in this house.

He stared up at where the paint was peeling from the ceiling, still trying to wrap his mind around this woman.

Everything about her said she wasn't a criminal. He'd been watching her for five days now. She was kind to other people. Zodiac Tactical had done their best to make things financially tight for her, but he'd still seen her pay for old Mrs. Sutton's food when the woman forgot her purse.

What sort of criminal mastermind did that something like that?

My family is the most exhausting thing in my life.

Her words from a couple of hours ago wouldn't leave his mind. What did that mean? That she wanted out? That she was about to make a move with the cartel?

He scrubbed a hand down his face. Regardless of whether Tasha was innocent or guilty, they still needed her for intel.

And Andrew had figured out the way to get it.

He eased back from her slowly so not to wake her. He needed to talk to Callum and discuss his plan.

He slipped on his clothes and shoes and grabbed his jacket as he headed to the front door. The snow had started shortly after they went to bed and was still coming down. He quietly opened the door, then walked out to his truck. He couldn't take a chance on Tasha hearing anything he was about to say.

Despite it being the middle of the night Callum picked up on the first ring.

"Is everything okay?" the other man said without greeting.

No. Everything definitely wasn't okay.

"Yeah, it's all fine," Andrew responded. "Except for the fact that I don't think we're going to get anything from Tasha the way things stand now."

"Have circumstances changed?"

"No, and that's the problem. Nothing has changed and I don't foresee it changing anytime soon. We need to make a move. We need to do something that will force Tasha into action."

"I'm assuming you have something in mind if you're calling me in the middle of the night."

Andrew didn't like what he was about to suggest, but he didn't see another way around it. "I think we need to leave Roman's calling card where Tasha will find it."

Callum let out an exhausted sigh. "Please don't tell me that you're suggesting we leave a dead body in her house. That's beyond what even I can arrange."

"No, I mean leave the calling card *electronically*. Something that makes her think something's wrong."

Callum was silent for a minute as he thought. "Okay, I can see where this could possibly work. Let's walk through the possible options for what might happen."

Andrew nodded even though the other man couldn't see him. "The way I see it, Tasha falls into one of three camps. One, she is part of the Volkov Cartel like we've always thought. She's their lookout person or whatever.

"Okay."

Andrew looked out at the snow. "The second option is that she knows about the cartel, but she's not actually one of them. Maybe she has turned her back on them and just wants to live her life. Pine Valley seems like a reasonable place to do that."

Callum made a murmur of agreement. "Okay. That's possible too."

"The third possibility is that she's not even aware of the cartel at all. Maybe her father kept her sheltered from it, she doesn't know anything about it, and she's a dead end."

Option two or three would mean she was innocent. Andrew couldn't let himself hope that was true.

"Okay," Callum said. "I agree those are the three most likely outcomes. So how does Roman's calling card help us?"

Andrew had already thought about this for a long time. "If she knows about the cartel and Roman's calling card, she is going to wonder what the hell it means that he's sending that image to her. She'll either contact him electronically or maybe even try to go to their next rendezvous point."

"Okay. Keep going."

"If she knows about the calling card but has nothing to do with her family maybe that will still compel her to contact them and find out why Roman is sending it. And if she doesn't know about it at all then it will just be a very weird thing she was sent and she'll ignore it. Whichever way she responds, I will be here to help with the fallout."

Callum let out a murmur of agreement.

"At the very least it will show us what she knows, even if it's only subconsciously."

Andrew waited silently as Callum processed what he was suggesting.

"The only downfall I see is that once we put this into motion, we can't stop it. We're either going to have to eventually explain that you're law enforcement or we are going to have to be ready to move if she does."

"Agreed. But anything is better than sitting around waiting for Roman to kill again."

"That sure as hell's right."

"My gut says she's innocent, Callum," Andrew said. "The more I'm around her, the more I think that's true."

"We've both worked this game long enough to know that a pretty face doesn't necessarily mean an innocent one, man."

"Yeah, I know. And if I'm wrong, I'm wrong. But I don't think I am."

"Okay," Callum agreed. "I trust your gut. Either way, we're

going to know more in a few hours than we do right now. I'll get Jenna to set up the calling card video and we'll send it to the chat room with ties to Roman that Tasha has visited periodically."

Andrew rubbed his eyes. "That's the big stickler, isn't it? Why would she be visiting that chat room at all if she's not part of the cartel?"

"It is damning, but there could be factors we don't know about. You just be sure to watch your back. If we lay this trap and you're wrong about her innocence, she may react in the same way Roman does: shoot first, sort out the bodies later."

"It's not going to come to that," Andrew said, praying he was right, but knowing he couldn't know for sure.

They finished up the rest of the details of the call then Andrew eased his way back inside the house.

He looked over at the couch where he and Tasha had kissed for so long tonight. Who would've thought that he'd reached the age of thirty-five and still be so damned thrilled by making out with a woman fully clothed.

But he had been. Thrilled by the soft, sweet kisses. Thrilled by the deeper, more passionate ones.

The soft little moans she'd made as he'd worked his lips down her neck had somehow been more intimate than the sex they'd had a month ago.

God, how he wanted to make that up to her. He'd wanted to do it tonight, had itched with the urge to slowly peel her clothes off of her and then make her understand how good it could be between the two of them.

But he couldn't, knowing that they'd bugged the house and there was a camera in both the living room and bedroom. Even though he trusted his colleague not to be a peeping Tom, he couldn't abuse Tasha's trust in that way.

He ran a hand through his hair making it stick up even

more on end. His priorities were fucked up. Innocent or guilty, Tasha's feelings shouldn't matter.

He needed to get his head on straight, but there was something about this woman that twisted him up inside.

Twisted him up in a way that he didn't know if he was ever going to recover from.

He walked in the bedroom and watched her sleeping. That itch to touch her was clawing at him again. He wasn't sure he was going to be able to keep his hands off her if he got back in bed with her. He should probably just stay out of it.

But then she wrapped her small body into a ball and put her arms around herself, obviously cold. The blanket around her was thin and didn't offer much warmth against the blasts of cold air seeping through the ancient windows, the heater was fighting a losing battle to keep her house warm.

Andrew couldn't leave her like that. He grabbed his phone out of his pocket and texted Isaac.

> I'm going to turn off the camera in her bedroom —something's blinking that's going to make it conspicuous if we're not careful.

> Roger that. I'll replace it next time she's out of the house.

> Callum is going to be coming at you with some new plans. Tomorrow we're going to have more information, so be ready.

> I was born ready.

Andrew rolled his eyes, then set his phone down and stripped back down to his boxers. He hated lying to Isaac, but if he gave in to this desire to do more than just hold Tasha in the morning, he didn't want any sort of audience.

He owed Tasha that much at least.

As soon as he got back into the bed, she snuggled into him as if they'd been sleeping together for years.

He couldn't doubt that her body felt so right next to his.

The question was, did he feel this way about a terrorist?

Chapter 15

Tasha woke trying to figure out why she wasn't freezing. The insulation in this house wasn't the best and she'd woken up cold all winter long. It took her a second to figure it out.

Andrew was here.

This time, he'd stayed. A giddiness she hadn't felt in years swept over her. She couldn't even remember the last time she'd slept all night with a man. She burrowed against him, never wanting this moment to end.

A soft moan rumbled from his throat and he shifted on the bed, unhooking his arm from her waist.

She wanted to tug it back in place, but now that she was awake, she had to pee. She knew better than to stay put and hope the irritating sensation would leave. Better to get up and get it over with. Then she could hop back in bed beside Andrew and maybe even wake him up. See where the rest of the night could lead.

Quietly, she slipped off the bed and grabbed her ratty, white robe. Goosebumps dotted her uncovered legs, now that she didn't have her own personal heater next to her. She ignored the bite of cold that shot up her feet—God she wished she had the money to buy some rugs—as she tiptoed to the bathroom and did her business.

Before heading back to her room, she made a detour to the kitchen for a glass of water, glancing out the window. The barest hint of dawn's light was starting to make itself known—muted in the snow that was still coming down.

It made her want to get back in bed even more. Maybe she and Andrew would be snowed in. The thought brought a smile to her lips.

Whatever would they find to do?

She turned back toward the living room, about to dart for the bed when she saw her laptop. It was sitting on her coffee table, the screensaver pattern floating across the screen.

In the top right corner a red cupcake icon was blinking. She knew what that meant. She had a message on the listserv she used solely as an attempt to try to monitor Roman's whereabouts and actions and to stay ahead of him.

The site looked like it was about baking hints, but she'd seen Roman use it on his computer and knew it was much more sinister than sharing pointers on making your cupcakes more chocolatey. It doubled for passing intel among the Volkov Cartel and others.

Honestly, she had no idea how it worked and hadn't been able to make much sense of anything. This was the first time she was receiving a message directly. It was probably some sort of mistake.

But still she slowed as she reached for the keyboard, trepidation coursing through her. She pressed the button to open her account.

It was a video file.

Her breath hitched in her throat. She slowly pressed play, only relaxing when the video started and showed a candle flickering next to some baked goods.

She let out a little laugh. Okay, she'd definitely let her

imagination get the better of her with that one. Someone had obviously mistaken this listserv as a true baking site.

She was reaching to shut down the page when the camera angle panned, moving away from the cookies. It zoomed out to show more of the room. The first object to come into sight was a shot of vodka sitting on the floor.

Then the dead body.

She saw the X's cut over the eyes and immediately knew it was Roman. Fear fisted her throat smothering the scream struggling to break free. She covered a shaking hand over her mouth and stumbled backward, unable to tear her eyes away from the footage.

Roman had sent her this.

Her head spun in panic. What did it mean? That he was coming for her? Could he track her computer?

She had to get out of here, right damn now.

She'd have to take the computer with her. She'd ditch it on her way. No way was she leaving it here with Andrew in the house if Roman was using it to track her.

She sprinted to the kitchen and got her phone from the drawer then hurried to the closet and grabbed the bugout bag, shoving the phone in the pocket, and set it by the front door.

Sweat coated her palms and her heart raced, but she couldn't slow down. Time was of the essence. Every second mattered.

She hurried for the bedroom silently. The sound of Andrew's heavy breathing stopped her in the doorway. He lay on his back, his chest raising and falling, and a forearm thrown over his eyes.

Regret twisted her insides. She'd give anything to forget what she'd just seen and be able to get back in bed with Andrew and cuddle against his warmth.

But that wasn't her life.

She'd let herself forget what her life was really like in the midst of last night's kisses, but there was no forgetting it now.

She mentally stomped down all emotions. Wishful thinking wouldn't help her now. She grabbed her yoga pants off the floor, shoved on a pair of socks and sneakers then made a beeline for the nightstand. She inched open the drawer, wincing at every sound and creak until she could slide out her Glock. The heavy weight in her hands loosened the pressure in her chest by a fraction.

But still, one gun wouldn't be enough if Roman was coming for her. If she wanted to protect the people she cared about, Andrew and all her friends in town, she had to get out *now*.

Get as far away from them as possible.

She gave Andrew one last longing look then moved soundlessly toward the front door. Shrugging on her coat, she scooped up her laptop and bag—shoving the gun in the pocket next to her phone—then hesitated for a brief moment. She took in the shabby living room one more time.

Her heart ached.

This rented space hadn't been fancy, but it'd been hers. These walls offered her comfort and warmth and protection. Had given her refuge and made her feel safe enough to be a small part of the community she hated now to leave behind. Her potted plants caught her eye, and she rushed over and grabbed the closest pot. One thing, so she'd always remember this place.

As if she was ever going to forget it or Andrew.

She stepped outside then turned and relocked the door pelted by freezing rain and snow the whole time. She gasped, the sudden cold burning her lungs. The combination of the freezing wind and rush of adrenaline made her teeth chatter. A blanket of white covered the ground.

Ice sealed her car door shut and inches of frozen powder

hid her windshield. Gritting her teeth, she yanked on her door until it creaked open. She started it, thankful when the engine sputtered to life. She blasted the heat, hoping the vents would pour out warm air soon, and let it run while she used her forearm to swipe away the snow from her windshield. A thin layer of ice remained, so she found an old credit card in her wallet and chipped the ice away until she cleared a tiny patch of visibility.

Good enough.

She jumped into the car, closed the door, and set the windshield wipers in motion to combat the remaining ice as she flew in reverse then sped off down the road. Her tires spun over the slippery street, but she didn't dare slow.

She gripped the wheel and shot a nervous glance in her rearview mirror. No headlights chased after her nor idling cars waited in the shadows to follow.

How far away was Roman?

She couldn't think of that now. Couldn't let the sadness threatening to swamp her take over. Couldn't think about all she was leaving behind.

She just had to get the hell out of town. Fast.

Her life here was over.

She could only pray her life wasn't over completely.

Chapter 16

"Not me. G-get them out. Leave—leave me—"

Smoke burned the back of Andrew's throat, searing his lungs. He couldn't shake the taste of it—that acrid weight on his tongue left behind by the flames licking up the walls and burning through throw pillows and the blue rug beneath him.

Fire. Fire everywhere. He couldn't see a thing in the smoky haze but he could feel the heat singeing his arms and legs. A woman hovered over him, her face distorted by smoke and flame. He could barely see her.

"Kylie?" His voice was hoarse and broken—he barely recognized it.

No, not Kylie. He already knew it wasn't her. The touch of the woman who hovered only inches away didn't feel like his wife. She gripped his shoulders and shook him, and he heard the faint sound of a voice breaking through the flames. He blinked, trying to clear his vision and mind enough to process anything but the agony overwhelming him.

He couldn't move.

He had to move.

The not-Kylie woman came into view, her large eyes reflecting the flames as she said something.

Tasha. It was Tasha.

No that couldn't be right.

The not-Tasha shook him harder, her face the only clear thing in his vision. Her eyes went wide with fear, her lips parting as she yelled something at him.

But there was nothing but roaring flames and crackling embers. He couldn't even hear the blood rushing through his ears anymore.

Tears fell down her cheeks, and for a moment she looked up and toward the window on the far side of the room. Her profile was smudged with dirt and soot, and her hair—dark and loose over her shoulders—was peppered with ash. She turned pleading eyes to him, saying something he couldn't hear.

"My wife. Kylie…" He tried to stand, but unable to make his body work. It was then that he felt it, something heavy over his legs and ripping, tearing in his lower back.

The pain was enough to numb his senses, his vision going cloudy and dark.

"Wait—the g-girls—. Where are they?" The ceiling above his head was nothing but smoke. The entire second level burned above him. Andrew's eyes fluttered as the woman holding him and shielding his body from the sprays of embers flinched, and through the flames he heard her cry out in desperation.

And then his blood rushed to his head, ringing in his ears.

Pain. All he felt was pain. His back stung as he was dragged across the floor. His lungs burned with each ragged breath.

"Stay with me." The words were a whisper, something he wasn't sure he actually heard. "Stay with me."

He tried to struggle. "Girls. Please, girls."

He didn't matter. The girls mattered. Kylie mattered.

"They're already outside," Not-Tasha said.

They were?

Yes. Right. The girls were outside. They'd gotten outside.

But how had they gotten outside? He couldn't have done it. He could barely move.

"Why are you here?" he asked Tasha.

Why was Tasha in his nightmare? She shouldn't be here at all.

She didn't reply. Just dragged them both inch by agonizing inch from the burning building. Reality blurred in and out.

The pain. The heat. Tasha sobbing as they moved. Andrew couldn't do anything to help her. The only sound louder than her sobs was the incessant thumping that hurt his ears and made his skin crawl with adrenaline.

Over and over. What was that?

Andrew sat straight up in bed, his heart racing as three loud bangs echoed through Tasha's bedroom. Someone was shouting his name.

His nightmare faded as he blinked into the dimly lit room trying to get his bearings. Why had he seen Tasha in his recurring nightmare this time?

He scrubbed a hand down his face, the hair on his arms standing on end as he reached across the mattress for her but found her side of the bed empty and cold.

Where was she?

Three more knocks thundered at the door.

"Tasha?" he asked loudly as he swung his feet from the bed. Where was she?

"Andrew!" The deep voice very definitely wasn't Tasha.

"Isaac?" Andrew rushed toward the front door and fumbled with the many locks before throwing it open. Cold hit him, making him fully aware of the fact he was in little more than boxers and a T-shirt. Snow ripped in every possible direction as Isaac glowered and pulled a snow-plastered beanie from his head and storming in.

"What the hell is going on? I thought you were fucking dead. What the hell happened?"

Andrew was blinking away the last of the nightmare and looking for any sign of Tasha. Where was she? Definitely not here. This place was too small to give her someplace to hide.

"What are you talking about? Where's Tasha?"

"I've been calling you for forty-five minutes. You disconnected the cameras last night. I didn't know what the hell was going on."

Shit. Right. "I'm fine."

Isaac rolled his eyes. "Yeah, I figured that out since you're here perfectly intact except for some hideous bedhead."

"Where is Tasha?"

"That's why I was calling, then drove through that fucking blizzard to get here. She left fifty-one minutes ago."

"*What?*"

"Right after we sent the calling card. She checked it at exactly 6:03 a.m."

Andrew glanced at his watch and cursed. He hadn't expected Callum to have it sent that soon. Tasha must haves seen it and bolted immediately. Glancing at the closet again, he noticed her bag gone. So was her laptop.

He bit down on a curse and planted his hands on the table, leaning down to look at Isaac's screen.

"The tracker's doing its job." Isaac pulled up the radar, a little blinking dot showing something moving west out of town. "So we at least we know where she is."

"Anything from her phone? Did she contact anyone?"

"No incoming or outgoing calls or messages."

"But she's on the move." Andrew stood to his full height and heaved a breath. He walked to the nightstand and threw the drawer open. Nothing. Empty.

This was not how he'd envisioned this plan going.

"You spent the night here with her. Wouldn't she have woken you up or said something if she was scared?"

"Obviously she didn't." The truth hit him in the gut. "How many eyes are on her right now?"

"Just tech."

Andrew eyed the locks on the front door. He'd had to open them before he could let Isaac in. She'd taken the time to lock every single one before she took off without a word.

Had she been closing him in to protect him from the threat she thought was coming her way, or locking him in here to give her longer to escape?

He needed to get to Tasha. "I'm going after her. Call it in so that Jenna can give me real time updates as I go."

"I'll come too—"

"No." Andrew walked into Tasha's bedroom and finished getting dressed, then walked back out to grab his jacket off the back of one of the rickety dining chairs. He pulled his boots on. "I need eyes on this house in the event she ditches her car and tries to come back, or if anyone else shows up."

Isaac shifted his weight, tapping his fingers on his laptop. "She's not going to get far in this storm. Look at how slowly she's going. Are you sure you want to chase her down?"

"She's running back to her brother, and because of that calling card she thinks this is an emergency." The words didn't feel right in his mouth. He swallowed thickly. "Or she's freaking out and is trying to find somewhere to hide. Either way it's a suicide mission in this weather."

Isaac nodded. "Okay, but be careful. Hang on so I can get you connected to Jenna."

Andrew walked to look outside where snow was pooled on the front porch and against the frosted windows, and let out a curse. Tasha's car with its bald tires was already a death trap. Now? At least they had a tracker on her car after her last disappearing act to visit her mother's grave. They'd be able to find her this time. He hoped.

"Okay, Jenna's ready." Isaac walked over and handed him an earpiece.

Andrew fitted it in his ear. "Jenna, I'm connected. Over."

"I got you linked up, Gemini." Jenna's voice cracked through the static in his earpiece.

"Why is it so hard to hear you?"

"We're experiencing some blackouts in your region

because of the storm, but I'll do my best." Jenna sounded a little worried, and one look at Isaac told him no one was too thrilled about this.

Andrew wasn't, that was for damn sure. He was either walking right into Roman's lair or setting out on a rescue mission.

He wasn't sure which option was better. Tasha working for her brother was clean cut and simple, something he'd expected when he first agreed to come here and do this. To weasel his way into her life.

But that was before. Now he could only think of her weight pressed up against him last night and the soft moans that left her lips when he trailed hot kisses up and down her neck.

Why hadn't she come to him when she'd gotten that calling card footage? That had to mean she was guilty, right?

If she was innocent, she'd left in a hurry, scared and desperate. And hadn't asked him for help.

That bothered him almost more than the idea that she was working for her terrorist brother.

"If anything goes online on the listserv," Andrew finished suiting up, "you let me know immediately."

"Got it." Isaac nodded, opening his laptop again. "Where's the thermostat in this place? It's freezing in here."

"Broken," Andrew winced, grinding his teeth. "You'll be fine."

Tasha had lived with it broken for long enough.

He didn't wait for Isaac to say anything else before he ripped open the front door and stepped into the storm, sprinting toward his truck.

∿

THICK, wet snow blanketed everything. It was the kind of snow that clung to every surface in big, slushy clumps once it hit the ground. Overhead, wind whipped in every direction sending sheets of white over a barren, silver landscape.

Andrew couldn't tell up from down as he inched along the road. Jenna directed him to turn off the highway after roughly an hour of driving through a blizzard like he'd never experienced before.

His fingers were white on the steering wheel and not just to try to keep on the road. All he could see was Tasha and her big eyes and that bright smile. All he knew was that she was out here, somewhere, freezing her ass off and trying to either get back to her brother, or away from him.

Andrew bit back on a pang of regret that hit him square in the chest at the thought. This mission should have been simple, easy, nothing more than fitting a few puzzle pieces together and bugging a woman's phone to get information on her brother.

It had become so much more than that.

"Gemini, Tasha's vehicle has stopped." Jenna's voice came over the speaker in his truck. The storm had been making communication more and more difficult.

"Where?"

"Roughly a mile north of your cur... location." Jenna's voice cut in and out as she spoke.

The question was: was Tasha meeting someone? Roman?

Andrew squinted into the storm, slowing down a bit to try to glimpse any nearby buildings, but there was nothing but a sea of white. "What else is out here?"

"Satellite footage picked up a few buildings. Warehouses. There's a farm roughly three miles north—" Jenna's connection cracked and filled with static, then came back on. "Can you hear me?"

"Jenna? Over. Come in, Jenna."

Nothing.

Wind whipped against his truck, rattling it violently. He felt the snow trying to suck the vehicle into the embankment to the left of him. He glanced out the passenger window and noticed a steep drop-off, but just how far to the bottom of the embankment was a mystery he didn't want to solve.

Shit. If Tasha's car had lost its momentum and got sucked into the deep ditch, she'd be stuck, not pulling into some safe house owned by the cartel like he told himself.

He'd been almost hopeful she was meeting her brother if only because she'd be safe from the storm. But now that seemed unlikely since there was nothing out here as far as he could tell. Nothing but snow.

My family is the most exhausting thing in my life.

Her words came back to him again. She wasn't meeting Roman. Not out here.

Something metal glinted against what little daylight made it through the angry cloud of bitter weather, grabbing his attention. He turned his head, eyeing a warehouse roughly three hundred yards from the side of the road.

"I'm passing a warehouse."

Jenna didn't respond.

"Jenna?"

Nothing. Not even static.

"Jenna, do you copy? I need an update on Tasha's coordinates." And his, if he were being honest. He'd lost track of direction the second he turned off the highway, which meant he'd been driving blind for almost twenty minutes.

A vacuum of silence filled the interior of the truck. He sped up, trying not to get stuck as the snow hugged each wheel and drew him closer to the edge of the embankment.

"Gemini—Can—hear—"

"Repeat," he shouted, as Jenna's voice cut in and out

again. It sounded like she was trying to talk to him underwater. "Jenna, I can't hear you! Say again, over."

Snow piled on his windshield, the wipers now stuck beneath two fresh inches of slush and frozen solid to the windshield. He couldn't stop now. If he did, he wouldn't be able to get going again, even in four-wheel drive.

What would he even do now if he found Tasha? Let the storm bury them alive, and sit in his truck with Roman Volkov's sister until they were rescued?

"You—passed—she's behind—" Static filled his ears and the connection went dead.

But Andrew had understood enough. He stopped then threw the truck in reverse and moved backward through the snow, cursing audibly as the truck fishtailed and one of the back tires slid over the edge of the embankment. He corrected, rolling the steering wheel all the way to the side and forcing the truck out of the ditch with his foot pressing to pedal to the floor.

A wave of snow spread over the road in his wake, but now he was facing the direction he'd come—at least he thought.

A break in the snow gave him a better view of the road ahead for a split second, and that was all he needed. He saw Tasha's car over to the side.

It was upside down at the bottom of the embankment.

Chapter 17

Andrew stuffed his keys in his pocket and grabbed his gun out of the glove box before bolting out into the storm. The snow immediately clung to his boots as he hurried toward Tasha's car.

"Shit." He slid down the steep hill, noticing the patterns on the snow from her vehicle. He could see where she'd tried to overcorrect and where it had picked up speed before rolling and landing upside down.

He prayed he wasn't about to find the worst as he rushed up to the driver's side door.

"Tasha!" He dropped to his knees, and peered inside.

He let out a hiss of relief when he found the car empty, her bag also gone. But his relief was short lived. He didn't know how long she'd been out in this cold or where she was. Even if he could get back in touch with Jenna, it wasn't going to help him now.

He stood and squinted into the blizzard, the cold biting his cheeks and stinging his eyes while wet clumps of snow hung off his eyelashes.

Through the dizzying haze of white he could barely make

out footprints leading away from the car. The only reason he spotted them made his heart sink into his stomach.

Blood.

Tasha was hurt.

He followed the drops of blood as quickly as possible, unsure of his direction. It became evident where she'd fallen a few times, and the footprints started to weave back and forth like she'd been struggling to maintain a straight line. Crimson splotches left a trail—the *only* trail—through a field of stark white nothingness.

"Tasha!" he bellowed, but her name was carried away by the wind. He shielded his face from a spray of icy snow, his fingers tingling from the bitter chill.

He stumbled down a sloping incline he hadn't seen until it was too late. Trees rose up around him, their branches covering in snow.

"Thank God," he grumbled, brushing himself off and blinking into the calmer shadows. The canopy was thick enough to shield the forest floor from the storm but made it nearly impossible to see where Tasha had gone.

This had not been the plan when he'd had the team send her Roman's calling card. Never planned that she'd be wandering around in this fucking blizzard, hurt.

All because he'd decided to push her into acting, to doing something.

His attention was caught by something on the ground against a tree. Her bag, the contents spilling out into the snow.

"Tasha?" He noted the bloody handprint on the tree and started looking around, but she'd moved on from the area. "Tasha!"

He shrugged her backpack over his shoulders, adjusting the straps to fit his frame instead of hers. It reminded him how petite she was, how thin, almost frail. The only coat he'd ever seen her in hadn't been created for this type of weather, nor were the sneakers she always wore.

He yelled her name again, hating that he was looking for blood to lead the way.

"Come on, sweetheart. Where are you?"

He moved quicker, following the footprints that faded in and out, and the blood splotches that were coming less frequently. Good news and bad news.

Good news, she wasn't bleeding out as far as he could tell.

Bad news, he was running out of ways to locate her, and the storm was keeping everything way too dark.

Wind ripped through the trees, sending sheets of snow down over his head as he continued on, ignoring the biting chill. He gritted his teeth when he saw blood near a small stream, and crossed through it.

If her clothes somehow hadn't been wet before, they were now. *Fuck*. Things had just gone from ugly to downright critical.

He sprinted up a small hill that gave him a visual vantage point of the area. From there he could make out the dark outline of a warehouse about half a mile away. Maybe she was heading for that.

He spun in a circle, eyes taking in as much of the terrain as he could. His heart stopped as he spotted what looked like a dark lump just past the creek.

That had to be Tasha.

He ran with reckless speed toward her, landing on his knees behind her still form—face down in the snow. He moved her immediately. Risky, since she might have some sort of injury, but right now that was secondary to hypothermia. Her lips were blue, her skin pale and cold to the touch.

A gash lined her forehead, the blood had dried but bruising had started to fade into view. Again, secondary.

He picked her up, cradling her soaking wet and nearly

frozen body in his arms. She mumbled something, her chest heaving as she took a shaky breath.

"Andrew?"

Thank God.

"Hang on, sweetheart. I'm going to get us out of here." He held her to his chest and started moving toward the warehouse he'd caught glimpse of on the hill. "Stay with me."

He didn't give a second thought to her weight as he moved them quickly through the snow. If it had been just a few degrees colder, the snow would have been a fine, dry powder. Now it just made everything miserable and wet.

Wet being the problem. "Tasha, talk to me."

"C-cold."

"I know you are. But we're going to get you warmed up, okay?"

With each step the sky seemed to get worse—nothing but a swirl of gray and white. He prayed he wouldn't miss the warehouse and that they'd be able to find a way to get inside. There was no way he'd be able to get her back to his truck and warmed up in time.

She'd stopped shivering violently, which was a bad sign. Her body was no longer trying to generate heat. He needed to get her warm, *fast*.

"Hang in there, angel. I've got you," he said, almost to himself, moving faster.

His arms were burning by the time he crested the hill and let out a sigh of relief, his breath coming out as a puff of mist that was carried away by the wind. The warehouse was in his sights—the metal building sterile and dark ahead of him, snowdrifts clinging to the side of it and icicles trailing along the roof's edge.

Andrew would take it. Anything was better than their current exposure.

He forced speed out of his legs and headed towards what looked like the door. Locked, but flimsy.

"Sorry," he murmured to whoever owned the building, then he kicked the door near the hinges with a single brutal movement that sent a spray of icicles cascading to the ground.

A moment later he was carrying Tasha inside. It had to be cold in here too, but compared to outside in the wind it felt downright balmy.

"Hello?" he called out.

Nothing.

It didn't take long for his eyes to adjust to the dim interior and notice the machinery and crates lining the walls. They were out of the worst of the weather but weren't out of danger yet. Tasha was way too still and he needed to get her out of these wet clothes.

"Tasha, look," he whispered, shaking her a bit. She didn't move, didn't make a sound.

Shit.

The only thing that kept his panic tamped down was that he could still feel her breathing. But that didn't mean the situation wasn't critical.

He spotted stairs that looked like they led up to some sort of office. The enclosed space would be warmer even if it wasn't heated.

He got them up the stairs and opened the door. The space was dirty and smelled like dust and oil, but it was a goldmine.

A desk sat facing the window looking down on the warehouse, a space heater on the ground next to it. On the adjoining wall was a couch, with multiple blankets thrown haphazardly over it. Evidently the warehouse manager was a napper.

He and Tasha could survive the night here no problem, longer if need be.

"We've got blankets, Tasha." He shook her slightly in his

arms, hoping to get her to wake up, but she didn't move. He turned to try to figure out where to set her so he could get her out of her wet clothes when he saw a door in the far corner.

It was a bathroom with a tiny shower. He muttered a prayer of thanks as he carried her through the door and used one hand to start the hot water full blast. The shower was small and grimy but that didn't matter.

"You're okay," he whispered as he started stripping her down. She didn't respond, but her eyes were blinking out at him and her teeth starting to chatter as warm, steamy air brushed over her skin.

"You're okay. We're fine. We're going to get you warm."

She said nothing as he slowly and carefully set her down in the corner of the shower. "Can you stand?"

The only response was her starting to slide to the floor. He helped ease her down then stripped out of his clothing and stepped inside with her.

He turned the heat down on the water so it wouldn't scorch her skin then sank down beside her, pulling her into his lap. Her head lolled against his chest, her rigid body beginning to relax as waves of heated steam prickled their skin. Andrew hadn't admitted how cold he was, but now his body felt like it was on fire from millions of pinpricks as his skin began to thaw.

And it was even worse for her. She would have died if he hadn't found her—a slow, painful death from exposure.

He shut his eyes and bit back the regret welling in his chest. He'd done this to her. He'd asked Callum to send the calling card video to force her to act on their suspicions.

But instead of running to Roman, she'd run for her life.

When Tasha's skin felt warm to the touch and had lost that bluish color, he carried her out of the shower and wrapped her in a thick towel. She still wasn't talking, but at least she was breathing more evenly. Just surviving had taken up all the reserves of her energy.

He laid her on the couch and made quick work of wrapping her in the thickest blanket he could find before pulling the space heater in front of her, putting it on full blast.

She didn't move, so he put his boxers back on then went back into the bathroom to lay out their clothes as best he could to let them dry.

He checked his phone, noticing the bitter cold had sucked the battery life down to practically nothing. Still no service, no way to contact anyone at Zodiac Tactical.

They'd send someone out to locate his truck. He glanced at the couch where Tasha was fast asleep and wondered if the tracker on her car still relayed a signal after the crash.

"Andrew?"

He glanced up from his phone to find Tasha's eyes fluttering open. He went to her, sitting down on the couch, waiting for her to say anything, but all she did was blink up at him with those big blue eyes.

Now that the head wound had been washed, it was looking much better. He doubted she even had a concussion, although the bruise was painful looking.

"Where are we?" she whispered.

"We're okay. It's all going to be fine." He pulled her into him, covering them both with the blanket. He lay on his side and pressed her to his chest.

"Just rest," he whispered against her hair. Her eyelashes fluttered against his bare chest.

He felt her drift off to sleep while the storm raged outside.

The storm raging inside him was no less violent.

Chapter 18

Tasha felt…*warm*. Blissfully, wholly warm and cozy. She purred as she snuggled deeper into the heater keeping her warm.

Wait, no, not a heater, a chest.

Andrew's chest. He was still here in bed with her after all those hours of kissing.

A soft sigh escaped her lips. Having him in bed made the whole broken thermostat thing feel like nothing. She couldn't remember being this warm and she liked it. She could definitely get used to this.

She breathed in deeply through her nose and froze. It smelled like…cars and dust and old cigarettes. This wasn't her house. And even though it was Andrew lying next to her, this wasn't her bed.

Everything that had happened came pouring back.

Roman finding her, sending that video. Rushing from her home. Crashing in the snow. Somehow getting here in this—she glanced around—*office*.

And somehow naked except for the blanket wrapped around her and the warmth of Andrew's body. She vaguely remembered a shower also.

Teeth gritted, she slowly peeled herself off him.

He'd found her. Somehow. She had no idea how. But he'd saved her life.

She gingerly pressed her fingers against her forehead, wincing at the pain. The car had flipped when it went down that embankment—she remembered the terror then just sitting there for several long, freezing minutes. Finally she'd figured out she had to move or she'd die.

She'd nearly done that anyway.

She'd always thought Roman would be the death of her, just had figured it would be by his actual hand rather than indirectly in a snowstorm.

But then Andrew had found her and she was here.

She swallowed hard and gently trailed her knuckles over his cheek, tears stinging her eyes. She had to go. Roman had found her which meant Andrew was in incredible danger being here with her. The greatest gift she could give him was getting as far away from him as possible.

She hadn't even made it off the couch before those brown eyes opened.

"Where are you going?" He sat up as she pulled away, and she was surprised by how quickly he'd moved.

He hadn't been asleep at all.

"I have to go." Tasha's voice wobbled over the words as she stood, pulling the blanket off of them and wrapping it around her naked body. Andrew sat back on the couch in nothing but his boxers, totally unfazed.

"We need to talk."

She swallowed against the hard lump tightening her throat.

"You almost died out there," he said, looking up at her. "What were you thinking driving out into the storm like that?"

"What was I thinking?" she squeaked, her voice rattling.

She couldn't tell him what she'd been really thinking—that she'd been trying to protect her and him both. Roman had already taken so much from Andrew. She couldn't let him take any more.

She tried to force her voice back to a more reasonable pitch. "It was time for me to leave, that's all. I was done."

He raised one eyebrow so high it looked like it might become permanently attached to his hairline. "*Right then?* In the middle of a blizzard after we'd spent hours kissing each other?"

Shit. Yeah, that didn't make any sense. But she was committed now.

"Yes," she forced out. "I knew it was time."

Now those eyes narrowed. "I don't believe you."

"It doesn't matter what you believe! I just have to go and you have to leave me alone!" She was back to hysterical but couldn't stop.

"Tasha…"

"No! You just need to let me go, Andrew! We had a little fun but now it's over. Enjoy your life, and I'll enjoy mine."

She backed further away as he stood up. He held his hands out in front of him, almost like he was trying to show her that she had nothing to be scared of.

God, if he only knew. She had *everything* to be scared of.

"I'm not going to hurt you, sweetheart," he said softly. "If you've got to go, then that's fine. But you need to think about this. It's still storming out there. Your clothes are still a little damp. Your car is upside down in a ditch, even if you could get to it."

He was right but that just built the panic inside her. "It doesn't matter, I have to go."

"Why, Tasha? What could be so important that you're risking your life for? Are you that desperate to get away from me?"

"No. No. I…" She rubbed her eyes with the heels of her hands. "I can't explain."

His fingers wrapped gently around her upper arms through the blanket. "Try. Please."

"There are things you don't know about me." She kept her hands up against her face so she wouldn't have to look at him.

"That's aways true with everyone though, right?"

"Not like this."

"Tasha, please tell me what's going on."

She was so tired. Tired of running. Tired of hiding. Tired of putting her needs aside. Tired of every part of her life being a secret to everyone.

"I'm not who you think I am." The words were out of her mouth before she could stop them.

"Tell me what you mean by that. You're not Tasha Bowers?"

"No." She dropped her hands from her face. She had to face him as she said this. "My last name isn't Bowers. It's... Volkov. Tasha Volkov."

He froze, eyes narrowing. "Volkov? That's an unusual name. I...knew someone with that last name before."

She'd known he'd put it together immediately.

"Roman Volkov," Andrew continued. "I found out later he was a criminal."

"Yes. Roman is my half-brother." She forced the words through a dry throat.

Andrew shook his head like he couldn't believe it. "Not just a criminal, Volkov was a *terrorist* from what I found out." He began pacing back and forth in front of her. "Are you a criminal, too, Tasha? Is that why you were running away?"

The chill in his eyes made breathing difficult.

She wasn't going to get into the fact that Roman wanted her dead, but she could at least answer this honestly. "No, I'm not."

"But your brother is."

"My half-brother." As if that made any difference.

Andrew obviously felt the same based on his bitter laugh. "Right. *Half.*"

"Andrew, I—" She reached toward him but he jerked away. Even though she'd been expecting that response, it still hurt.

"I was one of Volkov's bankers three years ago. Did you know that? I was providing him advice for how to set up off shore accounts most effectively. This was when I didn't know he was a terrorist."

She nodded, unsure of what to say.

"Did you know I worked for your brother? Did you know who I was when I came to Pine Valley?"

She didn't want to lie to him. "Yes. I knew you worked for him three years ago. I didn't know any specifics."

"Right." The word was short. Bitter.

"I found out Roman Volkov was a criminal right about the time of Kylie's accident. I probably should've gone to law enforcement with my suspicions but I had other things on my mind."

Accident. She rubbed at her chest. She had to tell him the truth.

"Your wife's death wasn't an accident. Roman had her killed."

"What?" Andrew roared.

Tasha stepped back. She didn't want to tell him all the details, but she had to tell him something.

"About three years ago Roman found out his business had been infiltrated by law enforcement. He basically ordered a hit on anyone he wasn't one hundred percent sure about."

"Including my wife?"

"No, *you*. Your wife was collateral damage. He had a dozen people killed that night."

The words made her ill—memories swamping her. It was the night Tasha had found out the truth about her brother and what her family truly was: *evil.*

That night had changed everything. When she'd come across the communication on Roman's desk with details of the plan to execute a dozen people, she'd tried to stop them. Stop *any* of them. She'd rushed from place to place but had been too late.

Even with Andrew she'd been too late to save his wife.

He backed up from Tasha as if he wanted to be as far away from her as he could get. "I need some time."

He walked to a door and opened it wide, revealing a bathroom. Dusty, amber-hued light flickered inside, casting him in shadow. She vaguely remembered the warmth of a shower in it.

He pressed a hand to the doorframe and sighed heavily. "Did you know Roman was a terrorist?"

"I'd found out he was a criminal a little earlier, but I didn't know how bad it was until that night. I would've done anything I could to stop him." She'd even put anonymous calls in to the police—although she hadn't had enough details to seem credible.

But that didn't bring Kylie back, did it? Andrew's daughters would never know their mother.

He said nothing further as he shut the bathroom door behind him, locking it.

She couldn't leave now even if she wanted too. Her clothes and shoes were in there with him.

Her legs wobbled as she walked back to the couch and sank down into the cushions. The tears came and she didn't even try to stop them.

She'd just lost Andrew forever...not that he'd really ever been hers.

Chapter 19

Andrew let the hot water wash over him wishing it would wash away the weight he felt at having to act surprised and angry when Tasha told him Roman had been responsible Kylie's death.

Andrew had lived with that knowledge every day for three years. And evidently so had Tasha.

She wasn't lying. He knew that in his gut. Every instinct that had told him she was innocent, and the fact that law enforcement hadn't even known she'd existed until a month ago just confirmed it.

The water rushed over him and steamed around him. Talking about Kylie's death still wasn't easy—would never be easy.

But knowing Tasha had nothing to do with it eased something inside Andrew. This changed everything between them. Ended all the reasons he'd been holding himself back from her.

He needed to report in to Callum Webb and Zodiac to let them know what he had found: Tasha wasn't their enemy. There was no love lost between her and her half-brother. But unfortunately, that also meant she wasn't going to be able to lead them to Roman either.

Andrew turned off the water. He couldn't yet tell her he was working for law enforcement. Not until he and the team had a plan. Once she knew exactly what he was, and what they were trying to do, there was no going back. And he would definitely tell her, he just needed more time.

He stepped out of the shower, drying off, and putting on his clothes. He needed to figure out what he could say to Tasha. Even though he couldn't admit he was working with law enforcement to bring her brother down, he could at least let her know that just because she was related to Roman didn't mean Andrew held her in any contempt.

There was no reason to keep such a distance from her anymore, not that he'd been doing such a good job of that anyway.

He opened the door silently and walked back into the office. Tasha was as far away from him as she could get, sitting on the corner of the couch with her back to him. Her head was bent and arms resting on her knees and he knew she hadn't heard him.

Because she was crying.

His heart broke. He'd played too tough when pretending to learn that Roman had killed Kylie. Made Tasha feel too guilty. That was going to come back to haunt him when she learned the truth that Andrew had known everything all along.

But no matter what, he couldn't leave her like this. He moved forward, ready to take her in his arms.

He stopped when he got close enough to see her skin clearly. The blanket had fallen off her shoulders, revealing her naked back to him.

His mouth went dry as he processed what exactly he was seeing. Tasha's back and shoulders were covered in scars—the kind that made her soft, smooth skin raised, uneven, and mottled in places. He knew exactly what those scars were. Had some himself.

Burn scars.

Andrew squinted, wondering if the dim overhead light was playing tricks on him. But another step closer assured him it wasn't.

"Tasha—"

She turned her head, her hair partially covering her profile as her teary eyes met his. Something about that movement— the way her hair shifted over her face and shoulder—sent a hazy flash of memory rushing to the forefront of his mind.

His dream this morning hadn't been wrong. It had been Tasha at his house the night Kylie died.

"You were there that night," he whispered roughly, meeting her eyes.

Tasha gave him a brief nod, tears spilling from her lashes as she blinked. She didn't break from his gaze as his world shattered and crumbled around him.

Tasha was his angel.

He sank onto the couch next to her, his hand still over her back like it bound them together in some way. Maybe it *had* bound them—some unseen tether that snapped into place that night Tasha saved his life and the lives of his infant daughters.

"It was you," he continued in a barely audible whisper. "You got me out. You got the girls out—"

"I tried to stop it." The column of her throat bobbed as she swallowed. "I swear. All I had was a list of addresses where Roman's hits were taking place. I got there too late."

"Why didn't you tell me you were there?"

"What was I supposed to say?" Tasha's laugh held no humor whatsoever. "Hey, it's me…the woman who dragged you out of your house after my brother tried to kill you." She shook her head, wrapping the blanket tight around her.

"But you saved me. Saved the girls."

"But I couldn't save Kylie. You begged me to, but I couldn't do it." Tasha turned to face him and her expression broke his heart into pieces.

"I couldn't find her," she breathed. "I tried, Andrew. I did. I heard the girls crying upstairs and knew—I knew I had to get them out. They were so little." She looked down at her arms beneath the blanket like she could still see them there. "I got them outside and the house just… erupted in flames. I heard you screaming for your wife."

Tasha looked up at the ceiling and blinked several times like she was trying to dry out her tears before continuing, "I left the girls in the grass and ran back inside because I couldn't—I couldn't let Roman leave them without parents, even if it killed me to try. You were in the living room when the ceiling came down. You kept trying to get back to Kylie. You kept fighting me and fighting me. My shirt caught on fire when I pulled you out from under the debris and dragged you outside."

Andrew remembered that. He remembered seeing the night sky moving overhead as he was dragged outside by what he believed was an angel.

It had been Tasha this entire time.

"I tried to find her, but the house caved in on itself before I could go back inside a third time. And my burns hurt so bad…" She shook her head and faded off. "I saw a car pull up and was afraid it was Roman or one of his men. I heard sirens, so I ran."

"What happened after that?" Andrew's hand still hovered just off her back. It was like he couldn't move it away or closer.

"I don't really remember." Tasha knitted her brows. "I woke up in a hospital. They asked me who I was but I gave them a fake name and ran the first chance I got. I knew Roman would be looking for me, would want to kill me for going against him. I went to California and got a job as a maid. I found someone who could make me some fake IDs and forge documents so I could get an apartment and try to move on, but…"

She sucked in a breath and shook her head.

"One of Roman's guys found me one day, followed me home. I went out a window to get away from him and ran. I bought a bus ticket, and I've been running ever since."

This was so much worse than Andrew had thought. She not only wasn't involved with her family's business, she was actively running for her life from them.

There was so much he wanted to tell her. That he and his colleagues at Zodiac Tactical would protect her, that she was no longer alone in this. But, goddamn it, he couldn't. Tasha was still the best chance they had at finding Roman.

He stared at her back. How had he missed those scars?

Because the night they'd had sex she'd insisted on going into the dark bedroom. And in the shower a few hours ago, he'd been too focused on making sure she kept breathing.

But still…he should've noticed. She'd gotten them by saving his life. His and the girls.

"Tasha," he whispered. "Thank you. I owe you so much more than I can ever possibly repay. Without you…"

"I was too late to save your wife and I think about it every day," Tasha whimpered, her entire body trembling.

Andrew roped his arms around her and pulled her to his chest. Tasha didn't protest. She melted against him, her warmth penetrating his skin.

Andrew's mind was a mess of conflicting emotions as he held her.

"You should have told me right away. You should have said something to me at the wedding—"

"It wouldn't have changed anything. You're in danger just being here with me. I have to go, Andrew. When the storm passes, I need to get out of Pine Valley. I'll be fine. I have some money saved. I know how to start over."

"Tasha…"

"I know you hate me for what happened and I'm sorry. I'm so, so sorry—"

He gave up the fight and kissed her before she could utter another word.

Chapter 20

The kiss caught Andrew by surprise. He hadn't planned to do that. But once his lips met hers, he couldn't stop.

There was still so much between them that needed to be said, explained, revealed…but all Andrew could do right now was drown in the desire he had for this woman.

Not just because she was his angel. Not because she'd saved his life and the lives of his daughters. But because she was *Tasha*. Because everything he'd learned about her—even when he thought she was a criminal—had appealed to him.

She was kind and funny and strong.

So turning away from her didn't seem possible at all. And pulling her closer seemed inevitable.

"Andrew."

God, he loved the breathy sound of his name coming from her lips. He picked her up and settled her, straddled across his thighs. Her moan as he pulled her down hard against him was the most beautiful sound he'd ever heard.

"Andrew, I—"

He moved his lips across her jaw. "I know, sweetheart.

Tomorrow brings things we have to deal with. But right now it's just you and me in here. And that's exactly how I want it."

He'd never spoken truer words. Tomorrow would have to fend for itself because tonight it was just them.

Just Tasha.

And she was so fucking beautiful staring down at him with those blue eyes.

"Just you." He placed a kiss against her neck. "Just me." Another one. "Just us."

He nipped gently at her throat again and her head fell to the side with a sigh. He threaded his hands into her hair and brought her lips back to his. God, he could drown himself in this woman and never regret a second of it.

"Hold on to me, sweetheart," he said against her lips. As soon as her arms were wrapped around his neck, he hooked his arm under her legs and stood, lifting her effortlessly with him. "Last time we did this—"

She shook her head. "Don't worry about last time."

Like hell. "I wish very much I could change last time, but I can't. All I can do is give you some new memories to replace those."

And pray it would be enough.

The blanket was draped over his arm, caught between their bodies. He spun then settled her on it, dropping to his knees between her legs.

"Andrew. You don't have to—"

"There's nothing *have to* about this, sweetheart. It's all *want to*." He kissed the inside of her knee then made his way slowly up her thigh, moving from one leg to the other. "You have no idea how many times I've wanted to do this. To be right here. To show you how beautiful and amazing you are."

She let out a soft sigh as he worked the rest of the way up her thigh, kissing the soft skin almost reverently. Because she deserved that type of care—care he very definitely hadn't taken last time.

He let her sighs be his guide, her moans drive his actions. Discovering what she loved at the same time he discovered her unique taste… he was getting just as much pleasure out of giving as she seemed to be receiving.

Every tremble. Every squirm. Every hitch in her breathing… He relished them all.

He didn't stop until she was crying out his name, her hands wrapped in his hair keeping him pulled against her.

As if he was going anywhere else.

He knew the second she came down from her high…felt her release him and try to scoot away, embarrassed.

There was no way he was letting that happen.

Without a word, he got to his feet and scooped her up, spinning them around until she was lying on the blanket on the couch.

"I…" She didn't finish her sentence, looking away.

He cupped her cheek until she was looking back at him. "I hope to hell you're not about to apologize. You're beautiful. You're passionate. You're giving. And I can't get enough of you."

He could see when she started to believe him and a feminine smile crept up her face.

God, this woman.

"I want to feel you inside me," she whispered.

His entire body tightened at her words. "There's nothing I'd like more."

He got a condom out of his wallet sitting on the desk, ignoring the tiny voice in his mind whispering why it was there in the first place, and stripped his clothes off.

No, he didn't need to sleep with Tasha to get information any longer. This was solely because he wanted to.

Tasha still had that smile as he walked back toward her. He

reached out and grabbed her knees, fingers spreading to cover as much surface area as possible. Sliding downward, he parted her thighs and fitted himself between them. Her eyes stayed locked with his as he eased himself inside.

Her smile turned into a gasp and he leaned his head against hers. This was how it should've been between them the first time—how he wanted it to be every time.

He began rocking his hips, each thrust a deliberate attempt show her how amazing she was. How special. He couldn't use words, but he could use his body.

Their breathing matched the pace of their bodies. Her hands clung to his back as if she was afraid of being swept away by what was happening between them.

Andrew understood that notion way too well.

He reached down and hitched her leg up over his hip, changing the angle of his penetration so the pressure began to build inside her again. He forced himself to move slowly—rolling his hips in a deliberate motion—until her moans were once again filling room.

Then he let himself loose.

She wrapped her legs around his waist as he thrust harder and faster. His fingers gripped her thigh and his groans were all he could hear.

Tasha was all he could feel.

The fervor built inside them until all it could do was crash and shatter. Andrew called out her name as he felt her nails dig into his back.

Then there was only heat. Only passion.

Only them.

Chapter 21

Twenty-four hours later the snow had stopped falling. Not only that, it had started to melt. It was like Mother Nature had totally forgotten that she'd tried to kill Tasha just the day before.

She felt Andrew's hand on her elbow as they walked the last steps through the slush to his truck. She liked feeling the protective gesture from him. Like feeling his hands on her.

She was exhausted but in a good way. Andrew hadn't been able to keep his hands off of her since he'd come out of that shower after finding out Roman was her brother.

When they'd used up the condoms Andrew happened to have with him they'd made love in all the other possible ways. Ways Tasha had never even considered.

He'd definitely more than made up for the first time they'd been together.

She never imagined this was how he'd react to the truth. It was more than she possibly deserved.

She offered him a small smile as he opened the door to his truck for her and got her settled inside. Her car was still upside down in the ravine. She had no idea how she was going to get it out—she had no money for a tow truck.

And no matter how gentle Andrew was with her now or how great the past twenty-four hours had been, Tasha knew she couldn't stay. She couldn't put Andrew in jeopardy like that. Him knowing that Roman was a criminal already made him a target. The best thing she could do for him would be to stay as far from him as possible.

But also, now that she'd had a chance to calm down and think about it, she knew there was something off about Roman's calling card.

Why had he sent it electronically? That didn't seem like something Roman would do if he wanted to kill Tasha for betraying him and the family. Showing up at her bungalow and putting a bullet in her head was more his style, not sending some video file.

If he knew where she was he would've already showed up to kill her. He must've been using the calling card to get her to give herself away. To do something stupid.

Case and point, her car upside down in a ravine.

She needed to remain calm, come up with a plan to quietly slip out of Pine Valley and reestablish herself somewhere else. Panic led to mistakes.

"You doing okay?" Andrew asked as he got in on the driver's side. She looked over at him but remained silent.

She very much wanted to tell him that Roman was toying with her, but what could Andrew possibly do? He was a banker. Not a cop. Even asking him to go with her to tell the police who she was and what she knew would put him in danger.

He had two young daughters. She couldn't take a chance on making Caroline and Olivia orphans.

The best thing she could do for Andrew was get out of his life.

She forced a smile on her face and reached over to grab his hand. "Yeah, I'm fine. Just a little worried about my car."

Yeah, she needed to get out of his life, but not just yet. Wrapping her fingers around his, she couldn't stand the thought of leaving right now. She had to get her vehicle situation figured out anyway, so she would give herself a little more time with him before walking away forever.

He reached over and kissed her forehead. "I'll get one of the Crossroads guys out here and they'll tow it back to town. You'll have it home and working in a couple of days."

A couple of days. That would be her deadline.

A couple of days before she'd need to leave him and all her friends in Pine Valley behind. She wouldn't even be able to tell anyone goodbye. Maybe she'd drop them some notes letting them know she'd moved on. Not that any of them would think much about it probably.

Her heart ached just thinking about it.

It didn't take long for Andrew's truck to warm up now that the weather wasn't quite so bad. Soon they were headed back towards town. When he reached over and put his hand over her thigh she let out a little sigh, and covered it with her own. She very much liked the feel of it there. Might as well enjoy it while she could.

Neither of them spoke as he drove, both wrapped up in their own thoughts.

Andrew's phone rang. She missed the heat of his hand as he let go of hers to answer it. Giggles erupted from his phone and he winced, holding it away from his ear for a moment.

"Daddy!" two sing-song voices shouted through the phone. Andrew's twins.

"Hey, there are my girls." He grinned, face softening. "Are you having a good time?"

Frantic squeals cut through their exclamations about their

Disney trip with what sounded like Andrew's brother and sister-in-law.

"So, so, so, so much fun!" Olivia said, each word barely more than a squeak.

"You sound sugared up." Andrew laughed, and a small argument ensued about not begging their aunt and uncle for sweets before breakfast.

Tasha couldn't help but smile at Andrew as he spoke to his daughters. His eyes were creased with pleasure and a wide grin touched his lips every time their little voices rang through the phone.

It must have been hard raising them on his own.

Tasha had never thought about having kids. That wasn't in the cards for her.

Keeping herself hidden was difficult enough. Bringing an innocent child into her nightmare? She winced at the thought and pretended like she wasn't eavesdropping on Andrew's call.

"What have you been doin', daddy?" Caroline asked with what sounded like a mouth full of food.

"I went camping with my friend Tasha." Andrew's eyes met Tasha's and she felt a warmth spread through her chest as he slowly looked back to the road. "We got snowed on pretty good."

"Snow? It's hot here!" Olivia yelled.

"I like snowball fights," Caroline cut in, before the girls began to bicker about who got to hold the phone.

"Alright, alright." Andrew laughed. "I have to go, but I'll give you a call tonight, okay? I love you."

After a few seconds of I-love-yous, kisses and then another couple of minutes talking to his brother and sister-in-law and Andrew hung up.

"They sound so happy," Tasha said as he set his phone down in the center console and plugged it into the charger.

"How can they not be happy? They're at the most magical

place on earth with two people who cater to their every whim." He chuckled.

"I'm sorry you're having to raise them on your own." Sorry that was her fault.

Tasha swallowed past the lump in her throat and refused to meet his eyes. She could feel him looking at her and hated that her words had wiped the smile from his face. She regretted speaking at all.

"And I'm sorry you've been running for three years all alone all because you tried to help my family," he finally said. "My girls are my life. They were the only thing keeping me going for a long time. I had to be strong for them, do what was best for them. If they hadn't been around, I don't think I…" he tapered off.

"They're so well-adjusted and happy."

"Thank you. I had family and friends to help me. It made a difference."

She glanced out the window. The only support she'd had at all she'd found in Pine Valley. And now she had to leave.

"Tasha, I…"

She waited for him to finish but he faded off again.

"Look," he finally continued. "I want you to know you're not on your own anymore. I promise."

Despair clutched her heart and refused to let up. She rolled her lip between her teeth and squeezed his hand back without looking at him. It sucked knowing she had to lie to him even more than she had already.

Telling him the truth about her brother felt like a weight had been lifted, but that was all she could share. She couldn't tell him that Roman was toying with her—trying to put her on edge.

It wasn't long before they were back in Pine Valley. She hadn't gotten very far in the storm. Running out like that had been a huge tactical error. She needed to be smarter.

Andrew was taking her back to her house. She had no problem with that now that she was convinced Roman wasn't really aware of her whereabouts.

When they pulled up in her driveway he jogged around to open the truck door for her, and helped her out. Once they were inside, he sat her down on the couch gently, moving her hair to look once again at the cut on her forehead.

"It's fine," she whispered. He'd already checked it a dozen times while they were at the warehouse. "Just a little tender."

"You should probably take it easy, just in case."

She nodded. "Although if it could withstand our shenanigans over the past twenty-four hours I'm sure it'll be fine."

He grinned at that, but she could tell there was something that was weighing on him. He looked around the house, then back at her.

"What?" she whispered.

He shook his head. "Nothing. I…just want to make sure you're alright. There are some things I need to take care of, but I'll be back in a little while."

"That's fine." She needed some privacy to get some stuff done too.

He crouched down in front of her, reaching to tuck a strand of hair behind her ear. "I'll be back soon, okay? There's stuff we need to talk about."

Not as much as he thought if she was leaving town for good in a few days. But she didn't want to think about that now. Couldn't bear to think about it.

"Yeah, okay. I'll see you soon."

ANDREW WAS on his phone to Isaac the minute he got back in his truck.

"Man, are you okay? Jenna could tell you'd stopped but we weren't sure—"

"We need to get Callum on the line," Andrew interrupted Isaac. "I found Tasha but we need to talk."

"Where were you? Where did you find her? What the hell happened?"

"Callum, first. Then I'll explain." He pulled out of Tasha's driveway and drove toward the RV where they were running command central.

A few minutes later he had both men on the phone.

"I'm glad you're alive, Zimmerman," Callum said. "That could've gotten ugly in multiple ways. We didn't know what was going on."

"The storm killed cell coverage. Tasha flipped her car and almost died of exposure before I found her."

"Were you able to ascertain any intel from her based on her reaction to the calling card?"

"Yes. She hasn't had any contact with Roman for three years. Since the night Kylie was killed."

"What?" Isaac asked. "Are you sure?"

"Tasha is innocent." There wasn't anything Andrew was more sure of.

There was a moment of silence before Callum spoke. "You're positive?"

"Definitely. It was her that pulled me out of my house that night and saved my girls. She has burn scars." He told them about the list she'd found on Roman's computer and how she'd tried to help.

He didn't mention any of the personal details between them, but he wouldn't be surprised if his friends had already put it together.

Right now he wanted all this behind him so he could tell Tasha the truth and start over with her from the beginning— no secrets this time. Pursue her the way she deserved.

"Roman is hunting her," Andrew told both men. "She's going to need our protection."

"Does she know you're working for law enforcement?" Callum asked.

"No, not yet."

Callum let out a sigh. "It's probably best not to tell her. It might spook her. You staying close and keeping the status quo is probably best."

Andrew ground his teeth. He could see Callum's point but didn't want to keep up falsehoods between he and Tasha. "Fine."

"What about the calling card? Has she mentioned it?" Callum asked.

"No. She probably believes it was Roman trying to taunt her. Definitely doesn't have suspicions we sent it."

"Maybe see if you can accidentally stumble onto it and ask for more information. That's probably our best bet for gathering intel."

Andrew agreed with Callum's assessment. "Roger that."

"We need her to talk, Andrew. Otherwise, we can't help her and Roman goes free."

"I know." Andrew hated to use Tasha but the truth was still the same: she remained their best bet for finding Roman and shutting down the cartel for good. "She may not want anything to do with Roman, but that doesn't mean she doesn't know stuff about him that won't prove helpful."

Andrew had to believe Tasha wanted to help. The more he knew about her, the more he knew she'd want to do the right thing.

The real question was whether she'd be able to forgive Andrew once she knew the truth.

Chapter 22

Tasha smiled down at her phone—she'd started carrying it on her after the recent turn of events. Andrew was at her house, and he'd let her know he'd brought a pizza and bottle of wine with him. She was walking back from town since her car was still out of commission. She was supposed to catch a ride from her friend but Laura had called and said she was delayed and she didn't want to wait.

She couldn't wait for a quiet, cozy night with Andrew snuggled up with her on the couch.

Tasha knew she was on the road to heartbreak but couldn't help it. Keeping her thoughts off Andrew and on the task at hand—preparing to run again—was damn near impossible. But she was trying her best.

She'd picked up an afternoon shift at Chill N' Grill. She needed every penny she could get. At least the band-aid on her head made the patrons at the grill more than sympathetic. She'd never made this much in tips before. She'd be excited about it if it didn't mean she was that much closer to leaving.

"Tasha, honey, why are you walking?" A grill regular, the elderly Mrs. Marceen pulled up in her car beside where Tasha was on the sidewalk. Mrs. Marceen and her husband had lunch twice a week at the Chill N' Grill.

"No car." Tasha shrugged. "I went into a ditch yesterday during the storm. My car's being towed back to Crossroads."

"Well, get in! Good gracious, you must be freezing!"

"I don't mind the walk, Mrs. Marceen. I'm watching my figure." Tasha wiggled her eyebrows at the older woman, who gave her a motherly look of disapproval.

"You young people. I'll never understand. Well, if you're sure. Bye now!"

"I'll see you on Thursday!" Tasha waved and chuckled to herself as the older woman drove away. She hadn't been the first person to stop and ask why Tasha was walking across town. People knew Tasha now, expected to see her at the grill and instructing her yoga classes.

Which made having to leave even harder.

She kicked at a rock as she continued down the sidewalk, blinking back tears. She couldn't stay. Staying put all these people in danger just as much as Andrew. Roman wouldn't hesitate to hurt or kill anyone in Pine Valley just to get back at Tasha.

Yet still, the thought of leaving left a gaping hole in her chest.

Two more days to get her shit together. Hopefully her car would be ready by then too. That's all she could afford to wait. Then she'd move on to the next town, to a new name, a new hair color—

"Hey!" Tasha stumbled, her breath catching in her throat as a hand came over her mouth and muffled the scream that left her lips.

"Roman's been looking for you, you little rat bitch," a grisly voice said into her ear, the man's breath tickling her cheek. She wriggled in his grasp, but he was a huge guy. The back of her head pressed against his chest as he dragged her into a darkened alley and out of the shelter of the streetlights that had just started flickering to life.

Fear was threatening to swallow her, freeze her into paralysis. She couldn't let that happen. If this guy got her much further down the alley she wouldn't be able to get away at all.

"Ow!" the man shouted as her teeth sank into the palm of his hand.

She didn't let go until she tasted blood and his grip on her body eased. She lunged out of his reach and ran, but he was fast, catching her by the wrist.

The self-defense she'd studied over the past three years kicked into place. Tasha whirled, her free hand forming a fist that she drove into the inside of his elbow. He staggered forward, thrown off-balance by the blow. Her knee met his groin with a crunch.

She didn't wait to catch a glimpse of his face before driving her fist into his nose. His yell filled the alleyway, and a light in a window above them turned on, casting him in a golden glow.

She bolted, her boots splashing water as she ran through icy puddles. She kept running, jumping up and over curbs and darting between buildings.

She knew this town. She knew it better than the man chasing her through its streets. She'd memorized every road, alleyway, and walking path for this very reason.

"Get back here, you stupid bitch!" her assailant shouted, but his voice was much further back. She was gaining distance now and turned to look over her shoulder only once before taking a sharp turn between two buildings and climbing up a fire escape.

She crouched, holding her breath as he ran by. Two minutes passed. Then five. Still, she waited.

Finally she climbed back down the ladder and dropped to the ground. She quietly crept through the alleyway and cut through two backyards, carefully confirming she wasn't being followed. She kept looking over her shoulder as she slowly got closer to the edge of town and her house.

Nobody. Then it hit her: what if Roman's man had gone to her house first?

Where Andrew was.

Panic caused her chest to convulse as she fumbled in her purse for her phone. "Please, please, please—"

"Hey, where are you? I thought—" he answered.

"Oh, thank God—" Tasha bent at the waist, struggling to catch her breath, tears leaking from her eyes. "Are you okay?"

"I'm fine... what's going on?" His tone changed abruptly. "Tasha, where are you?"

A crunching sound nearby caused her to move on instinct, pressing her back to a wall as a car drove by. She breathed into the phone, her eyes wide as she slipped further into the shadow of the building.

"Tasha—"

She disconnected the call, running the rest of the way to her house. She didn't care who might see her. If Roman's men were here in town, then Andrew was in danger. She needed to get him out. Get them both out.

She reached the door to her house just as it flew open, Andrew taking up the entire doorframe.

She skidded to a stop. "We have to leave." She could barely get the words out she was breathing so hard.

"Why? What happened?"

"Please we have to go right now. We need to go."

"Tasha. Take a breath and tell me what happened? What happened to your ride?"

"I'm so sorry. I was attacked in town. It was one of Roman's men." She ran to the window so she could look out it. "Laura called and said she couldn't make it and I didn't want to impose on anyone else. I'm so sorry, Andrew. I put you in danger. Roman's men are here to kill me but they won't hesitate to kill you too. We have to get out of here right now."

She expected a demand for more details or a panicked flurry from him, but he looked calmer than she'd ever seen him.

"Get your bag." He was typing on his phone as he said it.

Why was he so calm and collected?

She grabbed her bag out of the closet—silently thankful that he had found it when she was lost in the storm—and returned to his side just as he opened the front door. Putting his phone away, he clutched her shoulder, guiding her outside and toward his truck. He opened the passenger side and got her in before rushing around and getting in himself.

She yelped in surprise when he peeled out of the driveway before she even had time to buckle her seatbelt.

"Andrew—"

"How many were there?"

"I don't know. One guy grabbed me, but—"

"There's never just one," Andrew murmured, pulling out his phone again.

Never just one? Tasha's mind reeled as she looked over at him. Calm, cool, and collected.

He lifted the phone to his ear, his eyes on the road as he sped in the direction of leaving town. "Isaac. We're headed to Command. Roman's men were just spotted in town."

Tasha choked on a breath. *Command?* What the hell did that mean? And why would Andrew be calling someone about Roman's men? Who the hell was Isaac?

Panic started to well in the pit of her stomach as she sank into her seat, her eyes not leaving Andrew's face.

"Who are you?" she whispered, unsure if he'd heard her.

His eyes met hers, full of regret, before flicking back out to the road.

"I'll be there in five. Yes, I have Tasha with me," he said to

Isaac.

Andrew ended the call and set the phone down, then clutched the steering wheel. "I'm sorry—"

"What is happening right now?"

"I'll explain everything. Let's just get you somewhere safe."

She was still trying to wrap her head around what was happening when they came to abrupt stop in front of an RV.

"I— I don't understand what's happening."

"Come inside and I'll answer your questions.

Andrew kept his distance as they walked up to the RV.

Her hands shook. Her whole body trembled. She didn't know if it was from the adrenaline from the attempted kidnapping or if it was due to whatever she was about to see. She had a feeling it was both.

Andrew opened the door and Tasha stepped inside. She wasn't sure what to expect when she walked into the RV, but it wasn't this.

Screens were mounted everywhere inside the space. They were showing footage from all over town: the Chill N' Grill, the lodge, her yoga classroom...

She froze, staring. The images on the main screen were from...

"Oh my God, that's my house."

Andrew reached over and clicked a switch that shut off most of the images, but the damage had already been done. Her heart was pounding too loudly and too fast. Tension filled her whole body.

Tears welled in Tasha's eyes. "What is this?" Bitter cold reality crushed into her. "Andrew? What the hell is this?"

"I'm not a banker."

"What?"

"I've never been in International Finance. That was my role when I was undercover working for your brother."

"Then, then...what are you?"

"I work for an organization called Zodiac Tactical. We're partnered with law enforcement in an attempt to shut down the Volkov Cartel."

Tasha lowered herself into the chair in the middle of the RV. "I don't understand."

"I was undercover when Kylie was killed, but then got out of active-duty missions because of the girls. When Zodiac Tactical found out Roman Volkov had a sister…"

Her. He was talking about her. But his words were going in and out as her brain struggled to process.

"…best way to take Roman down for good. We had no idea that you were on the run from Roman."

"Roman found me," she finally got out. "I didn't tell you this, but he has this sick calling card when he kills someone— cuts X's over their eyes and puts a shot of vodka by their head."

Andrew nodded slowly. "Yes, we're aware of this. It's one of the reasons we want to take him down. He's sick and has to be stopped. The calling card just proves it."

"You don't understand. He sent me a video of his calling card the other day. And now that guy in town—"

Andrew shook his head. "No, that wasn't Roman. That was us. I had our team send you the calling card trying to jump start you into doing something. I wasn't sure if you were in on all this with your brother or not."

His words finally penetrated her brain.

Roman hadn't found her. The calling card hadn't been from him. Andrew and his friend had tricked her. And she'd nearly died in that storm because of it.

"Tasha, I'm sorry—"

She stiffened then pulled away as Andrew touched her arms. She couldn't bear to be touched right now. She felt like her heart was cracking in two.

Nothing was ever going to be the same again.

Chapter 23

Tasha sat at the far end of a long conference table at the Crossroads Retreat, her face void of expression and eyes totally, completely blank.

She'd been that way all day since finding out the truth.

Andrew hated that it was his fault. He wanted desperately to be able to take back how she'd found out the truth about him and Zodiac Tactical. He'd seen the devastation in her eyes when she'd understood how thoroughly her house had been bugged.

She hadn't said a word. Hadn't cried. Hadn't fought. Hadn't slapped him like he deserved. She'd just been…lifeless. He'd tried to interact with her but nothing he said could get her to engage.

Fury was eating at Andrew. At himself, at Roman, at the situation, at the fact that they hadn't caught the man who'd tried to take Tasha in town earlier.

Isaac had sped into town to try to apprehend the man, while Andrew had been dealing with the Tasha fallout, but hadn't been able to get there in time. And like Andrew had known, the man hadn't been working alone. Security footage had captured two men running through town and getting into a car, which had later been abandoned at a gas station a few towns over. They'd switched vehicles, but even Jenna couldn't find footage of the car they'd gotten into before fleeing town completely.

Callum and Ian had gotten in town a couple hours ago. Dawn was creeping up over the horizon of the Smokeys and everyone was aware that the window to catch Roman was inching closed by the minute.

Andrew hadn't slept or eaten, and knew Tasha had declined to go upstairs to a room to rest or eat herself. She'd been sitting in the conference room for hours, alone.

Nothing he could say or do would fix this. And right now he wasn't even trying.

His only priority now was keeping her alive, even if she hated him forever.

Tasha didn't meet his eyes as he sat down at the conference table. He didn't sit next to her. He wanted to be able to see her face clearly without the others noticing he was watching her. Isaac passed a few folders around, pausing for a moment before sliding one in front of Tasha too. She didn't so much as look at it. She wrapped herself tighter in the blue blanket someone had given her during the night and stared blankly ahead at the flatscreen TV on the far wall.

Callum came into the room, followed by Ian—both men looking grim. They nodded at Andrew before walking over to Tasha.

"Ian DeRose," he said, extending his hand to Tasha.

Tasha looked up at him, her blue eyes shining in the unforgiving florescent lights. She unwrapped herself from the blanket and gently shook his hand but said nothing.

Callum introduced himself formally as well, and Tasha responded in the same mostly-empty manner. It was more than she was giving to Andrew, but he didn't care. As long as she was responding to someone.

Jenna Franklin's face came on the big screen TV as she called in from home. The computer guru never left her house, for reasons that were totally her own. She was so good at her job nobody cared where she did it.

Callum started the meeting. "Jenna, get us up to speed."

The screen in front of them switched to pictures of two men side by side.

"This is William Murphy and Victor Sanders. Both known members of the Volkov Cartel. They were both in Pine Valley a few hours ago. Sanders now has a broken nose thanks to Tasha."

Andrew glanced over at Tasha. She was looking at the screen, more tense than she had been a few moments before. Andrew wasn't sure if that was better or worse than the dead, blank stare.

He wanted nothing more than to pull her into his lap and hold her to his chest. Shelter her. Ease her through every flinch and scary thought. If he thought there was any way in hell she would let him, he would've done it already—not giving two shits about what his colleagues would think.

He just wanted to hold Tasha. Assure her they would get through this. Her eyes flashed to him for just a second before quickly looking away. Getting near her right now definitely wasn't a good idea.

"We think the Volkov Cartel reverse-traced the fake calling card video we sent to Tasha's address at the listserv. Evidently they were already suspicious about the account if they were already watching it, but not suspicious enough to move on it." Jenna turned to Tasha. "We should've been more diligent about watching for a reverse trace. That's on me, so I apologize."

Tasha gave the other woman a small, forgiving nod.

Progress. Very little progress, but still better than the blank stare.

"Since they were watching that listserv," Jenna continued, "the calling card video Zodiac sent definitely let them know something was not right. They traced Tasha's computer to where she dumped it outside of town in the blizzard."

"So they didn't know where my house was?" Tasha asked softly.

Jenna shook her head from on the screen. "No. They were already looking at that address but didn't have a reason to act. They probably would've eventually anyway."

And Tasha would've probably been caught completely off guard. Never known Roman's men were coming until it was too late. A glance at her face let Andrew know she understood that too. It didn't change the current situation, but it did play a factor.

"Tasha," Callum said with cool calm. "We're sorry for how this played out. We were unsure of where your loyalties lied. We definitely didn't mean to bring the cartel to your doorstep."

"You were just doing your job." She didn't look at Andrew as she said it, but he knew she was questioning everything that had happened between them.

His hands clenched into fists under the table. He wished he could carry Tasha out of here right now and prove exactly how much *not* his job their time together had been.

The photos of Murphy and Sanders came back up on the screen. "Tasha, are you sure your brother wants to kill you?" Jenna asked.

Tasha sat up straight, more of freeze melting from her eyes. "Yes. I betrayed him. That's not something Roman will forgive or forget. He wants me dead."

"I'll show you why I ask." Jenna pulled up some grainy footage and began to play it. "Pardon the poor quality. This is from a mixture of traffic cams, security footage, and reflections in town this afternoon. Not my best work, but it will give you an idea of exactly what went down."

Andrew watched as Saunders grabbed Tasha and pulled her down an alley in town. Even through the grainy footage he could see the panic on her face behind the man's hand.

He also saw the moment she remembered how to fight back. She bit Saunders then got out from his hold. Every man in the room winced as she kneed him in the groin.

"Good for you," Ian murmured.

Whistles and laughs of appreciation filled the room a second later when she drove her fist into Saunders' nose. Definitely broken.

"I think I speak for everyone when I say, *fuck yeah*, girl." Jenna's face came back on the screen momentarily. "You handled him like a champ."

Tasha shrugged one shoulder, but Andrew caught the slightest hint of a smile on her face. Good. She should be proud of how she handled that.

"But this is what you need to be aware of." Jenna put more footage back on the screen. This was obviously from a different angle. Tasha was running off further in the background, Saunders was in the foreground.

And he was obviously pissed. Andrew tensed as he pulled out a weapon and pointed it at Tasha's fleeing back. If Andrew didn't already know Tasha had made it out of the situation safely, he'd be afraid they were about to watch her death.

But before Saunders could get a shot off the second man—Murphy—ran up and grabbed him. The angle of the footage switched again, Jenna making it so that it was close up on Murphy. He was saying something to Saunders.

"We don't have any audio," Jenna explained. "But I got some lip reading experts to confirm—"

"No. Boss needs her for…" Andrew said it out loud having

figured out what Murphy was saying before Jenna finished speaking.

Jenna nodded. "Yes, exactly. Murphy continued saying something else but he turned his head so we lost the ability to read his lips."

Callum leaned back in his chair. "So there was a no-kill order out on Tasha. Sounds like Roman needs something from her based on what Murphy said."

Ian turned to Tasha. "Do you have any idea of what that could be?"

Tasha rubbed her forehead. "The last time I saw Roman three years ago was in my rearview mirror while his men shot at my car. Not the tires, the windshield. He wanted me dead then, for sure. If something has changed I have no idea what."

"And you've had no contact with Roman or anyone from the cartel in three years?" Callum asked.

"No." Tasha's shrug was exhausted. "Only to run from them."

Once again Andrew was swamped with the need to pull her into his arms, if only to assure her she wasn't alone in this anymore. Not that she was going to believe him.

There was a soft knock at the door before Laura Metcalf stuck her head in the room. Andrew stood immediately and turned to Ian and Callum. "This is Tasha's friend Laura. I called her."

Because if there was one thing Tasha needed right now it was a friend. Someone she knew she could trust. So he'd called Laura a couple of hours ago and woken her up. He hadn't been able to give her many details, but he'd asked her to come in for Tasha.

She'd instantly agreed.

For the first time since she'd found out the truth, Andrew saw life in Tasha as she rushed toward her friend, still clutching the blanket around her. Laura wrapped Tasha in her arms and narrowed her eyes at Andrew.

"Thank you for coming," was all he said.

"I'm going to take her into the kitchen." Laura's statement wasn't a question—she wasn't asking for permission to take care of her friend.

Andrew nodded, but knew he had to say more. "Elizabeth and Tucker said to help ourselves to anything we need. I'm sure that includes the kitchen too. But for Tasha's safety, and in case we have more questions, we need her to not leave the house."

Tasha stiffened in Laura's arms but neither woman said anything as they exited.

Andrew turned back to find everyone staring at him. He gave them a shrug as he sat back down. He wasn't going to apologize. "Tasha needs a minute with a friend to wrap her head around everything. Finding out the truth has been…a lot."

Nobody argued. Probably because they'd all lived through tragedy themselves and knew what it was like to just need a moment.

And for some of them…to never get it.

"We need her, you know that, right?" Callum said softly. "In a different way than before."

Yes, he'd known it from the moment he'd found out Roman was after her and definitely knew it when they'd heard the no-kill order.

They were going to use Tasha as bait.

"We need her if we're going to bring Roman down." Ian sat back and crossed his arms over his chest. "Trust me, I don't like the thought of using your woman to lure Roman in any more than I would like the thought of using Wavy. But if he wants her alive then that's something we can use."

Andrew didn't even blink at Ian calling Tasha his woman.

It was nothing short of the truth—although she didn't see it that way.

"Do you think you can talk her in to helping us?" Callum asked. "Having her cooperation will make this a shit ton easier."

They could do it without her cooperation but it would be more dangerous for everyone involved.

He ran a hand through his hair. "I'll talk to her. Explain. Hopefully she'll be willing to hear me out." But the truth was, he couldn't blame her if she never talked to him again.

"Okay." Callum sat up straighter in his chair. "Then let's figure out our plan."

Chapter 24

"…and so I've been running for my life ever since."

Tasha looked over at Laura as she finished telling the story. The *whole* story—every bit of it.

Her family, and finding out the truth about them being a cartel. The fire that had killed Kylie. Being on the run. Meeting Andrew again under circumstances she thought were much different. Roman's men finding her again.

All of it.

Laura could've been mad because Tasha had been so dishonest, but she wasn't. She just sat there and listened for the past two hours. Listened, and fed Tasha damned near everything in the Crossroads kitchen—snacks, coffee, hell, Laura had even fried an egg for her.

It just felt so good to share it all. To let the pressure release for just a moment.

"So that's it," Tasha finished with a shrug. "You know everything there is to know about me."

Laura gave an unimpressed smirk. "That's all you got?"

"And I'm not a natural blonde."

"Oh, then we're done. I can look past your psychotic

family, but lying about your hair color?" Laura laughed and threw an arm around her. "I don't know that I can ever forgive that."

Tasha leaned into her. "Thank you for being such a good friend. For listening."

Tasha had had no idea how much she'd needed that: just someone to share the burden with who wouldn't judge.

"Really, you're not freaked out by all this?"

Laura reached for her glass of water. "Mostly I'm so sorry you've had to go through all this alone. That had to have been so hard."

Tasha shrugged. "I didn't want to put anyone in unnecessary danger. There are some things you just can't tell other people."

Laura looked away. "I know that feeling. Believe it or not, I've been keeping some secrets too."

Tasha smiled gently. "Oh yeah, is that not your natural hair color either?"

Laura touched her blonde locks. "Completely mine, I'm afraid."

"You know you're welcome to share whatever it is, especially since you know more about me than literally anybody on the planet." Tasha didn't want to push, but she wanted Laura to know that she could also talk about whatever was going on.

At first she thought Laura wasn't going to continue, but finally she blurted her news out. "I'm pregnant."

Tasha stood up, covering her mouth, eyes wide. "What? I didn't even know you were dating anyone!"

"I'm not." It took a second for Tasha to register that her friend was still sitting, features drawn.

"Oh." Tasha sat again. "I'm sorry."

"I've been hiding it from everyone. But I'm nearly six months along and I'm starting to show. The father is my ex-boyfriend. I'm glad for the pregnancy, because it made me realize I couldn't stay with him."

"Are you going to keep the baby?"

Laura put a hand over her stomach. "Yes. Yes, I am. I'm going to be a mom."

Tasha wrapped her arms around her friend. "You're going to be the best mom ever."

"Thank you. And while I'm glad I told you, I don't really want to talk about any more details right now if it's okay. I'm still trying to figure everything out."

Tasha nodded and grabbed her hand. They both sat back, staring out over the kitchen table, each lost in thought.

"What a day, huh?" Tasha finally whispered.

"You can say that again. You know of everything you told me what actually pisses me off? That Andrew used you like this."

"I know, but Andrew lost so much at Roman's hands—his wife and almost his daughters. It makes sense that he's willing to do anything to take Roman down." Tasha rubbed her eyes. She wanted to cry but was afraid if she allowed the tears to start they would never stop. "I just…"

"You just had real feelings for him," Laura continued for her.

"Andrew made me feel safe for the first time in my life, honestly. And now… Now I know all of that was fake. Him pursuing me, him being kind and protective. I was a pawn in a bigger game, and how he treated me has nothing to do with how he feels about me."

"You don't know that for sure."

Oh but she did. "I'm an idiot to have fallen for him, especially now that I know none of it was real on his part. But what Roman did…"

Once again Tasha found she couldn't really blame Andrew.

She felt like her heart was going to break apart in her chest, but she still understood why he'd gotten close to her.

Laura squeezed her hand. "You are not your brother and you are not responsible for other people's choices. I had to learn that the hard way so I hope you'll just take my word for it."

"You're right. I'm not responsible for Roman or anything he's done." Tasha knew that. "And in a lot of ways I'm happy Zodiac Tactical and law enforcement are now involved. At least it means I'm not alone in this anymore."

"Yeah, feeling like you're completely alone...that's some scary shit."

"Hey." Tasha turned to look directly at Laura. "You're not alone either. There are way too many people here at Crossroads that care about you for you to ever think you're truly alone."

Laura let out a little sigh. "I'm already six months along. I've been keeping it a secret from everyone."

"Why?"

"My father was abusive when I was growing up. How stupid could I be to have dated someone with the same patterns? My ex started out emotionally abusive then it turned physical."

Tasha's hands clasped hard on her coffee mug.

"I kept thinking it would get better, but it didn't. I couldn't seem to make the break for myself, but I knew I had to for the baby."

Tasha reached out and grabbed her hand, squeezing. "I have your back, Laura."

A knock on the doorframe on the far side of the kitchen drew their attention. "Can I interrupt, ladies?"

Andrew.

Tasha felt like all the air had been sucked from the room.

He stepped inside, his face hollow, eyes devastated as he looked at her.

Why was he still acting like he cared? It wasn't needed any more.

Laura stood and scowled at him. "You have some nerve talking to her at all."

He nodded solemnly and Tasha knew he understood she'd told Laura everything. "I can understand why you'd think that but regardless, Tasha, I need to talk to you."

Laura squeezed Tasha's hand. "I'm staying in one of the rooms upstairs. Come stay with me if you want. We can talk more or sleep or I'll supervise while you drink—whatever you want."

Tasha pulled her in for a hug. "Thank you for tonight. I love you."

"Love you too, sweetie."

She turned to the man who had broken her heart. It helped just slightly that he seemed as raw as her.

"I don't deserve it," he began, taking a step toward her with a hand raised in surrender. "But I want to be able to explain myself to you. I am sorry, Tasha."

Tasha said nothing as he dropped his hand and tucked both hands in his pockets, his face downcast.

"But I don't have time to lay all of this out right now." His shoulders stiffened. "We have a very narrow window to capitalize on the fact that Roman's men know you're in Pine Valley but don't know we're here."

"And you need me to do that?"

"I do." His eyes met hers as he took a few tentative steps toward her. "We do, I mean. Law enforcement and Zodiac Tactical needs you. I know you're upset and you have every right to be. I—"

She cut him off. "I'll do it."

"What? I'm not sure you understand exactly what we're asking of you."

"I'm pretty sure I do." She shook her head and walked by him from the kitchen into the hallway. No point in postponing the inevitable. "You need to capture my brother and the best way you have to do that is by using me as bait."

Chapter 25

There was no fucking way.

Tasha's words of acceptance as she walked by were exactly what they'd been hoping for. She understood using her as bait was the best way to capture Roman and was willing to help. He'd spent the past two hours with Ian, Jenna, and Callum coming up with the best way to do just that.

But as soon as he heard her say it and agree he knew he wasn't going to allow it. They would have to find another way.

"Like hell," he muttered, grabbing Tasha's elbow, opening the nearest door and pulling her inside.

The familiar smell of wine hit him and he knew he'd chosen the door to the wine cellar. He pulled Tasha further into the room and shut the door behind them, Tasha's arm still clasped in his hand. He led her down the dimly lit stairs to the room below.

"What are you doing?"

He didn't stop until they were at the bottom. "You can't do this, Tasha."

"Do what?"

"You're not going to offer yourself up as bait," he ground out, shoving his hand through his hair.

"It's the best option. The *only* option." Tasha shrugged, looking way too small there in the shadows. "Roman's men being in town looking for me is the closest you've ever come to him, isn't it?"

Yes, but it didn't matter. "I don't care. We'll have to find another way. I don't want you in danger."

She threw her hands in the air. "Your undercover work is over, Andrew. You don't have to keep pretending like you care about me. You've gotten what you want."

He resisted the urge to slam his fist into the wall. "It wasn't like that. Yes, we were hoping you would lead us to Roman, but what I felt for you—"

She shook her head. "Look, I get it. Okay? Your job is important. Roman is a terrorist and a murderer. Not mention you have a very personal reason to use any means necessary to take Roman down. Sleeping with me included."

He had no idea how to make the truth clear.

"Yes, bringing down Roman was an important job—*the* most important job. But you're also important to me. The lovemaking at the warehouse was real."

What he felt for her was fucking real.

She let out a sigh. "You don't have to keep saying stuff like that."

"I'm not saying it because I have to." His hands clinched tightly at his sides. His fingers itched to touch her; pull her into his arms. "I'm saying it because it's true. I'm saying it because I'm hoping you will give me a chance at some point. That I can sit down with you and answer every question you have and explain every detail I can about this operation."

It was more than he deserved but he prayed she'd give him that chance, and maybe they could start over from there. Because looking at her now in the dim light of the room he couldn't deny somewhere in the middle of all this crazy he'd fallen in love with this woman.

It wasn't what he'd been expecting when he came to Pine Valley but he wasn't going to deny his feelings. At least not to himself.

Of course mentioning it to Tasha now would be nothing short of stupid and cruel. She would think he was trying to further manipulate her. And he wouldn't blame her. Love was just a word without action and he was going to have to prove himself to her.

And damn it, if it took the rest of his life, he *would* prove himself to her.

However, all he could think about right now was making sure she didn't volunteer herself as bait, even though that was what he'd been order to get her to do.

Somehow taking down Roman was secondary to keeping Tasha safe.

She was shaking her head at him now. "I don't know if I want to know all the details. That first night we had sex after the wedding. Was that the night you bugged my house?"

He grimaced, but wasn't going to lie. "No, not that night. But I did tap your phone."

"What did you think I could do? Call Roman up? Ask him to come visit me?"

"At that time I didn't care what you were up to, or why, or whether or not you were in active contact with him. I wanted —want revenge. I want revenge for what he did to my family. Hell, I want revenge for what he did to you."

Tasha said nothing as Andrew stepped toward her.

"I've thought about what it would be like to have him cornered, to see him have to surrender. I've thought about it every day for three years. But I'm not going to do it by giving you over to him."

"I'm doing you a favor."

"You're putting yourself at major risk and I can't let you do it."

"Why?" she hissed. "This is the man who killed your wife!"

"And I spent three years living with that. I can't let it tear me apart anymore. There is so much more on the line now."

"I don't understand…"

"You. You changed everything for me. What happened between us in the warehouse, Tasha? That was real."

She swallowed, her eyes settling on his chest.

"I thought you were dead when I saw you face down in the snow in that clearing, and I… It would have been my fault. I don't want to put you back in more danger now."

"It's my decision. I'll never be free of him unless I do something."

"We don't know what he wants with you—"

"Then we'll use me find that out. He knows I'm still alive and I'm tired of being hunted." She closed her eyes, arms wrapping around her waist like she was trying to protect herself from a blow. "I'm tired of being used."

It was a kick to the gut. *He'd* done this to her.

"Tasha, I'm so sorry." He wasn't even sure he'd even said the words to her yet. He was damned sure it wasn't the last time he would say them to her.

"I know. It was your job, but—"

He couldn't stop himself. He wrapped his arms around her and pulled her against his chest. "You are not a job. Not to me."

He expected her to pull away, but she didn't. Andrew didn't know how long that would last but he'd count every second as a treasure.

"What I did to you was inexcusable," he whispered against her hair. "But please know I never wanted to hurt you. I thought I had more time to tell you who I really was and why I'd been sent after you, but I didn't. I'll find another way to get to him without needing you to draw him in."

"There is no other way, Andrew," she protested, looking up at him.

"I will find a way. I don't care…" They were so close now that his words brushed over her lips. He couldn't finish the sentence, not when the smell of her shampoo and soft, clean scent of her skin lingered in the air between them.

His lips were on hers before he could stop himself. Once again she didn't pull away and Andrew thanked every higher power he'd ever believed in for the blessing. He hadn't been sure this would ever happen again.

And he didn't fool himself into thinking anything was forgiven.

"Yo, Andrew, you down there?"

They stepped apart at the sound of Isaac's voice at the top of the stairs.

"Yeah, Isaac, I'm here. We're on our way up. I just needed to talk to Tasha for a second."

There was a moment's pause. "Yeah, no problem. We're ready in the conference room. I think we have a plan."

Isaac left without another word, leaving the door wide open.

Tasha was already moving toward the stairs, as Andrew gripped her elbow to slow her down. "You don't have to do this."

"We don't have any other options."

"There is always another way. I'll figure it out."

She met his eyes. Andrew knew once they set foot in the conference room, there wouldn't be another chance to have this conversation.

Andrew desperately wanted to kiss her again, to feel her in his arms. Had this horrible feeling it might be the last time.

"I'm sorry," she whispered, pulling away from him.

"Tasha—" He wanted to explain how he felt. Get her to believe him. How real this all was to him, but she was gone in a flash of blonde, and he was left alone in the wine cellar. There was nothing he could do to stop her.

Or to stop this feeling that he was about to lose her for good.

Chapter 26

Fifteen hours later Andrew watched the screens on the two laptops in front of him, each split into four different vantage points of the places Tasha was known to frequent in Pine Valley. Although there was no snow, it had turned cold outside again, and sitting in a parked van for surveillance was pretty miserable.

But Andrew would gladly freeze his ass off out here since Tasha was currently safe and warm in a cabin on the far side of the Crossroads property, almost as far away from this danger as she could get. Isaac was on guard duty.

Andrew had wanted to stay with her, but things were too tense between them right now. Plus, taking down Roman Volkov was something Andrew needed to see through. Everyone knew it.

And now not just to obtain justice for Kylie's death. Not even to shut down the Volkov Cartel once and for all.

But because Tasha would never be able to live the life she deserved until Roman was out of the picture. And damn it, whether Andrew was part of that life or not, he was going to make sure she had it.

He looked back at the screens in front of him. The Chill N' Grill was the most active, and through the camera he watched a thin blonde woman lean across the bar, a black apron tied around her waist.

Tasha, except *not* Tasha. Zodiac Tactical team member Sarah Hayes, the closest they could get to Tasha's weight and build, had taken Tasha's place for her shift. She wouldn't hold up under close inspection, but hopefully it would be enough to get Roman's men to make a move.

Tasha's boss, Wade McKenzie, was in on the ruse, as were a number of others who were attached to the Crossroads Retreat. When they'd found out the truth about Tasha they'd wanted to help.

Wade nodded as Sarah pushed off from the bar and untied her apron—preparing to get off shift. This was it. This was when Roman would go after Tasha if he was on the offensive.

Sarah was careful to keep her head down until she reached the employee locker room which was out of view of the camera. Andrew scanned the patrons in the grill, glancing down at the mugshots on the tablet in his lap.

"Anything yet?" Callum asked from the front seat, his eyes on his phone.

"No, not yet. Sarah's just getting off shift."

Ian nodded from next to Callum. There were three other vehicles around town ready to make moves as needed—all with Zodiac Tactical or Crossroads Retreat team members.

Jenna's voice came over a speaker in the van, "Sarah's leaving the bar."

A camera located in the back lot behind the bar picked up Sarah's movements as she walked toward her car, which was the same make, model, and color of the car Tasha had nearly totaled and was still being repaired. It should be enough to fool Roman's men.

Andrew reached above his head and pressed a button on

the radio before replying, "Have her drive back to Tasha's house, slowly. We need to see if anyone comes out of the bar and follows her."

They'd been doing this for hours now—watching, waiting. Sarah had a similar lean build like Tasha, honed by yoga, pilates, and martial arts. The blonde hair was a wig, but it did the job. It was eerie, honestly, watching the woman act like Tasha, because from a distance the two were exactly alike. Sarah studied the way Tasha moved from table to table. She'd practiced Tasha's careful grace and perfected it down to the smallest of details, like the way Tasha slightly hung her head when shrugging into a jacket and the way she tucked her hair behind her ears while talking to patrons.

Andrew hadn't realized how many little things he'd noticed about Tasha and buried in his subconscious until he watched the agent pretend to be her.

"Jenna, can you patch us in to Sarah," Callum said from the front seat.

Andrew leaned back in his chair and watched the screens above his head as Sarah started up the car and pulled out of the parking lot. A few quick motions of his fingers brought up several different camera angles situated around town.

She wasn't followed back to Tasha's house.

"Sarah, go ahead and drive out of town and get on the highway. We'll have drones tailing you."

Sarah's voice cut through the speaker as she acknowledged Callum's command.

Andrew stood and stretched as best he could in the tight space of the van. "Okay, I'm getting into the other vehicle with Chet and Tucker. Let's hope this works."

He nodded at Callum as he left the van and walked the hundred or so yards down the side of an open, snow-dusted gravel road to the car Chet and Tucker waited inside. They were all about ten miles outside of Pine Valley and, if Sarah was followed like they hoped she would be, would form a barricade from the opposite direction.

"How's it going in there?" Chet asked as Andrew climbed into the backseat and shut the door against the cold.

"The trap is set, and now we wait." Andrew pulled a tablet out of his inner jacket pocket and brought up the drone footage, which showed Sarah driving out of town. Once she was a mile out, they would all follow discretely.

They'd left as many clues as possible that "Tasha" was leaving tonight. They were almost certain Roman's men were surveilling the town so made it seem like this was their last chance to grab her. Sarah had told Wade that she had to quit and was leaving and she'd packed up everything in her house.

It made the most sense that the cartel would make their move once they thought Tasha was out of town on the relatively isolated road.

Tucker started the car, glancing over his shoulder at Andrew. "Everything in place?"

"Yeah. Hopefully they take the bait."

"If they do, they're going down," Chet said. "They shouldn't have messed with one of ours."

Because Tasha, despite what she thought, had made a name for herself in this town. She had no idea how many people were helping her right now. Wade, her boss at the grill, had been more than willing to play the game with Sarah in order to make this all look real. And her friends from Crossroads were loaded up with an impressive number of weapons and ammunition.

Through his earpiece, Andrew heard Callum tell Sarah to take the next exit and head west.

"Okay," Andrew said to Tucker. "Let's go. Sarah's on her way out of town. You two are wearing vests, right? The Volkov Cartel are a shoot first, sort out the bodies later, type of organization."

"Hell yeah" Chet responded. "Our women would skin us alive if we didn't."

"This is about to get serious. I need you both to keep your heads on straight."

"You got it, Boss." Chet reached out his fist to Tucker and they bumped knuckles with a smile.

At least they were enjoying themselves. There was a point in time during Andrew's early years in Zodiac when missions filled him with a primal excitement that had him buzzing with adrenaline for days before and after the mission.

Now he just wanted it done. Wanted Tasha safe.

"A car followed me off the exit. Black Suburban." Sarah's voice cut through the earpiece.

"We've got visual on you through the drones. We have two vehicles behind you and one in front," Ian's voice replied.

Their biggest advantage right now was that Roman and the cartel thought Tasha was in this on her own. Thought she was running by herself.

They were about to find out otherwise.

"Another Suburban just pulled up behind me. They're trying to box me in. They'll make their move soon." Despite the stress of the situation, Sarah's voice was calm and collected.

"Andrew, let's roll," Callum said sharply.

"Go," Andrew commanded and Chet ripped out of the snowy field and onto the desolate road, ready to intercept Sarah and the cars trailing her. This was the bigger advantage of having Chet and Tucker with them: they knew this area better than anyone.

Everything was going as planned. They'd spent the entire afternoon planting clues Tasha would try to leave tonight. They sent Sarah walking around town buying supplies for a road trip—snacks, fuel, water. They'd had her load up a suitcase and put it in the car before driving to work, parking near the camera in the parking lot at an angle the suitcase was visible in the backseat. The curtains in her bungalow had been left open so anyone walking by could catch a glimpse of the interior—empty now, save for the furniture.

It looked like the cartel had bought it.

Sarah maintained her normal speed despite the tails through the discreet and rural area just out of town. No street-lights, just open road. The people following her had no idea they were about to run into a trap.

Everyone drove for a few tense, silent minutes then two more Zodiac vehicles pulled in behind Sarah and her tails. Between those cars and Andrew's team, the cartel members were about to be trapped.

"I see you," Sarah said a few moments later. Andrew could make out her headlights in the distance.

"Just keep moving," Ian said. "We'll cut them off as soon as you've passed."

The second Sarah's vehicle went by them, Tucker pulled their car to a hard stop. Callum did the same in the van, creating a barricade. They all jumped out, weapons raised.

The two cars that had been following Sarah were forced to stop, unable to go any further with Andrew and the other agents blocking their way. Tires screeched as both enemy SUVs turned around and sped in the direction they'd come.

It didn't take them long to realize they were boxed in.

Then all hell broke loose.

Gunfire rained down on Chet's car as multiple members of the cartel got out of the Suburbans and started firing. Andrew and his team returned fire, quickly taking out two of the cartel, both men slumping to the ground.

One of the gunmen got back in his car and started to drive away, cutting through a field.

Chet and Tucker wasted no time. They climbed back in

their vehicle and sped off after him, snow spraying in their wake. Andrew had no doubt they would stop him.

He looked over to where Callum and Ian were both returning fire. Ian signaled toward the car to his right then gave another hand motion. Andrew knew exactly what his boss was saying. They would lay down cover fire so Andrew could make it over to the other vehicle and have a better vantage point.

Ian signaled the countdown and Andrew moved on his mark. Both Callum and Ian provided the cover he needed so Andrew could run across to the other vehicle. Now that they had the enemy flanked and trapped.

It didn't take the cartel members long to realize that either. Four of their men were down already. And while Zodiac had taken some injuries too, it was clear who was going to come out on top.

"Lower your weapons," Callum called out, still behind the protection of one of the cars, when the shooting had lulled. "There's no way out."

There was some brief talk between the remaining cartel members before one called out that they would surrender.

Once again Ian signaled with a hand gesture. *Prepare for fire.*

Ian didn't trust them. Andrew didn't either.

"Drop your weapons and put your hands up where we can see them," Callum continued. "I'm coming out at the count of three. Three. Tw—"

Ian and Andrew jumped up from their positions in the middle of the word, weapons drawn. Sure enough all three of the remaining cartel members were pointing their guns in the direction where Callum would've been standing a moment later.

Andrew didn't hesitate to fire, nor did Ian. Two of the three men fell. The other dropped his weapon and ran towards the woods.

Neither of them was going to shoot a fleeing man in the back. Ian rolled his eyes. "Up for a run?"

"Yeah, I've got him." Andrew took off before the statement was finished.

Adrenaline made short work of the chase and the run felt fucking good. Andrew tackled the man to the ground, dodging his fists as they tumbled on the ground. He finally got the man on his stomach and subdued him long enough to fasten zip ties to his wrists behind his back and drag him back toward the vehicles.

Local law enforcement was showing up now, having honored Callum's request as a federal officer to stay in reserve until the mission was completed or they were needed. The officers handcuffed and carried off the uninjured members of the cartel while paramedics attended the wounded.

"Roman's not here," Callum said as he walked up to Andrew.

"Shit." Andrew ran a hand through his hair. "Not totally surprising. We knew Roman being here himself was a long shot."

But damned Andrew had hoped for it.

Ian joined them, looking around the frenzy. Chet and Tucker had made it back with their bad guy in custody too.

"No Roman," Andrew muttered. "Do you think he knew it was a trap?"

Ian shook his head. "Not necessarily. I think he has minions to do work like this. That's how he's stayed in the game so long."

"Doesn't matter," Callum said. "We have too many of his men now. Only one of them has to talk. We pit them against each other—whoever talks first gets some sort of immunity deal. Someone will offer details about how to get to Roman."

Andrew didn't doubt that was true. He'd seen Callum work an interrogation room. He would get someone to flip.

All Andrew needed to do now was keep Tasha safe in the meantime.

He continued to watch the chaos around him, his mind already formulating a plan. The girls would be coming home soon, so staying here in Tennessee wasn't an option. But bringing Tasha back to Wyoming with him? Very definitely an option.

All he needed to do was convince her. She wouldn't need to stay with him, there were plenty of fortified locations within the tiny town of Oak Creek, home of Linear Tactical. Andrew had family there that wouldn't blink at a request to help keep Tasha safe.

And it might allow her to get to know his daughters at a pace comfortable for everyone. Although he had no doubt Olivia and Caroline would love Tasha.

He certainly did.

They would get Roman—bring him down. And until then, Andrew would make it his own personal duty to protect Tasha.

By keeping her as close as possible.

Chapter 27

Tasha stared out the window of the cabin even though she couldn't see anything in the darkness outside. She seemed to continuously come back to this window although she didn't know why.

All she knew was that she couldn't sit still. Couldn't keep from fidgeting. Couldn't focus on anything but the knowledge that Andrew was out there in possible danger and she was sitting safe and sound on the other side of town.

"I don't know why you keep looking out that window when you can't see anything." Isaac had tried to engage her in conversation multiple times from where he sat at the table.

She didn't respond, although she had to give the man credit, he was charming and gorgeous. Normally she wouldn't mind spending a few hours with someone as easy-going as him. No red-blooded woman would.

But she was exhausted and worried and despite the fact that she wasn't sure exactly where her relationship stood with Andrew, he was still more appealing to her than her current movie-star looking bodyguard.

"You're scared," Isaac said.

She turned from the window, her eyes falling to the gun Andrew had given her lying on the table. "I'm not scared. I'm bored."

"Andrew and the rest of the Zodiac Tactical team are very good at what they do," Isaac continued as if she hadn't spoken.

"And Roman is very good at killing people. Andrew has experienced that first hand."

"But we have the upper hand because Roman assumes that you're on your own and you're not anymore. You understand that, right? Not just with this particular takedown, but with it all. You're not alone in this anymore."

She started pacing again. "I appreciate what everyone is doing to help keep me safe. But that doesn't necessarily mean I'm not alone."

Isaac leaned back in his chair. "I don't know Andrew very well, but I do know that he's a good guy. He's saved the lives of multiple people on the Zodiac team over the years."

"I don't think he's a bad guy."

"He never meant to hurt you. As a matter fact he tried to protect you even from our eyes. That night before you took off into the blizzard he shut down all the surveillance equipment in your house. That's how you were able to get away without us knowing it. Andrew wanted you to have privacy if the two of you were being intimate."

It did make her feel somewhat better that the kisses they'd shared and sleeping with him in her bed had not been recorded by the rest of the team.

She shrugged. "I said this to him and I'll say it to you. I get it. He had a job to do, an important one. But really there is no need to pretend like it was more than that."

She turned back to Isaac.

He raised a single eyebrow. "That's just it. I don't think Andrew's pretending at all. As a matter fact I'm not sure he knows how to pretend. Yes, taking Roman down and getting justice for Kylie's death has consumed him for the past few years. But what he feels for you…he's not making that up. If this had just been a mission and it was over now, he would be professional but distant. Andrew is anything but that when it comes to you."

Tasha couldn't allow herself to believe it. It would make her a fool. Again.

Regardless, hopefully after tonight she at least wouldn't have to run for her life anymore. Things with Andrew were secondary to that.

Changing the subject seemed like a good idea. "Do you wish that you were where the action is tonight rather than babysitting me?"

Both Isaac's eyes got wide in an exaggerated fashion. "Me? Hell no. I try to stay away from danger as much as possible. As a matter fact when we were drawing straws to see who would stay with you, I cheated and made sure everyone else's straw was longer than mine. I'll let Andrew dodge bullets any day. Definitely not for me."

Tasha couldn't help but smile. Obviously Isaac was lying. Just as obvious was the fact that he respected Andrew.

Andrew had offered to stay here at the cabin with her, but she'd said no. He thought it was because she didn't want to be anywhere around him, but the truth was she wished he was here right now. Both because that way she would know he was not in harm's way but also because she just wanted him to wrap his arms around her.

No matter what the state of things were between them, she would take the comfort of his arms if he was here to offer it. She wasn't sure exactly what that said about her, but it was still the truth. She missed him.

She turned back to the window. Then almost immediately turned back and started pacing.

"Should we have heard something by now? What if Roman didn't take the bait?"

Isaac wasn't ruffled. "No news is good news in a situation like this. If there was a problem they would let us know immediately. The fact that we're not getting any intel from them probably means that everything is going the way we hoped."

Tasha prayed that was true but she still couldn't stop pacing. She walked by the table and grabbed her cup of coffee, glancing at the gun once again, remembering how Andrew's arms had felt around her as he showed her how to use it properly.

"Are you sure you don't want to switch to wine?" Isaac asked. "You're already pretty tightly strung and caffeine isn't going to help."

She shook her head. "I definitely don't want to have any alcohol in my system. But maybe I'll switch to water."

She looked at Isaac more carefully. He was calm and charming when he talked but his eyes were in constant movement around the cabin. He was on edge to but was doing his best not to allow any of it to affect her.

An alarm chimed on his watch. "I'm going to walk the perimeter. I'll be back in a few minutes."

He had done that every thirty minutes since they'd gotten there. As he left she took her coffee and poured the rest in the sink. She definitely didn't need any more caffeine in her system.

She grabbed a water bottle from the fridge and tried to sit down at the table but immediately jumped back up. There was no way she could sit still. A couple minutes later there was a tapping on the door. She rolled her eyes as she went to answer it. She appreciated Isaac trying to distract her, but this was a little juvenile.

"Really Isaac? Don't you think—"

She caught him as he collapsed into her arms.

"Isaac!" She struggled under his weight as he fell through the doorway barely conscious. Her hands were immediately covered in blood.

He'd been stabbed.

"Oh my God, Isaac." She had no choice but to lower him to the floor. He was too heavy for her to do anything else.

"Ru—R…"

She couldn't understand what he was trying to say.

"I think your friend is trying to tell you to run."

Tasha's blood froze in her veins as she heard Roman's voice from the doorway. Still clutching Isaac in her arms, she looked up at him.

Roman waved with all his fingers like he was a schoolgirl. "Hello there, sister. How long has it been?"

Every instinct in Tasha's body screamed for her to run, but she couldn't. If she took pressure off of Isaac's wound he was going to bleed out.

And it wasn't like Roman was going to let her get away anyway.

He was flanked by one of his men, Saunders, the same guy who had grabbed her in the alleyway. He sported two black eyes and a bandage over his broken nose as he stared down at Tasha.

She really wished she could break it again.

Roman smiled, but nothing about it seemed friendly. "It's so good to see you again, Tasha. I've been looking for you for a long time."

"How did you find me?"

"We were concerned that something wasn't quite right when it became so obvious that you were leaving town tonight. Why didn't you leave town right away? That would've made more sense."

Because Zodiac had needed some time to get the decoy in

place. It had tipped him off. Tasha should've insisted on being the bait herself.

Roman walked further in the cabin as if he owned the place. "We had our tech people reverse pinpoint tracking frequencies, and lo and behold it led us here."

Tasha didn't know what tech stuff Roman was talking about and ultimately it didn't matter. He had found her.

He was going to kill her. She was a little surprised she was still alive.

She peeled off her lightweight jacket and pushed it against Isaac's back in an attempt to stop the bleeding. She had no idea how bad the wound was but there was definitely too much blood.

"Hang in there," she whispered in Isaac's ear. "You're going to be okay."

Without her jacket on some of her scars were visible.

"Look at your skin. That's disgusting," Roman sneered. "You were a disgrace to the family before, but at least never physically. Now you don't even have that."

"These scars are your fault." She kept her eyes on Isaac, but couldn't bite back her words.

"You were right, Saunders." Roman turned back to the man standing in the doorway. "I should've known Tasha would be working with the very people who infiltrated the family three years ago. She betrayed me then, so why would it be any different now?"

Tasha tied the arms of her jacket around Isaac's torso and pulled it tight. He groaned in pain but she hoped it would staunch the flow of blood.

"Let's go," Roman said. "You're coming with us."

"The hell I am," she said with a bravery she didn't feel. "If you're going to kill me you can do it right here and get it over with." She didn't even want to think of the torture he might have in store for her if she left with him.

Roman walked over to her and grabbed her by the hair making her gasp from the sharp sting of pain. "If I wanted you dead you'd already be dead. I have need for you, dear sister. But don't worry your death will come soon enough."

Enough, damn it. She had to be brave, make a stand. No more cowering.

She jerked her head out of his hand and dove for the table. The gun Andrew had given her was still sitting there. She swung it around and pointed it at Roman.

Immediately, Saunders pulled up his own weapon and pointed it at Tasha. "Drop it."

"Evidently I'm not allowed to be killed so I don't think I will. You drop your weapon before I kill your boss."

It would mean the end of her own life but maybe that would be worth it.

But instead Saunders turned his gun on Isaac. "Drop your gun or he gets one in the head."

"No, Tasha…" Isaac's voice was weak. "Let him. I'm not going to make it anyway…"

But she couldn't do it. It was one thing to be willing to lose her own life but another thing completely to cost Isaac his. She lowered the gun.

"There's a good sister," Roman said condescendingly. "And besides you didn't just think we came out here unprepared, did you?"

Roman pulled his phone from his pocket and held it in front of Tasha. "Why don't you take a look at this?"

It was some sort of security camera image. It took her a second to realize exactly what she was looking at. Then her heart threw itself against her ribs when she recognized the house on the Crossroads property immediately.

It was Elizabeth and Tucker's place. The windows were slightly foggy from the cold weather, but the camera view offered clear footage from inside. Elizabeth rocked in a chair next to a fireplace, a sleepy little girl in her arms. Elizabeth leaned her cheek against her daughter's head as she read *Goodnight Moon*.

"Daddy's not home tonight," Roman whispered in Tasha's ear. "He went after my men who I was willing to sacrifice if it meant getting to you. It's just Mommy and Daughter at home, all alone."

He used his finger to zoom out on the window. A small black box clung to the shutter, a red light blinking.

"We've gotten quite a bit more sophisticated in the past few years from the Molotov cocktails. One press of a button and this beauty and her baby girl meet a fiery end."

"Don't," Tasha begged, whimpering. "Please. I'll do anything. Don't hurt them. They have nothing to do with this."

"If you don't come with us now, they will die. It's as simple as that. Give me your gun."

Defeated, she handed it to him. She had no doubt Roman would sacrifice Elizabeth and Audrey to get what he wanted. She glanced down at Isaac, who was now unconscious on the floor in a pool of blood. She prayed the jacket tied around him would be enough to keep him alive until someone got here.

And they would get back here eventually.

But she knew it would be too late for her. Once Roman got what he wanted, whatever that was, he wouldn't keep Tasha around anymore.

She winced as he grabbed her arm in a firm hold and yanked her out the door.

"I'm sorry," she whispered to no one in particular, then closed her eyes and let the tears fall.

Chapter 28

Andrew watched Callum drive away with the last of the cartel that had been arrested. He was overseeing everything himself to make sure nothing went wrong.

Andrew tried Tasha's number. She didn't answer, although that did not necessarily mean anything. She may just not want to talk to him.

More than anything he just wanted to hear her voice right now. Wanted to put this new plan of taking her back to Wyoming with him into action. Wanted her home with he and the girls so he could not only protect her but could infiltrate himself into her life.

He wasn't above using any means necessary to prove to her how important she was to him.

He tried her number again but still no answer.

Fine. He could wait. Speaking to her face-to-face was probably better anyway.

"You talk to Isaac?" Ian walked over. "I was going to update him but he's not answering his phone."

Andrew stiffened. "Not at all?"

"I knew he'd want to be updated so I first tried him about twenty minutes ago."

Andrew met his friend's eyes. "I'm not getting any answer from Tasha either. That didn't surprise me at first but—" He broke off with a shake of his head.

Both of them not answering? That was a problem.

He and Ian immediately turned and ran for the car. Andrew jumped behind the steering wheel as Ian got in on the passenger side. They were both on their phones trying to redial Isaac and Tasha as Andrew sped back towards town.

"Still nothing," Ian said. "He looked down at his phone. "I'm going to call Tucker. See who's at Crossroads that can go see what the fuck is going on."

A moment later he had Tucker on the phone and had explained the situation. Andrew could only hear half of the call but could tell that Tucker would be calling someone named Cruz Sawyer who was already on property to go check it out.

"Don't send him in alone," Ian told Tucker as he disconnected the call. He glanced over at Andrew. "I've got a bad feeling about this."

So did Andrew.

Gripping the steering wheel tighter and clenching his jaw, he pressed the pedal to the floor.

Both of them knew there were no good circumstances under which Isaac would not be in communication. The younger man had been a little pissed not to be part of the action. He definitely would've had his phone right next to him for an update.

Andrew and Ian continuously tried to get through all the way to the Crossroads property. With each passing moment the cold dread in Andrew's gut spread. Yes, he'd showed Tasha how to use the gun he'd left her, but honestly that had been more of an excuse to put his arms around her than anything else.

He'd damned well be teaching her how to use it for real.

They blasted by the main house to the cabin on the rear side of the property. As they approached, they saw two vehicles outside the building and the door was wide open.

This was not a good sign.

Andrew threw the car in park and leapt out, Ian on his heels. They both had their weapons raised as they entered the cabin.

It only took a second for Andrew to put together what was happening. Isaac was on the floor, unconscious, bleeding. A man was crouched over him, phone in his hand.

A second man spun and raised a weapon at them.

"We're on the same side," Andrew said, lowering his own weapon as the man lowered his. "I'm Andrew Zimmerman. This is Ian DeRose. We're both Zodiac Tactical."

"Cruz Sawyer," the man on the ground replied as he disconnected his call and applied pressure to Isaac's back. "Tucker told me you were on your way. We found your man like this. Stab wound. Emergency services are incoming."

"He still alive?" Ian asked.

Cruz nodded. "For now."

"Where is Tasha?" Andrew asked.

But he already knew. They all already knew.

He looked over at Ian. "I'm going to look around outside to see if there's…"

He didn't even know how to finish that sentence, but Ian just nodded.

The first thing Andrew looked at was the door. It was still on his hinges and had not been tampered with in any way that he could see. That meant someone had opened the door from the inside.

"I'll come with you. Name's Zeke Friedman."

"Andrew."

"Yeah, I've heard quite a bit about you."

Andrew looked around the cabin. "I want to walk around to make sure there's not any intel to be had."

Zeke nodded. I'll circle to the east and we'll regroup when we meet up."

"You understand what we're probably looking for, right?" Andrew asked.

Tasha's dead body. Andrew tamped his emotions all the way down as he thought it. He could not allow himself to even think that Tasha might be dead. But he had been in this business long enough to know that was the most likely scenario.

"I understand," Zeke said with a nod. "But there could also be other clues. Let's just hope for that."

And not for Tasha's body with X's cut on her eyelids and a shot glass of vodka next to her head.

Andrew moved in the opposite direction of Zeke, looking for anything, any sign of struggle, any blood, *anything*. When he met back up with Zeke coming from the opposite direction neither of them had found anything.

For the first time Andrew had a glimmer of hope. Tasha wasn't dead. At least not yet.

But Roman had definitely outsmarted them. *Again.*

Andrew grabbed his phone and called Jenna Franklin.

"Gemini! Please tell me you're calling to say Callum already got one of the Volkov Cartel to flip. I have a bet going with Outlaw on—"

"Roman outsmarted us, Jenna." Andrew cut her off. "I'm at the cabin. Tasha is gone and Isaac has been stabbed."

"Fuck," Jenna muttered. "Hang on."

Andrew and Zeke both walked back to the cabin door.

Jenna came back on the line. "All the trackers have been disabled by a third party. That means the cartel used our own equipment against us again. Goddamn it."

"I need whatever help you can get us, Jenna. Tasha is gone. Roman has her."

"I'm on it. I'll be back in touch."

Andrew disconnected the call, frustration having him clinch his phone in his hand.

"Isaac! You fucking hold on!" Ian's tight voice cut through the night.

There wasn't much that made the owner of Zodiac Tactical seem panicked but Andrew could hear it clearly in his voice now. Cruz was yelling at Isaac too. Andrew caught sight of flashing lights headed their way and rushed inside.

"Ambulance is almost here."

Ian began yelling at Isaac again. All Andrew could do was watch helplessly as a couple minutes later the EMTs got there and started working to save Isaac's life. It wasn't long until they had him loaded up in the ambulance.

Andrew's phone rang in his hand and he looked down hoping it was Jenna, but it was Tucker.

"Please tell me you have some good news man," Andrew ran a hand down his face.

"How is everyone?"

"Isaac's on his way to the hospital. Alive, but barely. Tasha's gone and there's no sign of her."

"I'm afraid my news isn't very good either. I just got home and when I let Otto out of my truck he went bat shit crazy."

Andrew bit down his frustration. "I don't know what that means."

"Otto is a retired law enforcement dog. He worked as an explosives detection K9 with me back in the day."

"Was someone around the house? Is that why he was freaking out?"

"Not people. But explosives. I found two bundles—enough to blow my house, my bride, and my daughter to kingdom come."

"Shit. Are they okay?"

"Yes, they are safe and we are searching the rest of the property. But the Volkov Cartel was definitely here."

Roman had used their decoy as his own decoy. And Andrew had no idea where he had taken Tasha.

∾

TASHA PULLED at the painful zip ties that bound her arms behind her back. There was no give in them whatsoever.

Roman was grinning at her from the front seat, the lights from the dash casting a devilish glow over his face. Not that that was necessary. He was the epitome of evil.

"It won't be long now, sister. I have to admit it's been a thorn in my side knowing you were still alive and I couldn't get to you. I'll enjoy when I finally know for certain that you'll never bother me again."

Tasha didn't reply. Nothing she said would make this any better. Begging for her life most definitely wouldn't do any good.

"When I heard you had gotten involved with the group that infiltrated the family I thought it would be more difficult to get to you. Evidently I underestimated your value to them."

"Why haven't you just killed me already?"

"Trust me, I want to, you little bitch. Unfortunately Marcus' last attempt to control me means I have to have you alive."

Marcus—their father—trying to control Roman? What did that even mean? "I have no idea what you're talking about. I have no idea why you've always hated me so much."

Roman made a tsking sound. "Does the princess want me to fawn all over her like a good little stable boy?"

"Since when am I a princess and you're a stable boy? We're siblings."

"I should have been the only child. Our father should have never slept with your mother. She got pregnant with you and then all of a sudden my mother wasn't good enough for him anymore."

Tasha blinked out at him. "What? Your mother died."

"My mother died because of mixing pills with too much drinking. And that was because of Marcus' unfaithfulness. That's your fault."

"Roman, listen to yourself. You can't blame me for our parents' mistakes. I wasn't even born yet. And I didn't even know about any of this until right now."

Her words were obviously falling on deaf ears, not that she expected anything different from Roman. He'd never been stable.

"Oh it goes way beyond our parents. Marcus always treated you like a you could do no wrong. He sent you to the best schools and he gave you everything you ever wanted."

She shook her head trying to reason with him again. "I was a little girl without her mother. I think Marcus didn't know what to do with me."

Roman turned more fully around in his seat. "He gave you everything. And most importantly he sheltered you from everything. Meanwhile he always treated me like shit. Never trusted me to run the family business correctly. Can you believe he said I was too violent?" Roman let out a mocking laugh. "We were running a cartel for fuck's sake. How the hell could I be too violent? Too psychotic?"

"Maybe it's your sick calling card making people think that you're a psycho." The words were out before she could stop them. "That doesn't exactly scream mental stability."

His backhand caught her across the face and sent her slamming into the door. Blood pooled in her mouth until she had to spit it out.

Why don't you just kill me?" She asked again.

"Oh I will, dear sister, and I'm going to take great joy in it. But I need you first."

"For what?"

She could feel blood dripping down her chin but couldn't do anything about it.

"Marcus, in his final attempt to control me before he died, bound the family's money to you."

What? "I have no idea what you're talking about. I've been living on the brink of poverty for years. If father did that then he didn't tell me. I can't help you."

"Actually you can. Even if you don't know it."

Fear froze Tasha's gut. Did Roman think she was just holding out on him? Did he plan on torturing her to get information she didn't have?

"Roman, I'm telling you the truth. I have no idea what you're talking about. Marcus never said anything to me. I swear."

Roman's face turned almost kind which was almost more frightening than the cruelty that normally sneered it. "I know you don't know. It took me three years to discover exactly what Marcus had done with the family's income. It's ironic that I would discover you so soon after finally figuring it out. And here in Tennessee of all places."

Tasha still didn't understand what he was talking about.

"I need you to access it but we can't do anything until Monday at 9 AM."

Glancing at the time on the dash, that was thirty-six hours from now. She didn't know why it had to be at that time but she wasn't going to question the fact that it at least gave her that long to live to figure out something.

To hope that Andrew would come for her. She bit back a sob. Had Isaac survived? She had no idea.

Moreover even if Andrew and the Zodiac Tactical team did want to find her they had no way of doing that.

She was on her own. Just like always.

"I don't want the money." She spat blood out of her mouth again. "I'll get it for you and then you can have it all, just let me go."

"I don't think so, little sister."

He was going to kill her no matter what.

"Then at least don't hurt Elizabeth and Audrey. Disarm that explosive."

"On Monday, if you do exactly what I ask you to do, then they are of no consequence to me. They won't be harmed."

Tasha had no idea if she could believe him but she didn't have any choice.

"Where are we going?"

"That's nothing you need to worry about." Roman turned back around to face the front and settled into the seat. Evidently this conversation was over.

That was fine with Tasha. The less she had to talk to Roman the better.

But the silence left her alone with her own thoughts and they kept coming back to Andrew.

She wished she had taken one more chance to kiss him before he left her at the cabin. He tried to get close but she pushed him away. Things weren't all right between them but she at least wished she'd taken one last moment to connect with him. To let him know she wanted to try.

To let him know that if he truly meant it when he said what he felt for her was real then she would give him the opportunity to prove it. Because she knew what she felt for him was definitely real.

If she only had thirty-six hours left to live she wished she could've let Andrew know that the time she spent with him had been the best of her life.

Chapter 29

Andrew's eyes were gritty as he watched the footage of Tasha in Pine Valley fighting Roman's man.

Again.

At this point he'd watched it at least a hundred times. Watching her break Saunders nose somehow kept Andrew connected to Tasha's strength. He had to hold onto that.

He knew it was possible she was already dead. He'd been doing this job too long to not know that it was a possibility. But until they had proof—and he chose to believe that Roman, bastard that he was, would definitely send them proof of her death—Andrew was going to continue as if Tasha was alive.

It was the only way he could function.

Everybody had been doing everything they could for the past twenty-four hours since Tasha had been taken. Isaac was in critical condition, but alive.

Tucker and the rest of the Crossroads team had been scouring the property looking for any signs of explosives, but fortunately had not found any more.

Jenna and the tech team had been looking for any sign of

Roman on the roads via cameras but without knowledge of what type of vehicle they were driving it was like looking for a needle in a haystack. Or as Jenna said, a needle in a stack of needles.

More Zodiac Tactical agents had arrived and every document related to the Volkov Cartel was now inside the Crossroads conference room. Nobody had slept. Everyone was on high alert.

And they all knew it didn't mean shit unless they could get ahead of Roman in some way.

Andrew rewound the footage and watched Tasha break the man's nose again. "You stay alive, sweetheart," he whispered to her image. "We're coming for you. I'm coming for you."

Callum came and sat down next to Andrew. "I know this is a dumbass question but are you hanging in there?"

Andrew rewound the footage again. "Watching her kick this guy's ass helps me remember how strong she really is."

"She's definitely a fighter."

But what neither of them needed to say was that even the strongest fighters couldn't cheat death.

"Let's not give up on getting one of Roman's men to turn on him," Callum continued. "I made it clear to everyone that whoever talked first was the only one not spending the rest of their life in prison. One of them will break."

Andrew nodded. "Good."

But it wouldn't be in time to save Tasha. Andrew leaned forward to tell Callum that exact thing when something from the footage caught his eye. It had played further than Tasha breaking Saunders nose to where the other cartel guy, Murphy, had walked up to him.

But over in the corner was a reflection Andrew hadn't seen before.

He grabbed his phone and called Jenna. "Can you look at

the footage of Tasha's attack in town. Four minutes and thirty-seven seconds in, bottom left corner there's some sort of window that I think might catch the reflection of what Murphy said."

Jenna didn't take offense at the lack of greeting. "Give me fifteen minutes."

It actually took twenty. When Jenna called back it was on the speakerphone so that everyone could hear.

"Okay people, we have a break. Granted, it's not much of one but it's better than nothing. A new reflection means we could tell a little more of what Murphy said to Saunders."

The footage popped up on the largest screen and everyone stopped what they were doing to watch it.

Boss needs her for...

That's where they'd lost the footage of him before but now Jenna had been able to loop it with the new reflection.

Boss needs her for...the bank.

"For the bank," Jenna repeated for everyone's clarity.

"Do we know which bank?" Callum asked.

The small image of Jenna in the corner of the screen shook her head. "No, we don't. Like I said, it's not much."

"It's more than we had before." Ian stood up. "Okay people let's focus our efforts. Anything to do with any bank the cartel has had ties to—that's where we look."

Andrew stood up and grabbed a file. "This is good. If he needs Tasha for a bank then she's definitely still alive. It's Sunday, so no banks are open. Let's figure this out before they do open."

"DRINK this and don't pick up another file until that sandwich is gone."

Andrew looked over at Laura who set a cup of coffee and a ham sandwich on a plate in front of him at the conference room table. He hadn't left except to go to the bathroom since they'd started looking at banks last night.

"I wouldn't think you would care if I was hungry or not after what I did to your friend," he told Laura.

She raised one eyebrow. "Don't get me wrong, I think you were an asshole. But I also see how hard you are working to get her back."

He scrubbed the hand down his face. They'd all been scouring over files—both electronic and paper–for the past eight hours. They were running out of time.

"I would do anything I could to get Tasha back. Don't doubt that. And once I do, I'll spend the rest of my life making sure she never doubts I would do anything for her either."

Those were some pretty grandiose words. He wondered if Laura would mock him for them.

She didn't. The opposite in fact. She laid a hand on his shoulder. "You get her back. Tasha will forgive you. Probably already has."

"I'm not so sure about that."

"Well, I've seen the way she looks at you. So, you fight for her and I have no doubt you will win her back. But sandwich first."

Before Andrew could say anything else Laura had walked away to hand a sandwich to someone else. There were plenty of people to hand sandwiches to — nearly the entire damn town of Pine Valley were either in here or at the Chill N' Grill reading over data.

Callum and Ian hadn't fought to keep the information private. They needed every set of eyes they could get, especially since these were people who wanted to help.

Tasha was one of their own.

"Andrew." Ian waved Andrew over to where he was sitting with Callum. "I think we've got something."

Andrew stuffed the last couple of bites of the sandwich into his mouth and grabbed his cup of coffee before rushing over to where Ian sat at the head of the conference table.

"Marcus Volkov died six months before Roman ordered the attack that ended up killing Kylie," Ian said.

"Okay," Andrew responded between chews. "How does that help us?"

"Jenna found this." Ian turned his computer tablet so Andrew could see some sort of communiqué from Marcus before he died.

"Who is this to?" Andrew asked.

"Jasper Millington. He was one of Marcus' trusted men. He was also one of the people who were executed the night Kylie died."

"Roman had one of his father's men killed? Why?"

"Because Marcus said this to him." Ian pressed a button so that Andrew could read the full message from Marcus to Jasper Millington.

In it, Marcus claimed that Roman wasn't fit to run the family "business" and that Marcus would be shifting all accounts to other, more neutral and hidden members of the family.

Andrew looked at Callum and then Ian. "More neutral and hidden members of the family? He's talking about Tasha."

Both of the other men nodded.

The message continued with instructions on accessing a security deposit box at *the bank that tied everything together*."

Andrew shook his head. It was all making sense now. "This is what Roman needs Tasha for. To access this security deposit box. That's why Roman couldn't get to it online. She has to go to the bank in person."

Again, both men nodded.

"That's what we think too," Callum said. "The question still is—"

"What bank," Andrew finished for him.

"As we already know, the Volkov Cartel literally has holdings spread across hundreds of banks all over the world," Jenna's image popped up in the corner of Ian's computer. "I've reduced that list to banks that have security deposit boxes, but it's still over thirty."

Ian nodded. "Let's keep digging through the financial data. Look for any clue about what bank Marcus might've been referring to when he's saying *the bank that ties everything together*. What the hell does that mean?"

Nobody knew, but at least now they had something to turn their attention to.

But a few hours later as time started to wind down, things got more and more grim. The Zodiac team called in as many favors as they could with colleagues they had to get as many eyes on the various banks as possible. The banks would open in just a few hours—international ones were already open.

The people of Pine Valley and the Crossroads retreat wanted to help. Callum made a list of banks that were possibilities that were in driving distance and everyone was given a bank they could get to before nine o'clock with instructions to not do anything but keep an eye out for Roman and Tasha.

Andrew wondered if Tasha was scared. Hurt. He wished she could see how many people had banded together to try to help her. That she meant so much to everyone.

And that she meant everything to him.

By seven o'clock the conference room was pretty much clear. They had hedged their bets as much as possible, sending as many people to as many different banks as they could.

Callum walked in. "Which bank are you going to? Ian has

made the Zodiac jet available for which ever one you want to be at."

At this point it was still anybody's guess. The only thing they knew for certain was that Roman wouldn't keep Tasha alive very long once she got him what he needed.

Andrew looked through the list of banks again—New York, Paris, Lima, Miami, Rio... All of them made sense, but none of them felt right to him.

He leaned back in his chair about to make a random choice when he looked at the secondary list of banks that had been eliminated. One town in particular caught his attention. Martinsboro.

Why had he heard of that town before? It took him a second to remember that that was where Tasha's mother had been born.

Andrew froze.

The bank that ties everything together.

He grabbed his phone and called Jenna asking for more information on that bank. She had it almost instantly.

"There are no safety deposit boxes there, so we eliminated it."

Damn it. "I really thought this was it. It would make so much sense that Marcus thought of the bank in the town where his wife was born as being the one that ties everything together. Are you sure we didn't miss anything?"

There were a few moments of silence before Jenna spoke again. "Shit. You're right, Andrew. They don't have safety deposit boxes there now but they did a few years ago. If Marcus left something in a box for Tasha, they would still have it."

Andrew turned to Callum. "This bank is it. I'm positive. It has to be. It's the only one with a personal tie to the cartel."

It was only an hour until the bank would open. Andrew

didn't have time to try to convince anybody else that he was right. He knew he was.

He was going to be there for Tasha. He didn't care about getting revenge against Roman anymore, didn't even care about getting justice for Kylie's death.

All Andrew cared about was making sure Tasha was safe.

Chapter 30

In the end Andrew didn't have to convince anyone that the Martinsboro bank was the way to go.

"If your gut says this is where Roman is going to show up, that's good enough for me." Ian had told him.

Ian, Callum, and Andrew had arrived in Martinsboro a few minutes ago and the bank was set to open in less than half an hour.

Andrew was sure this was where Roman was coming, but it was going to take a fucking miracle for them to be in place enough to take him down.

"I'm sorry, I can't legally give you access to Marcus Volkov's safety deposit box without a warrant," the manager was saying to Callum.

Callum looked like he was two seconds away from putting his fist through a wall, or the manager's face. Andrew understood that feeling.

But ultimately getting to the contents of the box right now were secondary. They just needed to be here when Roman came for it.

"We have a warrant incoming," Callum explained to the bank manager.

The man nodded. "And as soon as you have it in hand, I am more than happy to cooperate, but until then I'm afraid my hands are tied."

Callum looked at Andrew and Ian. Anger flared in the man's eyes but they knew there was nothing he could do. Things had to be handled legally so that Roman didn't get out on any loopholes once they took him down.

"I don't understand why there's so much sudden interest in this box," the manager continued. "You guys now. The call last week asking for details."

Andrew struggled to keep his patience and could see Ian and Callum were struggling to do the same.

"Somebody called about the security deposit last week?" Callum asked with exaggerated tolerance.

The manager looked a little sheepish. "Yeah. We haven't had security deposit boxes for a couple of years now. People just don't need them the way they used to and it wasn't a good use of the bank's space. When we decided to shut them down we helped owners find another location to transfer their valuables. There were only two box owners that we were unable to contact."

"And one of those is the box we're talking about." Andrew confirmed.

"Yes. Haven't heard a word about this box in three years since it was first established and then last week someone called asking if they could get into the box with the death certificate of the person who first opened it."

"And what was the answer?" Ian asked when the man trailed off. All three of them were trying not to pummel him.

"I told him the truth. That he could access the box to see the contents or add anything to it but he could not remove anything from the box, as per the original instructions. Only the listed recipient was to have access to the contents."

If Marcus Volkov had made Tasha the listed recipient, that definitely explained why Roman wanted her.

But again, none of this mattered. What mattered was being in place and ready when Roman and Tasha showed up.

The bank manager let out an exaggerated sigh. "Honestly, without a warrant I'm not sure you should even be here at all. We need to open in just a few minutes so I'm going to have to ask you to leave.

Andrew was done with this shit.

He grabbed his phone and turned to the bank manager. He brought up the file containing images of Roman's various murders and the calling cards he'd left, then spun it around to show the manager. "Do you see this? *This* is who we are up against. *This* is what he does to anybody he doesn't like. I don't give a shit about the contents of that safety deposit box but you're going to need to let us fortify this place. We need to replace your employees with our agents."

The manager looked a little green. This wouldn't be how Andrew would normally handle a situation but they were out of time and out of options.

The manager nodded. "Ah, oh my. Okay, yeah, I can get my people out. I'll need to stay to supervise, but everyone else can go. I don't want anyone getting hurt."

Ian nodded. "Make it happen, right fucking now. But we don't want to cause any panic. Tell them there is free breakfast down the block at the diner while some employees from a different branch come in for a few hours of training."

The manager nodded and scurried off, gathering his employees.

Callum, Ian, and Andrew looked at each other. There was way too much to do and not enough manpower or time to do it.

"We need people in here acting as tellers. Can't be you"—
Ian pointed at Andrew— "Roman will recognize you."

Callum nodded. "We also need to replace the guard at the
door with one of our men and ideally would have another half
dozen agents placed around as customers so it doesn't seem
too quiet coming in."

Andrew ran a hand through his hair. "We need snipers too.
We can't take a chance on him getting spooked and hurting
Tasha."

"You looked out that window?" Ian asked. "We've got an
elementary school across the street and we don't have time to
evacuate it. We can't take any chances on getting into a
shootout here."

Andrew gritted his teeth. "Understood."

And he did understand what Ian was saying. If it came
down to it, they were going to have to let Roman escape. Let
Tasha remain in his clutches.

Andrew wasn't sure he could do it. But he wasn't about to
say that now. He'd burn that bridge if it came to that. They
had enough to worry about in the next twenty minutes.

"Do we have anyone we can call in?" Ian asked Callum.

The other man shook his head. "I've got a full department
on the way, but they're not going to get here in time to do any
good."

Ian nodded. "Same with Zodiac team members."

"We could possibly get some Pine Valley civilians." Callum
rubbed the back of his neck.

None of them wanted to put untrained civilians in the
middle of this shitshow. "I don't think we have time, anyway."

"I'll get local law enforcement in here," Callum said, grabbing his phone. "Better than nothing."

"A bunch of cops hanging out in the bank is going to freak
Roman out."

Andrew didn't like this plan at all. But what were their

other options? He tamped down his panic. All the Crossroads guys were at other banks, and only having him, Callum, and Ian to try to fortify this whole bank and take Roman down would be nearly imposs—

"Uh, we heard there was a party here and I'm going to assume our invitations were lost in the mail."

Andrew spun at the sound of his twin brother Tristan's voice in the door.

And not just Tristan… a half dozen Zodiac and Linear Tactical guys were with him.

"What the hell?" Ian asked. "How'd you guys get here?"

Tristan grinned. "Cade O'Conner says to tell you you're not the only one who has a jet at your disposal."

Ignoring the laughs about Cade's message—who was a country music superstar and billionaire in his own right, Andrew rushed over to hug his brother. He shook hands with Sarge McEwan, and his wife Bronwyn. Landon Black, and Mark Outlawson—also Zodiac team members, were behind them.

Plus Zac Mackay and Finn Bollinger, two of the founders of Linear Tactical.

Andrew broke into a grin. There were no other people on the planet he'd rather have in this bank with him. For the first time, he had a sense of hope.

"I'm glad you're here," he said to Tristan.

"Wouldn't miss it, brother. Let's get your woman back."

Chapter 31

As far as undercover operations went, this was pretty much a shit show.

As highly skilled as the team was, they didn't have a plan or any sort of intel. Hell, they didn't have enough comms units for everyone, so they were relying on generalized hand gestures that everyone knew.

There were way too many fluctuating variables for this to go smoothly.

Landon and Tristan who were behind the counter as employees weren't even in suits—just some ill-fitting blazers they'd found in the back. It would not take much sleuthing to realize they didn't actually work there.

Sarge and Bronwyn were standing in the middle of the building at the island available for customers to fill out paperwork. Sarge in all his bulking hugeness was going to look out of place damned near everywhere, but at least his petite wife helped balance that out. Bronwyn didn't do active missions any longer, but she was still a highly trained field agent.

Sarge's protective closeness of Bronwyn wasn't any sort of

undercover work. At this point it was part of his very DNA. No one was ever going to hurt her again while he was alive.

Mark Outlawson—Outlaw—was over by the brochure rack as if he was deciding what sort of account he wanted. Andrew wasn't sure why a bank would even have paper brochures any longer, but was thankful for the cover.

Callum and Ian were acting as bank guards at the door. It gave them the excuse to be overtly armed.

The hopes were that they could shut the door once Roman was in the building with Tasha, then disarm him and his men while they held the element of surprise. Surprise was their most valuable asset.

Zac and Finn were outside—Zac to make sure no towns-people happened to wander in while the mission was going down. Finn somewhere with his sniper rifle—the skill which had gotten him the code name Eagle—to be used as a last resort.

Andrew was around the back of the bank in his car, able to enter the building if needed. Thanks to Jenna he had the security footage from the bank looped into his laptop so he could see what was happening. He could speak with Ian and Tristan who had the other two comms units. The rest of the team would take their cues from them.

Yeah, definitely not an optimal way to run a mission. There were a lot of things that could go wrong.

"Okay we've got two SUVs rolling in. That's got to be them." The angle of the outside security camera wasn't great, but two SUVs pulling up at the same moment? Had to be the cartel.

Andrew heard Ian announce the arrival to everyone inside the bank. They were as ready as they were going to get.

The security camera lost sight of the vehicles as they parked and the passengers got out. Andrew bit back a curse of frustration.

"I can't get a head count," he told Ian and Tristan. "The cameras aren't in line correctly."

This was where Zac or Finn could fill in with intel from their position if they had actual comms.

And most of all Andrew just wanted proof Tasha was alive.

"Roger," Ian said. "Whatever the number, we'll handle it."

Andrew tamped down the adrenaline coursing through his body as the interior cameras caught the entering party and Andrew finally had eyes on them. He shook his head as a cold sweat broke out along his spine. There were five people who entered the bank.

Tasha wasn't one of them.

"Fuck," Ian muttered under his breath into the comms unit. He realized the problem too.

"I'm going around front to see if they have her stashed in one of the vehicles." Andrew prayed that would be the case.

"Roger," Ian whispered.

Andrew dashed out of the car and ran around to the front of the bank only slowing to a walk when he was in visual distance of the SUVs parked out front. There was a man leaning on the hood of each vehicle, surveying the surrounding area. Andrew casually walked by giving them a nod as if he was on his way to the post office next door.

He caught a glimpse inside both SUVs. There was no one. Shit.

Zac saw Andrew from his post across the street, and started to make his way over. With a flick of his wrist Andrew waved him off. Zac immediately turned and focused his attention somewhere else so it wouldn't look like they'd been communicating in any way.

As soon as Andrew cleared the building and was no longer in sight of the SUVs he dashed back around to his car so he could see the video feed.

"Tasha is not with them. I repeat, Tasha is not with them."

Andrew resisted the urge to slam his hand against the steering wheel.

Was she hurt? Or worse, dead?

This also meant they were going to have to let Roman leave the bank today.

Andrew knew the team inside would assess the situation and come to the same conclusion he had.

He watched as Roman and his posse crossed to the bank manager's desk in the far corner of the building. Everett, the manager, was the only actual bank employee left. And the guy did not look like he was going to keep it together. Maybe showing him Roman's calling card had not been a good idea.

"Yes. Hello, gentlemen. Yes. How can I help you? What can I do for you today?" Nervousness fairly oozed from Everett.

Andrew scrubbed a hand down his face. This was going to be over before it began if they weren't careful.

"My father procured a security deposit box here three years ago. I'd like to access the contents."

"I. Um… Okay. Are you listed as a recipient?"

Neither the security footage nor the audio Andrew was getting second hand was great, but he could tell that Roman recognized a weakness in the bank manager and was going to attempt to exploit it.

"No, I'm not, but I have my father's death certificate. He was not of sound mind when he placed the contents of the box with you, so if you could allow me to access to the contents, that would be perfect. Thanks."

Everett swallowed hard and began nodding.

Shit. That same punk bastard who wouldn't give them access to the box without a warrant was about to hand it over free and clear to Roman, instructions and laws be damned.

But then again Everett had already seen the proof that

Roman would carve his eyes out and set a shot of vodka by his head given the slightest provocation, so maybe it was understandable.

If Roman made it out of this bank with the contents, Tasha's life wouldn't be worth much.

"Tristan..." Andrew muttered into the comms unit. His brother had been brought up to speed on the specifics of the safety deposit box, but Andrew wasn't sure how he could intervene.

Just knew he needed to do it.

"On it."

A few seconds later Tristan was in the security camera image next to Roman and the bank manager.

"Everett, are you still feeling poorly?" Tristan slapped Everett on the back then turned to Roman with a smile. "He was in the bathroom all morning throwing up. Such a trooper to still come in to work. How can I help you?"

Roman and his men shifted back a little. Nothing like the threat of vomit to make grown men uncomfortable.

Roman held out the death certificate. "I'm here to access the contents of my father's security deposit box."

Tristan's smile remained in place. "As I'm sure Everett was just telling you, the terms of that box are very specific. Only the named recipient—a Tasha Volkov—can retrieve the contents of the box. She'll need to be here in person."

Roman's jaw got tighter now that he realized he was dealing with someone who wasn't just going to fold and give him whatever he wanted. "I was told I could access the box."

"Let me just double check the details." Tristan pretended to look at something on Everett's computer. "Yes, that's correct. According to the terms of the box, you can see what is inside, and add anything to it, but nothing can be removed."

Roman didn't like that. "Look, the contents of the box

were left to my sister. I have her ID also, but she's ill and it will be difficult for her to come in here."

Everett was visibly shaking. Tristan stepped further in front of him. "Unfortunately, our hands are tied by the constraints under which the box was originally contracted. She'll have to be here."

Roman squinted his eyes at Tristan. "Do I know you from somewhere?"

Andrew tensed. He and Tristan weren't identical twins, but they were definitely brothers. Would Roman put it together?

Tristan didn't lose his cool. "Hazard of being a banker— everybody thinks they know me. Would you like to witness the contents of the box?"

Roman obviously wasn't happy. "Yes."

"If your...*friends* could stay here, that would be great. Only one person is allowed into the vault."

Andrew lost audio as they entered the vault, Tristan sure to keep himself between Everett and Roman, but he could see the footage.

Tristan stood to the side as Everett managed to open the box and give the contents to Roman without passing out. Roman stood at the small table and went through it.

There was no cash, no jewelry. Just a letter and a list of accounts.

Andrew couldn't see what the letter said, but it obviously made Roman furious. He slammed the contents back into the box and stormed out without a word.

Shit.

"Ian, Roman's going to be leaving. And he's pissed."

"We've got to let him go. If we arrest him now that could be it for Tasha."

"Yeah, I know." At one point Andrew would've taken his chances—bringing down Roman would've been the most important thing. But not now.

Nothing was more important than getting Tasha back safely, even if Roman got away.

But damn it, Andrew wasn't going to let that happen either.

"Stall him for a second if you can," he said into the comms unit before dashing out of the car again and back around to the front of the building. He wasn't going to let Roman leave without a way to follow him.

Zac saw him as soon as he rounded the corner. This time Andrew motioned him over, signing D-I-S-T-R-A-C-T with his fingers. Zac gave a brief nod then his gait changed immediately into someone who was drunk. He was across the street a moment later.

"Hey man. Hey my man!" Both drivers straightened from their perch on the hoods, turning to Zac as he came closer. They didn't draw their weapons, but they definitely went on high alert. "Listen, can you guys help a brother out?"

Andrew crouched down as they moved to the rear of their vehicles to assess the threat there. Zac continued to talk about needing a couple dollars so he could get some breakfast. The men obviously weren't interested, but Zac didn't let up.

Andrew cracked open the passenger door of the closest SUV and slipped his phone under the seat. Jenna would be able to track it. It wasn't a great option—so many things that could go wrong and it would be found immediately if they did a scan on the vehicles—but it was the only option they had. He closed the door silently.

"Roman's on his way out. We couldn't stall him any longer," Ian's voice barked in his ear.

Shit. Andrew dropped and rolled under the truck parked next to the SUV. A moment later Roman and his posse stormed out the door. All Andrew could see were feet.

"Let's go. I'll fucking drive." Roman's clipped words filled the air and doors opened, his men following his order quickly.

A moment later both vehicles were squealing out of the parking lot.

Andrew waited a few seconds before rolling back out. Zac was standing there watching the vehicles go. The other members of the team filed out the bank's door.

"They'll have to come back with Tasha to get the contents," Callum said. "I'm afraid they're going to be more prepared though. It's going to get bloody."

Andrew shook his head. "That's why we're not going to wait. I put my phone in the vehicle to track them. We're taking the fight to Roman."

Chapter 32

Tasha blinked into soft daylight, her eyes struggling to adjust. Her shoulders ached with the strain of her wrists being bound behind her back and secured to a rickety wooden chair. Everything hurt. Her head throbbed and her joints felt like they were coming undone. She couldn't remember much of anything.

How the hell did she get here?

More importantly, where was she?

A wave of nausea rocked her and she slumped forward in the chair, closing her eyes tight to ride out the rolling sensation in her body. The chair screeched, and before she knew it, she hit the ground face-first, her nose crunching against dusty wooden floorboards.

"Shit," a gruff voice said from across the room. "Untie her and get her up. Roman's going to be here any minute now. He said to make sure she wasn't bruised."

Tasha felt like she was moving through water as she was untied and lifted upright. She swayed, the floor coming ridiculously close again.

"She's barely lucid," another unfamiliar voice said nearby.

"What the fuck is wrong with her?"

"I told Boss he was being too rough," a third, scratcher voice mumbled from somewhere in the room, but Tasha couldn't tell which direction the voice came from. The whole room was spinning.

"Just get her on the couch. Throw some cold water on her. I don't give a fuck. Just keep her alive."

Something soft enveloped her body before a rush of pins and needles crept over her skin as icy water was dumped over her head. She gasped, crying out as the throbbing pain in her body erupted into something sharper.

"W-where am I?" Tasha choked, frantically rubbing her eyes. The room came into focus, nothing more than grimy paneled walls and an old dining room table. Yellow curtains hung still against three frosted windows, and the air inside the room was stale and cold.

Four men lingered nearby, all of them watching her.

One of them stepped forward and crouched in front of her where she sat on the couch. She drew her knees against her chest and shivered against the cold.

Tasha recognized him: Saunders. His nose was still bruised and slight off-kilter from when she'd driven her fist into his face.

She spit on him, pulling her teeth back in a sneer that made two of the men watching the exchange take a step back.

"Don't touch her," one of the men said as he stepped forward. His salt and pepper hair was swept back away from his face, his beard trimmed and dark brown eyes shining in the yellow-hued light from a dusty, dated overhead light.

Tasha's memories came rushing back to her, stabbing through her aching head. She fought back tears as she remembered Isaac lying on the ground covered in blood. She looked down at her hands—still stained red with his blood. She curled her fingers into her palm as she shook with both rage and fear.

They'd thrown her into a car and then her memories went black. She gingerly touched her forehead and pulled her fingers away when a stinging sensation throbbed over her skin. Fresh blood marked her fingertips.

They'd knocked her out.

She had no idea where she was now, or how much time had passed. But if she had to guess, it was now Monday. Whatever Roman needed her for, her time was up.

Before she could ask the men where she was, the front door opened and Roman stalked inside. He pushed back the men and grabbed Tasha by her hair. She yelped as he pulled her upright and dragged her toward the door and down the porch steps.

"Cars. Now. And somebody give her a towel to clean up. She has to look presentable." He turned his head to shout at the men now funneling out of the house.

Tasha bit back a sob as Roman threw her into the back of an SUV. His muffled voice outside the vehicle was hard to hear, but everyone was rushing around to do his bidding.

Tasha crawled across the seat to try to open the other door but it had some sort of childproof lock and wouldn't budge.

Roman got into the driver's seat in front of her, one of his men in the passenger side next to him. Roman turned around, tossing a towel back at her. "You look like shit. Wipe yourself off. I told the people at the bank you were sick, but you can't go in looking like you're Typhoid Mary."

Tasha bit her lip, as he looked her up and down. She used the towel to wipe her face as best she could without any sort of mirror.

"This is what's going to happen now. We're going to Martinsboro. You're going to go into the bank there and give them this." He handed her a piece of paper before turning back to the steering wheel and peeling out of the driveway.

Tasha stole a glance out of the window before the landscape turned to a white and gray blur. A small farmhouse disappeared from view behind them.

They were still in Tennessee? "Why are we going to Martinsboro?"

"Fucking Marcus. I finally found the bank where he decided to store the information about the other accounts. Accounts only you have access to."

"What?"

"He left a little letter to you inside the box. One last note voicing of his disapproval of me. Telling you to take the money, do whatever you wanted with it, but make sure I didn't get it."

She looked down at the paper Roman had handed her and ice filled her veins. It was a power of attorney that gave Roman full access to any bank account where she was the primary recipient.

It had already been signed by a notary. One Roman obviously paid off.

A pen ricocheted off her face as he threw it at her and she gasped, fresh tears stinging her eyes.

"Sign it. Right fucking now. Then when you get to the bank, you will smile and stay quiet and do exactly as I say. We'll get the accounts and that will be it."

She reached down and grabbed the pen. It didn't matter, did it? She wasn't going to get out of this situation alive.

But her hand stilled before she signed. She thought of the explosive device on Elizabeth and Tucker's house. "You have to promise me you won't hurt anybody else at Crossroads or Pine Valley."

Or Andrew, but she didn't want to give Roman more ammunition. Maybe he didn't know about Andrew at all.

Roman looked at her through the rearview mirror. "Sign. It." Each word was clipped.

"Promise me," she repeated with force.

"Whatever. Fine."

A tear fell onto the paper, blurring the ink as she scribbled her signature and threw it into the front seat.

Roman chuckled. "See? That wasn't so hard, was it? Follow instructions in town and I'm sure nothing will happen to your friends either."

He smiled at her in the rearview mirror and with one look into his icy eyes she knew.

She was going to die today.

That part she could even accept.

But Roman was going to kill people she cared about too. Elizabeth, Tucker, Audrey...and maybe there were more explosive devices she didn't know about. Maybe there were people he would kill just because they knew her.

She clenched the pen in her fist, rolling it back and forth. It was a sharp ballpoint. She dragged her tongue over her teeth as she watched Roman drive in silence.

The man seated in front of her was not a brother. He was a monster. And he'd continue to kill if she didn't stop him.

She lunged forward and drove the pen into his neck.

"ROMAN'S VEHICLE is headed back toward you." Andrew heard Jenna's report through the speakerphone as he, Ian, Callum, and Tristan sped toward the house twenty miles out of town where the tracker had stopped.

"Already?" Callum asked. "Shit."

They'd hoped to have more time and manpower. Right now it was only supposed to be a reconnaissance mission to find out the details about where the cartel was holed up and the best way to rescue Tasha.

"I've picked him up on satellite," Jenna continued. "You've got two SUVs headed your way."

"Do you think he's going back to the bank?" Andrew asked. "If so, Tasha will be with him."

Tristan pounded his hand against the steering wheel. "Probably so. He's not wasting any time. I was hoping we had until tomorrow."

They'd all been hoping they could breech the house tonight and end this far away from innocents being hurt. It looked like that option was being taken from them.

Andrew could see the SUVs cresting a hill in front of them.

"There they are," Ian said as the vehicles barreled toward them like it was a game of chicken. "We're not going to have a better time than right now to stop them."

The other three men glanced at Andrew. It wasn't his call to make, but they knew Tasha was in the most danger if they made this into a vehicular shootout.

If Andrew said no then these men—all of them his brothers in one way or another—would find another way to stop Roman. Even if it meant they lost the tactical advantage.

Callum made the choice for him. "No, we won't risk Tasha. We'll find another way—"

"Shit!"

Andrew watched in horror as one of the vehicles speeding toward them suddenly lurched to the side, swerving and riding the shoulder before sliding over the edge and flipping onto its side. The other SUV was obviously caught off guard by what had happened too. It sped past only to slam on its breaks and turn around.

Andrew caught a flash of blonde climbing out of the flipped SUV's window. "Fuck, that's Tasha!"

Tristan hit the gas speeding toward the other cars. Tasha managed her way out of the flipped vehicle then began half running/half staggering away as the men in the other vehicle began firing at her.

"Shit!" Andrew rolled down the window of the passenger side and began firing as Callum did the same from other side in the back. They were too far to be able to do much damage, but they at least gave the cartel something to worry about that wasn't Tasha.

But they were still gaining on her.

"Everybody in and hang on," Tristan yelled as he hit the gas and the car sped forward. "We're going to take them out of the equation."

Andrew and Callum had barely pulled themselves inside when a few moments later their vehicle slammed into the side of the SUV.

Everyone grunted at the impact as Tristan yanked the steering wheel away then slammed them back into the cartel's vehicle. One last swipe had both vehicles damaged enough that they couldn't go any further.

Tristan, Callum, and Ian jumped out of the car, laying suppressive fire. Andrew was running before his mind had a chance to catch up to his body, straight towards Tasha. He could hear guns being fired from either side of the fray.

It was a full-on battle and he was running right into it. It didn't matter. All he could do was get to Tasha.

"Tasha!" he cried out. "Get down!"

She heard his voice and turned to him. He waved his arms in a downward gesture, relief flooding him as she dropped to the ground. The shooting was slowing—undoubtedly because the Zodiac Tactical team was doing their job—but she was still in way too much danger.

One of Roman's men popped up out of the window, obviously dazed from the crash. It didn't take long for the man to get his bearings and point his gun at Tasha. It took Andrew even less time to pull the trigger on his own weapon at a full run. The man slumped over dead.

Andrew continued sprinting until he was right over Tasha.

JANIE CROUCH & DANIELLE M. HAAS

He crouched down and pulled her into his arms. "Are you okay?"

Tasha wrapped hers around him, yanking him to her. "Yes. Yes, I'm okay."

There were still some bullets flying so Andrew pulled Tasha back to the SUV that had flipped so they had cover. "Where's Roman? Do you know?"

She nodded, leaning up against the vehicle. "I stabbed him in the neck. With a pen. He was driving. That's how we flipped."

He reached over and planted a kiss on her lips. "That's my girl. Now, stay down."

Using the turned over vehicle as cover, Andrew straightened and started firing, helping to even out the odds for his friends. He ran out of ammunition just as it all ended. All of the Volkov Cartel were either dead or in handcuffs.

Callum was busy sorting the bad guys out as Ian and Tristan jogged over to Andrew, as he helped Tasha to her feet. He ignored the rage her bruises wanted to bring out.

She was alive. That was the most important thing.

"You okay?" He pushed a strand of hair gingerly back from her cheek. "EMTs will be here in a few minutes. We'll have them check you out."

"I'm okay," she whispered. She still looked dazed, but no one could blame her for that. "I just need a second to pull myself together."

He nodded and kissed her forehead careful of her wound. With a stroke of his thumb down her cheek, he walked over to meet Ian and Tristan.

"Nobody has seen Roman yet," Ian said.

"Tasha stabbed him in the neck with a pen. Caused him to wreck and flip the vehicle."

Tristan didn't even try to hide his delight. "Good for her. I'm only sorry one of us didn't get the oppor—"

Over the back of Tristan's head the dead man Andrew had shot *moved*.

"What the fu—" Andrew shoved his brother and ran the few steps toward the vehicle as he realized it wasn't the dead man at all.

Roman Volkov, covered in blood, stood from behind the body.

His gun was aimed right at Tasha.

"I won't let you win."

Andrew had no more ammunition, so did the only thing he could…he dove for Tasha.

He crashed into her, taking them both down hard. He felt an agonizing burn at the same time he heard shots. Breathing became impossible.

But all he cared about was keeping Tasha safe. He wrapped both arms around her head and buried her against his chest.

He couldn't lose her. He wouldn't survive.

"Andrew!"

He could hear her voice and see her big blue eyes in front of him, filling all of his vision. But focusing on them was becoming harder.

"Andrew!" She was crying now. That wasn't what he wanted. He never wanted to see her cry again. He tried to force the words out to tell her that but they wouldn't come.

"Hang on, brother. Help is coming." That was Tristan. He was next to Tasha now. Good.

Tristan would like Tasha. Would understand why Andrew had fallen in love with her. Tristan would love her. The whole family would.

How could anyone not love Tasha? She was kind, beautiful, gentl—

Everything faded to black.

Chapter 33

The hospital waiting room was packed.

Andrew's friends, family, colleagues—although honestly they seemed interchangeable—all spoke in hushed whispers to each other as they waited for permission to go back and see him.

Two of Roman's bullets had caught Andrew in the chest. If he hadn't been wearing a Kevlar vest, he would definitely be dead now.

If he hadn't jumped on Tasha, she'd be dead now too.

Ironically it was the bullet that caught Andrew in the fleshy part of his upper arm that had caused all the problems. He'd been fine as they'd removed the bullet but then had crashed and coded. A second emergency surgery had been required.

Everything had gone fine. All they needed now as for Andrew to wake up.

Tasha had missed most of the excitement. First she'd been having her own wounds—which were mostly superficial—treated then answering all the questions law enforcement had for her. Her cooperation, coupled with the fact that she didn't want a single dime of the money her father had tried to leave her in the accounts, had gone a long way on her behalf.

There would still be more questions, but she would gladly answer those also.

"You're going to be the first one he asks for, you know."

Tasha turned to find Andrew's brother Tristan standing next to her in the doorway. She'd met him on the way to the hospital. They'd only talked a little.

"I'm not sure about that."

"He was already wanting to know if you were okay when he was awake before. You are the most important thing to him right now."

She shook her head. "Do you know who I am? That I'm Roman's sister?"

Tristan shrugged. "I've read the reports. Both the first one when we didn't know if you were working with Roman and the most recent one where Andrew was adamant of your total innocence."

"His wife is dead because of me." She rubbed her burning eyes.

"That's not how Andrew sees it. He sees it as he and his daughters being *alive* because of you. Kylie is dead because of Roman. Don't take that on yourself."

Hadn't Laura told her the same thing? That Tasha couldn't hold herself responsible for what Roman had done?

"I feel like all I do is bring him pain."

Tristan smiled, and it looked so much like Andrew's for a moment that it took her breath away. "I'll admit, you two definitely haven't had a traditional start. But that doesn't mean you can't have your happily ever after."

Tasha's stomach clenched. There was nothing she wanted more than that—a chance to allow the feelings between her and Andrew to grow and flourish.

But this wasn't a fairytale.

"What sort of happily ever after can there be for us? My family killed his wife. His daughters will never know their mother because of the people I am related to."

"But that wasn't you." Tristan shook his head. "Plus, you have things to forgive my brother for too, if I'm not mistaken. So maybe you could both agree on a re-start."

Tasha wanted to believe it could all work out. Wanted to believe it more than she'd ever wanted to believe anything in her whole life. Looking at Tristan's smiling face, she almost could.

Andrew didn't hold her responsible for Roman's sins. She didn't hold Andrew responsible for doing his job. Maybe they really could start over. Get to know each other with no secrets between them.

Ian DeRose entered the room from the other end. "Good news on two counts. Isaac is awake and going to be fine and Andrew is waking up too. Isaac is already asking who's willing to sneak him in some steak."

Everyone let out a cheer and a bunch of the guys started looking up the best steak restaurant in the area.

"I know my twin," Tristan continued in Tasha's ear. "He doesn't fall easily and when he does, it's for good. Just you wait and see if you're not the first person he asks for when they allow him visitors."

Tristan squeezed her arm then went fully into the waiting room to celebrate with his friends.

Tasha didn't go in, but she did stay in the doorway. Maybe Tristan was right. Maybe it could work out between her and Andrew.

She rubbed the heel of her hand against her chest. Maybe, besides his daughters, she was the most important thing in Andrew's life. He was certainly the most important thing in hers.

When the nurse came in a little while later and announced

Andrew was conscious and able to have visitors, another cheer went up. Tasha took a deep breath and pushed away her nervousness.

She just wanted to see him. Kiss him. Let him know that she wanted to try.

The nurse smiled and shushed everyone. "Andrew said he'd like to see an Ian DeRose as his first visitor."

Disappointment flooded Tasha's system. She told herself that it didn't mean anything that Andrew hadn't wanted to see her first. There could be a number of very important reasons why Andrew wanted to see his boss first.

It didn't mean anything. She knew that.

But if Tristan was wrong about this, maybe he'd been wrong about everything.

Maybe she and Andrew just weren't meant to be. Maybe she needed to just let it all go.

She melted back from the doorway and left without a word.

ANDREW WANTED TASHA. She'd been the last person on his mind when he'd went under and the first on his mind when he'd come back up.

"Although flattered, I've got to admit I didn't think I would be the first person you wanted to see, Gemini."

Andrew sat up a little straighter as his boss walked in. He didn't remember any of scary stuff that had happened to him since he'd been brought in to the hospital, but his body was stiff and sore enough to let him know it hadn't been an easy process.

"Oh yeah?" he asked Ian. "Who did you think it would be?"

Ian shrugged. "Your twin, for sure. But also, Tasha."

Andrew's fingers itched to touch her. "She's okay, right?"

"Yep. Some bruises and cuts, but nothing major. Why didn't you ask for her yourself? Did you not know she was in the waiting room?"

"I needed to talk to you first."

Ian raised an eyebrow. "Oh?"

"I quit."

Ian actually laughed. "You're quitting Zodiac Tactical because you got shot in the arm?"

"I'm quitting Zodiac Tactical because between my daughters and the woman I'm going to marry, I'm not interested in active duties anymore."

Ian walked over and took a seat next to Andrew's bed. "Woman you're going to marry, huh?"

Andrew shrugged. "Yeah, well, I'll have to let Tasha in on the plan and give the girls a half-second to fall in love with her, but…yeah, marry."

"Brother, you know we'll find you a desk job if you don't want active duty. You're too skilled to give up this line of work completely."

Andrew nodded. "Actually, I was thinking I might use my skills at the Crossroads Retreat. Help people who've suffered losses like mine."

"So you're going to move out here to Tennessee?" Ian smiled.

"This is Tasha's home, Ian. The only one she's really known. You saw how everyone banded together to help her. I want her to have that, to know this community thinks of her as one of their own. But I also don't think I can live without her. So…yeah, Pine Valley."

Ian smiled and crossed his arms over his chest. "You know what? I've been thinking that maybe we should open a remote

Zodiac office in Tennessee. Think you might be interested in sticking around and training the next generation of Zodiac Tactical agents part time while also helping at Crossroads?"

Epilogue

One year later

"NAMASTE. Thank you all for a wonderful class."

Tasha walked around talking to the class participants for a few minutes. Her Saturday morning yoga by the lake class at Crossroads had become one of the most popular. It was definitely Tasha's favorite.

She looked across the field at the little girls running towards her.

Maybe her second favorite.

Caroline tripped carrying her mat, but Olivia and Audrey quickly stopped to help her pick it up and right herself.

"Hi Tasha!" Olivia yelled the moment she was in ear's reach. "We waited until your other class was done before coming down here."

Olivia looked back at the two men walking behind the girls, also carrying yoga mats—Andrew and Tucker. The men had obviously been the ones giving them instructions to wait quietly until Tasha's class was done.

An exercise in torture for these little rugrats.

There were other men and their children crossing from the parking lot for the next group: an adult/child combo class that had turned into the local men in the community bringing the kids out so the women could have a little time for themselves. Kids of all ages from teenagers right on down to Laura's nine-month-old brought by the man she never saw coming and fell in love with showed up each week.

They generally started with some stretching but it didn't take long until more physical activities were needed to keep everyone's attention. Tasha didn't mind it at all.

Andrew walked up to her and hooked an arm around her waist before kissing her forehead as the girls set up their mats. "I missed you. This damned situation has to change."

She couldn't help but break into a smile. "It will in two weeks."

Their wedding.

"If you don't run away again. You're my first choice, I promise."

She buried her face in his chest. "I'm never going to live that down, am I?" Everyone teased her about slipping out when Andrew said he needed to talk to Ian in the hospital that day.

She felt his lips on the top of her head. "You're never going to have to. I am going to spend every day of the rest of my life making sure you know that you are my first pick."

"You've been doing that every day since you and the girls moved here."

She had snuck out of that hospital that day a year ago thinking there would never be anything between them. Had thought it even more when Andrew had left town without a word a few days later.

Well, without a word to *her*. Evidently he'd talked to damn near everybody in Pine Valley because a month later he and his girls were permanent residents. He'd bought a house, enrolled his girls in preschool, started working at Crossroads.

And started showing up at every yoga class she taught again.

But this time it had been different. This time after each class he'd taken the time to tell her something about himself.

Something real. Something true.

They'd spent hundreds of hours over coffee getting to know each other. The *real* each others.

He'd told her about Kylie and the life they'd shared—the things he missed most about her. Tasha had told him of her frustrations that she hadn't realized the truth about her family sooner. Told him how she struggled with reconciling the killer her father had been with the man she'd simply known as *Dad*.

She'd gotten to know Andrew's daughters too. Daughters that would soon be hers. Daughters that had come to Tasha while working in their section of her little garden and asked if they could call her *Mom* after the wedding.

They'd sat down that night as a family and looked through all the pictures of Kylie they could find. Tasha would be honored to be their mother, but wanted them to know that they had a biological one who had loved them literally more than life.

"I can't wait to wake up beside you every day for the rest of my life. And to make sure you fall asleep each night moaning my name." He kissed her chastely on the cheek, the action in complete contrast to his naughty words.

They hadn't lived together, deciding instead to wait until they were married.

Tasha couldn't wait.

With one more kiss, Andrew took his place with the girls. Tasha winked and smiled at all three of them before turning to glance around.

The sleepy town of Pine Valley hadn't been where she'd

thought she'd stay permanently when she arrived here. But friends that had become like family had shown her the truth.

This was her home. An she couldn't imagine being anywhere else.

Also by Janie Crouch

All books: https://www.janiecrouch.com/books

HEROES OF OAK CREEK

Hero Unbound

Hero's Flight

ZODIAC TACTICAL

Code Name: ARIES

Code Name: VIRGO

Code Name: LIBRA

Code Name: PISCES

Code Name: OUTLAW

Code Name: GEMINI

NEVER TOO LATE FOR LOVE (with Regan Black)

Heartbreak Key Collection

Ellington Cove Collection

Wyoming Cowboys Collection

Holiday Heroes Collection

RESTING WARRIOR RANCH (with Josie Jade)

Montana Sanctuary

Montana Danger

Montana Desire

Montana Mystery

Montana Storm

Montana Freedom

Montana Silence

Montana Rain

LINEAR TACTICAL (series complete)

Cyclone

Eagle

Shamrock

Angel

Ghost

Shadow

Echo

Phoenix

Baby

Storm

Redwood

Scout

Blaze

Hero Forever

Major Crimes

Armed Response

In the Lawman's Protection

Also by Danielle M. Haas

check out these other great romantic suspense stories from Danielle M Haas:

-

Injured Heroes Series

Crossroads of Revenge

Crossroads of Delusion

Crossroads of Redemption

Crossroads of Obsession

Crossroads of Betrayal

Crossroads of Innocence

Safe Haven Women's Shelter Series

Laura's Safe Haven

Murders of Convenience Series

Matched with Murder

Booked to Kill

Driven to Kill

-

Stand Alones

Bound by Danger

Girl Long Gone

About the Author (Janie)

"Passion that leaps right off the page." - Romantic Times Book Reviews

USA Today and Publishers Weekly bestselling author Janie Crouch writes what she loves to read: passionate romantic suspense featuring protective heroes. Her books have won multiple awards, including the Romance Writers of America's coveted Vivian® Award, the National Readers Choice Award, and the Booksellers' Best.

After a lifetime on the East Coast, and a six-year stint in Germany due to her husband's job as support for the U.S. Military, Janie has settled into her dream home in Front Range of the Colorado Rockies.

When she's not listening to the voices in her head—and even when she is—she enjoys engaging in all sorts of crazy adventures (200-mile relay races; Ironman Triathlons, treks to Mt. Everest Base Camp...), traveling, and hanging out with her four kids.

Her favorite quote: "Life is a daring adventure or nothing." ~ Helen Keller.

facebook.com/janiecrouch

amazon.com/author/janiecrouch

instagram.com/janiecrouch

bookbub.com/authors/janie-crouch

About the Author (Danielle)

Danielle M Haas is a stay-at-home mom turned author. When she isn't writing fast-paced romantic suspense novels with mysteries to live for and romance to die for, she's busy being a taxi driver to her two busy kids and forcing her introverted self to talk to other soccer moms. Her kids and husband are her world, which is also shared with her hyper Bernie doodle, two sassy cats, and one leopard gecko who's happy to chill on a rock all day. Her days are packed with cuddles, kisses, and a brain constantly thinking of new ways to create danger and romance for her next book.

Made in the USA
Columbia, SC
28 November 2023

27282026R00178